BLOOD
IN THE
SAND

Seth Sjostrom

*wolfprint*Media

wolfprint, LLC
P.O. Box 801
Camas, WA,
98607

Blood in the Sand: a thriller / by Seth Sjostrom. - 1st wolfprintMedia edition

Trade Paperback
ISBN-13: 978-1-7349376-9-5

1. Sean Kendall (Fictitious character)-Fiction. 2. Terrorism-Ecological-Political-Fiction. 3. Blood Series-Fiction I. Title.

First wolfprintMedia Digital edition 2020.

For information regarding bulk purchases, please contact wolfprintMedia, LLC at wolfprint@hotmail.com.

United States of America

Acknowledgements

My deepest appreciation to those who have supported me and the development of the Sean Kendall series:

Kathi Sjostrom for her fuel to my dreams,

Hayden Sjostrom for his inspiration for me since the day he was born,

Tom and Linda Sjostrom for their eternal support and belief in me,

Kiara Hansen for her delightful, earnest enthusiasm for my stories and their success.

And to the Elstuns for being wonderful hosts on an amazing Mazatlan trip and adventure. Family forever.

One

The patter of rain against the cement of the sidewalk was broken up by a soft cry drifting down from the front steps of Ambassador Gutierrez' Manhattan townhome. The thirteen-year representative from Mexico turned to see his four-year-old daughter standing on the front stoop with outstretched arms, tears adding to the rain sprinkling her rosy cheeks.

With a sigh and a warm laugh, Ambassador Gutierrez retreated to the porch and kneeled to wrap his arms around the sad little girl. "Sienna, Daddy has to go to work," he cooed as he kissed his daughter on the cheek. Behind the toddler, a frazzled woman appeared in the doorway.

Looking over Sienna's shoulder, a rambling apology met the ambassador's glare, "Senor Gutierrez, I am so sorry. I turned to put away the breakfast dishes, and she was gone!"

"Consuela, if you hadn't raised both me and my brother…," he started and then took a deep breath, "It was as much my fault. I should have locked the door behind me. We must be careful. New York can be a very dangerous city."

"Yes, Senor," the nanny responded with her head bowed, her hand stretched out to collect the sobbing child.

Gutierrez planted another kiss on Sienna's cheek and gently prodded her forward to the waiting Consuela, who scooped her up and disappeared behind the heavy door of the townhouse. Despite his irritation with the elderly caretaker, he smiled at the surprise opportunity to steal another moment with his baby girl. Whistling, he strode to the Lincoln SUV that idled double-parked in the street in front of the brownstone. A soaked personal assistant, who at least wore the air of patience, opened the door for him, and the black car quickly sped away from the curb.

Shrugging off his annoyance for the delay and having to wait in the rain, the assistant looked at his boss with a gleam in his eye, "It is a big day, Senor Ambassador."

"Indeed, it is Sebastian. The economy of Mexico is about to enter a new era," grabbing the file folder that his aid had been clutching, "The tallies still show a consensus?"

"Near enough. The council will approve the agreement in time for an announcement at this week's World Trade Conference in Mazatlan," Sebastian Cortez confirmed.

"I can't believe they got the Golden Zone Conference Center completed in time."

"I think everyone in Mexico City knew what an opportunity it was to herald in the "modern Mexico" with the state-of-the-art facility. The revitalization of Mazatlan is the perfect statement of what the rest of Mexico could look like with the right U.S. trade agreements in place. The Americans see a chance to curb immigration and tap into cheap labor that can keep them competitive with China," Cortez rambled excitedly.

"And Mexico won't ever be called third world again."

"And they will credit you as the architect that made it happen," the aide gleamed over the documents in his hand.

"More importantly, Sienna can return to a respectable country someday. Hopefully, a less corrupt country," Gutierrez sighed.

"That would indeed be a *nuevo* Mexico, sir."

The delivery truck came to an abrupt stop outside of the townhouse. Two men in gray uniforms burst through the doors and scrambled up the cement steps. Giving several sharp raps on the door, the men waited to be greeted. In moments, Consuela's face appeared in the slight crack the chained door allowed.

"Pardon us, senora, we have a pick up scheduled," one man declared.

"I am sorry, Senor Gutierrez said nothing about a pickup," Consuela admitted, a confused expression washing over her face, "What was the item?"

"Her," the second man snarled as the tiny figure of Sienna emerged behind the nanny. Before the caretaker could respond, the man fired several shots from a silenced pistol into the head and chest of the nanny.

The first man kicked the door open, tearing the brass chain from its moorings. The heavy door flew wide, revealing a fear-stricken child, standing motionless beside the body of her caretaker. While the shooter holstered his weapon, his partner snatched the girl and retreated through the entryway door, sprinting for the van. Before both men could get inside and slam the door shut, the gray-paneled van sped down the street and disappeared into the thick traffic of Manhattan's commuter streets.

"Hurry, we'll miss the shuttle!" Sean called to Miranda, dragging his sizeable green suitcase behind him.

"We're fine, relax," Miranda grinned, fending off Sean's anxious pleadings, "Our flight doesn't take off for over an hour." A mere grunt met her reply.

Sean Kendall did not tolerate lengthy lines well. Wading through crowds and idling patiently were absent virtues that led him to leave the city for the more tranquil lifestyle of his home in the remote North Cascades wilderness. Abandoning a successful career in his prime, he cashed out his 401k, affording him the luxury of early retirement.

Now here he was, dashing into the throng of travelers converging on Sea-Tac's busy international terminal. This trip signaled the forced end to his retirement. In retribution for taking the law into his own hands against a terror cell, he could avoid prosecution by agreeing to work on a special task force led by Oregon Senator Rick Johnson. The Senator, whose life was spared twice by Sean's timely yet foolhardy exploits, convinced a federal judge that the extensive list of weapons and police interference charges Kendall faced were not fitting with the "spirit" of the law. Acknowledging that vigilantism should not be tolerated, it would better serve whatever sentence that would be handed down by putting Sean to work for the public good.

The judge agreed with Senator Johnson, sentencing Sean to eighteen hundred hours of community service–all served under the Senator's task force. Whether or not he wanted it, Sean was back to work. His role would be to aid the senator as an analyst on his pet project, the North American Ecological Alliance–a joint program between Canada, the U.S. and Mexico to align commerce and conservation policies to create maximum impact. Sean preferred to avoid politics but accepted his fate in joining the senator.

As Miranda caught up to Sean, she snaked her arm in between his, slowing him to a more leisurely pace. Sean looked at the smiling woman next to him. The trip signaled something else, a chance to rekindle the relationship that ignited with searing ferocity before hitting an emotional wall when Sean was forced to kill Miranda's cousin in self-defense. The event that nearly landed Sean in prison was the same that forced the two back together. A member of a dinner cruise held hostage, Miranda was rescued by Sean when he impulsively rappelled off a bridge as the boat passed underneath. Kendall's willingness to dive into trouble when people needed help was a trait that Miranda both adored and yet was extremely fearful of.

Sean had been afraid that the relationship would never survive, yet here he was with the auburn-haired biologist by his side. Feeling her hand run along his arm sent a surge of warmth through him.

Entering the terminal, James Wilkins, Senator Johnson's principal advisor and manager for activities related to the commerce and trade conference, met them. He met them with a broad smile, offering that they stop at the coffee kiosk before they move on to their gate.

"Well, Ms. Shaw, Rick tells me you are a marine biologist. Your research has even made the senate floor a time or two," Wilkins noted.

"Most of my work has been testifying on whale species populations and the implications on the International Whaling Moratorium. Recently, I helped create the protocols for the seals that migrated up the Columbia River and were harming the salmon runs," Miranda replied, shrugging modestly.

"A most accomplished young lady," Wilkins replied and turned to Sean, "And you sir, have a track record navigating bureaucracy yourself - securing over 100,000 acres of wilderness in the Pacific Northwest for the Conservancy."

"My model in working with the Conservancy was largely avoiding politics and *buying* the land they wanted protected. I don't see a ton of value in protesting and grandstanding when you make change directly and permanently. Most of my work was making business deals that exchanged land between the government, and commercial groups. I just had to find compromises that made all groups happy," Sean confessed.

"Still, any experience in negotiating with government and large private sector groups can be a test of one's devices," Wilkins continued smiling. "The senator also tells me you are quite the swashbuckler—literally swinging from ropes to stow away on boats, taking on crowds of bad guys. I sincerely look forward to working with you. I think it shall be rather interesting, to say the least."

"Keep in mind, that 'swashbuckling' as you call it nearly landed me in prison and is a primary reason I am now in your employ," Sean replied, not nearly as impressed with his decision making in those prior exploits as the senator's aide appeared to be. "If it's all the same, I'd just as soon restrict my efforts to the boardroom."

Wilkins laughed, "Wielding a pen as your trusted weapon. Very well."

Miranda put down her coffee cup and looked sternly across the table at the two men, "If it had not been for Sean's... somewhat hasty actions, I wouldn't be here today. Neither would the senator... or a hundred other people. As impulsive as he is, he is a good man, and I am sure he will serve your staff well."

"From all the wonderful things the senator says about him, I am sure. In fact," Wilkins continued, "You two have a wonderful opportunity while we are down in Mexico. We have set up a press day where the senator and his Mexican counterparts will help release recently hatched Loggerhead turtles into a preserve off of the coast just south of Mazatlan. This is the second joint venture with groups in the States. In fact, the first was from right in your backyard. Wolf Haven worked with the Mexican government to reintroduce nearly extinct Mexican red wolves back into their native habitat. That venture worked so well. They joined forces on this sea turtle project out of North Carolina. These are exactly the mutual ventures we hope to continue with our neighboring counterparts."

"These programs work better when everyone in the geography is on the same page," Miranda agreed, "And we get to be a part of it while down there?"

"A nice statement in front of the media," Sean agreed, seizing the obvious bid for positive public relations. "Good press, positive relations, better for the tourism industry."

"And that is why Rick brought you aboard. You have a nose for opportunity," Wilkins laughed.

"And a nose for trouble," an authoritative voice behind them said. The threesome turned to see Senator Johnson smiling at them, "I see you all made it all right."

"Are you kidding? If Sean had his way, we'd have been here three hours early," Miranda chided.

"Always the Boy Scout," the senator replied, "Sean, are you ready to take on the Canadian and Mexican negotiators?"

"I'm ready to do the most with what we're offered," Sean admitted.

"No explosives this time, right?" Senator Johnson ribbed his newest employee.

"Well...," Sean grinned, his face drawn in a wry smile, "You *did* hire me to make an impact."

"That I did," the senator laughed, and glancing at his watch, "Should we head to the gate?"

The gavel repeatedly banged to quell the uproar that erupted on the Senate floor. The Senate Majority Leader pleaded to his colleagues to allow him to proceed with the next presenter in the debate. The two sides were at deep odds on deepening the alliance with their neighboring countries, in particular, Mexico.

When the outbursts quelled enough where he could readdress the senate appropriately, "Honorable Senator from Idaho, you have the floor."

Senator Timothy Small strolled comfortably up to the podium. As the ranking minority group member, he had made the trek to the front of the room hundreds of times in his career. It was only in this most recent term that he had come out of the shadows and taken on a more leadership role. He turned to face his audience. Roughly half of the Senate was in attendance for the day's debate. His aide had informed him that his greatest rival, Senator Johnson, was on his way to Mexico and would not return for a week–the very reason Small's party rushed the debate for a vote in his absence.

"Fine members of the Senate. We have too many issues on the floor to manage in a single bill. Let's review the fundamentals of what the committee led by Senator Johnson would have us enact. First, United States citizens would have to abide by Canadian and Mexican conservation statutes. Let's be honest, I can hardly keep our own straight, but now I need to abide by what some French-speaking farmer from the north stipulates about a bird that flies in from across the border? I can't tell a U.S. born goose from a Canadian goose, but we better be damn sure whatever animals we hunt don't migrate from a few miles upwind.

Second, we are supposed to mix our economy with that of the third world to our south? Is Senator Johnson really that fiducially suicidal? The United States has been the most robust economy for the last century because of free enterprise, *not* freeloaders. Why do you suppose those Mexicans and Central Americans come up here? Because they want to share the wealth? Heck no. My fellow senators, if you love America the way I do, a shared economy will kill us. Kill us! We are strong because we are hard workers. We are strong because we do not placate to handouts. If we make trade deals on a weaker dollar for "fairness", it dooms us as a superpower.

Finally, Senator Johnson's view of managing the immigration problem is to let them stay, open the borders to all because we will spread our social system to Mexico, so why should they flock here to our God's country? Because their corrupt government will take the aid, we provide and shove it in their own pockets, and the lowest of their low will continue to slink across our borders.

No, I implore you, my fellow senators, a vote yes on this bill will be a no to the future of America!" Senator Small slammed the thick bill prepared by the Trade and Commerce committee down on the floor and walked back to his seat. At first, the stunned audience paused in silence to take in the Idaho senator's comments. After several moments had ticked by and Senator Small retreated to his seat, a trickle of applause led by the senator from Alabama, and then Texas until nearly half of the members of the Senate were clapping and cheering Senator Small's remarks.

The other half of the senate floor, the half that read the docket in front of them, flipped through the committee's recommendations with puzzled looks as they struggled to find the verbiage that Small had cited. There were elements of each of the scenarios explored. Still, the resulting bill did not grant asylum to immigrants, did not force the U.S. to adopt environmental treaties that they did not ratify, and did not establish the North American equivalent of the euro. It suggested that we would enforce the uniform laws of conservation that were endorsed by all three nations; it opened lines of trade and granted reasonable rights for investors who elected to do business in either Mexico or Canada. The committee recommendations, not reflected in the bill, suggested that improving the economies of the U.S. neighbors would bolster a total improved economy of all of North America as well as reduce the pressures of Mexican citizens to drive northward in search of a better life.

Despite the facts of the bill, Small's rant resonated with enough of the senate to elicit a "Nay" vote on Senator Johnson's bill.

Retreating to his office, Senator Small welled up with his victory. Sometimes a little fear could overcome reality. As far as he was concerned, the bill would have made Mexico the fifty-first state if they had ratified it. And Canada, he would welcome them if they would rid themselves of the French socialist influence. He reveled in the hunting available to him in the British Columbia province to his north. Chuckling to himself, he reckoned, he'd run for the senate there if that ever happened.

Entering the Idaho offices, Small snapped his fingers for his aide, Jerry Rhinehart, to bring him a scotch as he pushed his way into the back room. Tossing the Commerce file onto his desk, he turned to see a guest waiting for him on his leather sofa.

"Harold, this is a pleasant surprise. You have come on a victorious day," the senator smiled at the oil tycoon. Harold Billings and his family had been Senator Small's greatest financial benefactor over his political career.

"Really? I could use some pleasant news. Lately, I am questioning those who are running this once great nation," Billings scoffed, "So, what have you got for me?"

"We have squashed the Johnson Border Bill," Small boasted happily.

"That won't stop him. I hear he's down in Mexico singing *Cumbaya* with the wetbacks *and* the Canucks. Worse, he has President Marshall backing him on his brief adventure," Billings glared at the senator.

"Johnson's a punk. He has no genuine power. If he did, his bill wouldn't have fallen so easily," Small argued.

Billings shot a glance at Jerry Rhinehart, "What was the tally?"

Flipping open his notebook, the aide found the final vote, "73 nay, 68 yea, 69 abstain."

"That doesn't sound overwhelming. If that liberal fool from Oregon had been there to defend the damn thing, it might've passed," the codgerly oil tycoon barked at Small.

"Who cares if it did? It didn't have any teeth. All the bill said was that the three countries would hold a caucus once a year and yap about trade and saving furry creatures. They essentially already do that anyway," Small defended his position.

"You know as well as I do, this is all about perception. You give those yahoos traction, and they will make life more difficult for us, honest, hard-working Americans. We want to know you will take charge, Tim. Don't go soft on me," Billings warned the senator.

"Just picking my battles, Harold. You know diplomacy, these are a bunch of babies we have to manage. We just happen to need most of those babies on our side," Small said coolly, deflect his backer's negativity.

"All right, Small. This zoo is your world; just know you are being watched carefully. We are starting to think those waves you made in Seattle didn't have the impact promised," the oil heir continued his scrutiny.

"I have thought it about too. I think maybe we need to up the ante," Small confided.

"What are you thinking?"

"A lot of unpleasant things happen in Mexico. Senator Johnson may have placed himself and his family in harm's way," Small mused.

"I thought you said he was small potatoes," Billings questioned suspiciously.

"No, it goes way beyond Johnson. I am talking about a big foreign relations incident with Mexico. Stir the pot before that cesspool becomes a goldarn state!" Small bellowed dramatically.

Once Harold Billings felt like he had had his say with the politician whose campaign his organization had bankrolled, he excused himself to tend to other business he had in the District. Small watched the weathered Texan leave the office. As soon as his financier cleared the doorway, the senator pointed towards his aide, "Get Tug Gaskill on the line."

Rhinehart looked up at his boss, "The mercenary? Are you sure, sir?"

The look Small shot across the room to his subordinate snapped the senatorial aide into action. Within moments, the speakerphone indicated the call had been placed.

After several rings, a gravelly voice responded over the speaker, "Gaskill."

"Tug, good to hear your voice?" Small sang out, his inflection overly rosy.

"Senator Small, I was wondering when I'd hear from you," Tug grumbled into the phone.

"You still in the market?"

"I am. All the money that the Hasegawa heist was supposed to provide me was frozen and ultimately seized by the U. S. government," Tug replied.

"I had heard about that. Honestly, I had mixed feelings about the demise of our Japanese friend. That Chavez fellow you hired cocked things up pretty good. Nearly brought down the house with him," Small remarked, a tone of sarcasm ringing through his voice.

"Chavez was all right. Greed can make a man stupid," Tug replied flatly.

"Perhaps. I can't help but think of all the problems that he could have taken out on his way down...," Small lamented.

"Yes, I commissioned him to remove those problems, but obviously he failed," Tug admitted, "Small, not to be ungracious of your call, but... what do you want?"

"I love that about you, Tug, straight and to the point. Listen, I have a job. A big one," Small filled the mercenary in, "How do you feel about war?"

"I've been in a few, but what...," Tug began.

"Have you ever started one?" the senator asked.

"What?"

"I need you to start a war with Mexico…"

Two

The sounds of rapid gunfire resounded in Colonel Reyes' head like a sweet symphony. To the career militant, Mexico had long been the economic stepchild of America, and the World Trade Organization and other treaties only threatened to continue that burden. The one stock and leverage that Mexico had was its alliance with the drug trade that flowed from within and up through its bowels from Central America.

The North American Ecological Alliance would force the government to crack down on the illicit drug market. That was a proposition that the cartel that funded Reyes' group could not tolerate. Clenching a freshly lit cigarillo in his teeth, Reyes walked toward the range as the fifty well-armed soldiers honed their skills.

The targets on the far side of the range tattered into insignificant bits as shells rapidly ejected from the chambers of assault rifles. His employers had weaseled themselves onto the Golden Zone Convention Center project, giving them intimate access to the creation of the structure. Their architects had spun off an exact duplicate of the scale model of the massive contemporary structure. That model sat in Reyes' office as he planned his response to the delegates pouring into the conference.

He had considered an all-out attack on the convention center. Ultimately, he decided that might only draw the two countries even closer together. What they needed was an incident *between* the nations. That is where his group would best deploy. The cartel had mules and plants scattered all over the U. S. They would be called to act, while his assault team would stir up trouble in his own country.

The list of delegates arriving from both nations was quite esteemed. Reyes smiled. The opportunities were abundant in that guest list. Scratched his chin as he withdrew his pen and circled one name in particular–Senator Rick Johnson.

Miranda's grip tightened on Sean's hand as the wheels of the 737 hit the runway of the Mazatlán International Airport. The contingent from the northwest slid out of their first-class seats and meandered down the Jetway. The moment they left the bowels of the airplane, they were hit with the oppressive heat and humidity of the Sea of Cortez funneled coast air.

As they collected their baggage, a barrage of drivers offered to taxi them into town. Wilkins waved the drivers off until he found the one who was waiting patiently behind the throng of drivers. With a slight nod of his head, Wilkins summoned the youthful man forward. In an instant, the fit steward collected the group's baggage on a small cart and whisked them away from the crowd and to a waiting van.

Minutes later, the van was whisking down the highway. The driver leaned back, "Senor Wilkins, it is good to have you back. And Senor Johnson, it is an honor to welcome you to Mazatlan."

"Silverio, it is good to see you again, my friend. I fear it has been too long," Wilkins replied, clapping the driver's shoulder.

"You come back at a marvelous time. Mazatlan is buzzing with renewed zest. The conference center is beautiful, you will love it!" the driver replied and glancing at the mirror, "And who are your friends, the beautiful lady and the… gentleman?"

"Two extraordinary people. Miranda Shaw and Sean Kendall. Ms. Shaw is going to help with the loggerhead turtle reserve being set up south of town. Sean is helping us with public relations for our Alliance," Wilkins responded.

"Mexico is grateful for the work you do. We are hopeful for the chance to grow into a better neighbor, a proud country," Silverio beamed.

"With Senator Johnson's efforts, the entire continent will be the most powerful economy in the world," boasted the senatorial aide.

"We always have been," Senator Johnson cut in, "We just haven't put all the pieces of working together into place before."

"You guys have entertainment set up? I can recommend a fantastic fiesta, or snorkel trip…booze cruise…." the driver offered.

"We will all take part in the conference's fiesta as part of Secretary Lamarillo's guests tonight. Beyond that, I am afraid I will be in meetings most of the week. I do, however, insist my friends take part in some excursions," Senator Johnson smiled.

"Yes, tomorrow, you should have some free time and again on Wednesday during the day," Wilkins said, flipping through his agenda.

"What would my friends like?" Silverio asked, his eyes flitting up to the rearview mirror.

"I would love to go snorkeling!" Miranda exclaimed.

"Ah, yes, turtle lady. I can recommend some delightful spots. The Sea of Cortez emptying here stirs the waters, but there are some secret spots I can have some friends take you to," Silverio informed the group, and turning his attention to Sean, "And for *you* senor? You like tequila? My cousin Frederico runs up to the tequila factory on Wednesdays for a tour. It is a lot of fun. You'll have barbecue, skeet shooting, and the best tequila you will ever put to your lips."

Smiling, Miranda squeezed Sean's hand, "Sounds like fun."

"Let's play Wednesday by ear, I would like to be available if the senator needs me," Sean replied reluctantly.

"I am quite sure your time will be free, Sean, but I am sure Silverio can pull some strings if you go last minute," Wilkins added.

"Oh yes, senor. My cousin, he'll take care of you. You just give me a call, and I'll set it up," Silverio beamed.

"Thank you very much," Sean replied as he took a business card from the driver's outstretched hand.

Looking outside the window, Sean watched the barren land beyond the airport transition into small communities of ramshackle housing with children stirring up dust as they chased each other around the streets. To his eyes, it seemed nearly every house had some deficiency- no windows, no doors, no roofs. Some buildings were little more than concrete walls with tarps strung over the top to provide sun cover. Strings of clothesline ran along the side walls, with clothes collecting as much dust as they probably had before they were washed.

As the van sped along the highway, past the oil derricks, they closed in on Mazatlán. With each passing mile, the buildings became more robust in structure. Dirt roads were replaced by pavement. Neatly pressed school uniforms replaced children's soiled clothing. Still, there was a glaring disparity amongst the residents. The fishermen lined the bay with their tiny skiffs, eking out a subsistent living for their families, mixed in along the street vendors, most of which hailed from the hovel towns Sean had viewed along the highway. Bookending the bay was large, gleaming high-rise hotels where tourists from America, Europe, and Mexican elite, primarily from Mexico City, came to vacation.

It was clear to Sean that the class differences among the residents of Mexico were vast. He wondered what the people who were bussed in from the ramshackle towns to work in the hotels and the new billion-dollar convention center felt. His excitement for the trip was mixed with a feeling of respect for these hard-working people who were so welcoming, despite their disadvantaged versus those that they served.

Pulling into the circular drive of the hotel, the van was instantly met with both hotel employees eagerly collecting their baggage as well as members of the Mexican delegation greeting their visitors. Parting the crowd, a smartly dressed man in a tan suit approached them.

"Senator Johnson, it is an honor to see you again," the man smiled under his thick mustache.

"Secretary Lamarillo, it is always a pleasure," Senator Johnson replied, shaking the Mexican Secretary of Commerce's hand, "The Convention Center looks… magnificent."

"Si, we are very proud. It is the jewel in the center of the Golden Zone. A gleaming symbol of the prosperity of Mexico's future," the commerce secretary cooed and with an outstretched arm, herded them into the lobby, "Come, we must get you comfortable, the afternoon sun in Mazatlan can be quite warm!"

Sean quietly agreed with the diplomat. He felt overdressed for the heat of the tropics, his shirt under his sport coat was riddled with rings of sweat. Following the cheery diplomat, the travel-weary group entered the lush lobby, a miniature rainforest of palm trees and foliage surrounded by a babbling brook that was the home for hundreds of Koi. Sean was relieved as they were met with the breeze from the open veranda that ran the entire expanse of the ocean side of the hotel. Before he could even be greeted to check-in at the front desk, a server was beside them with a tray of frozen margaritas.

"Hola, Senor!" the desk clerk said behind a broad smile, "You are checking in today?"

Sean nodded, stepping up to the desk.

"Welcome to Mazatlan. The beaches are golden, as are the fruits of our ocean. You will have the best seafood in your life," the clerk declared emphatically as she punched in the information for Sean's reservation. Looking up and seeing Miranda sipping her margarita a few steps behind Sean, the clerk added, "The girl, is she with you? She is *muy bonita*."

"Indeed, she is…," Sean replied softly, shifting his weight subconsciously.

"Let's go, Kendall!" Senator Johnson called, "We have a reception to get to, and you need to get out of that monkey suit and into something more tropical." The tall, handsome politician called as he followed the entourage of bellhops toward the bank of elevators.

Sean thanked the check-in clerk and grabbed his bags as he followed the senator. Miranda giggled, as a young man eagerly snatched her bags from her and wheeled them after the group. "I can't wait to change, I'm melting," the marine biologist sighed.

"We cannot have that, *senorita*. I have something sent to your room to refresh you," the smiling boy promised.

"Oh, that's okay. We are going to attend a reception. I am sure I can make it until then. That was very sweet, though," Miranda replied. She swore that the young bellhop blushed.

The senator and Wilkins were led down the hall to their respective suites, and the bellman stopped to open the door to Sean's room. Pausing, he turned to Miranda, "The *senorita* stays here too?"

Uncomfortably, Sean cut in, "No, she has her own room."

"I'm right next door," Miranda beamed, eyeing the number of the adjacent suite.

"Thank you, I can take it from here," Sean said to his bellhop as he fished a handful of pesos from his pocket. Leaning across, he offered bills to the young man toting Miranda's luggage, "Here is for the lady."

"I'll see you soon!" Miranda called as her door was opened.

Inside, a spacious suite welcomed Sean. The bedroom was immediately inside the entry, a compact kitchen and sizeable living room sprawled in front of an enormous bank of sliding glass doors. Pushing aside the layers of pinned up gauze fabric covering the doors, he found the impressive view of the Pacific Ocean rolling to the beach at the foot of the hotel. Quickly, he cast aside the window coverings to open the view to his suite.

As much as he loved the mountains of the Pacific Northwest, the ocean had always called to him. Growing up on the beaches of the New England coast, he thought he would live in a setting such as this. The warm sun beating down on the golden sand, the blue-green waters lapping against the shore, the breezes, the sounds...all of it made him feel so at peace.

The sun streaming through the glass reminded him he had to get out of his clothes into one of the many linen outfits he had packed for the trip. Eager for a post-flight shower, he tossed his jacket on a nearby chair and ripped his shirt off over his head. Moving swiftly through the trail of clothes he was leaving, he startled by a soft but steady knocking. Head cocked, it puzzled him as the knocking did not seem to come from the door, but rather the wall near the door. Leaving the running shower, he turned the corner in the hallway to find a second door. Bursting through with full regalia of luggage, he hadn't noticed when he first entered the room.

As he placed his hand on the doorknob, the gentle rapping continued. Cautiously, he turned the handle and pulled the door slowly open. The image before him was one that Sean had not expected, not so soon. Miranda, her humidity teased auburn hair flanking her shoulders, her brilliant glacier blue eyes, her lips parted in a smile that consumed him in a wave of heat. Silently, he stood there, paralyzed. Their wounded relationship was on the mends, but he had little idea of how to proceed. Now here she was standing in his doorway and...

"Can I come in?" Miranda's voice broke his trance, "Isn't this great? I had the girl at the front desk put me in an adjoining room. We don't need no stinking walls between us."

Dumfounded, Sean's eyes followed her into the room. Miranda raised an eyebrow as she placed a hand flat on his bare chest. "I didn't know that adjoining door would provide so many perks, so quickly," Miranda giggled mischievously.

"I...I was just getting cleaned up," Sean stammered.

"Well, don't let me stop you," Miranda looked at Sean with a playful look that he hadn't seen in some time.

Sean's mind temporarily highjacked at Miranda's affect, he stood with indecision.

Laughing, she waved him off, "Go take your shower. I'm not going anywhere."

Those last words hit Sean square in the chest.

Sean's eyes fixed on hers, the cool pools of blue danced wickedly spirited, finally, words met his lips, "You not going anywhere is exactly where I want you to be."

He moved to kiss her as she continued to press into him.

The dark faded in and out, but the oppressive heat remained constant. Sienna Gutierrez struggled to remain conscious. The box she was in had several small air holes drilled into it, but through the rag that had been stuffed and tied to her mouth, she still found it difficult to breathe. The heat…the heat ailed her the most. Her body felt as though it would explode. Sweat dripped relentlessly off of her forehead, streaking down her face. Each knew winding trail of the salty liquid made her skin itch terribly, though her bonds left her tortured without relief. The sweat pooled to the floor, once mixed with the tears that had long dried up.

The little brunette five-year-old dreamt of being in her daddy's arms – so warm, so safe- and then the image of Consuela collapsing to the floor, blood seeping from her forehead. Those awful men snatching her. She wanted to be home.

As her thoughts drifted in and out of pleasurable and nightmarish postcards, it startled her as her prison walls shook. The wooden crate she had been stuffed in moved like this once before. It seemed like days ago to Sienna. That was when she went from cold to hot. When the men first tied her up and placed her in the box, she was freezing. The air that came in through the holes was so cold, so damp. Countless hours later, it was as if a blast of air from an oven had streamed in. Disoriented, she could hear voices. They were all speaking Spanish. She listened intently to what the voices were saying.

"It is my shipment, I want it now!" one man bellowed in Spanish.

"You must wait for customs clearance just like everyone else, *amigo*."

"I'm not your *amigo,* and I do not want to wait for frigging customs. This shipment is a priority for Tiburon LaCosta. We are taking it," the first voice demanded.

"I don't care if it is for President Lopez, you have to wait."

A third voice could be heard coming closer. The voice rattled quickly. To Sienna, the man sounded nervous. "*Senors,* forgive me for this inconvenience, this case has customs approval, it can be released!"

Without another word, the crate again was shuffled around before being placed down once more. The sound of van doors closing followed by high pitched squeals of nails ripped through wood. Soon Sienna was straining through her weary, dark brown eyes. The light was all-consuming at first. Her dark prison engulfed in a blinding blast of white. Slowly, blurry images of faces staring at her began to take shape. Her gag and bindings were quickly removed. The relief was immense for the frightened little girl. Just to have the freedom of movement and air other than the super-heated oxygen in the box was enormously comforting. But yet, the faces...

"Here, drink this, you'll be okay," one of the faces said to her, holding an opened bottle of water to her lips. Her sore, cracked skin eagerly lapped up the water provided to her.

"Not too much all at once, it will make you sick," the voice said to her.

As she drank the water, her senses seemed to flood back to her. She found herself surrounded by a ring of onlookers. One man had a delivery uniform on; the others wore military-style clothing, though not of either the Mexican or U.S. uniforms she had seen on trips with her father. These were different. Not as neat and crisp, the emblems and badging seemed all wrong, but she couldn't quite figure out why.

"I am sorry you had to go through that. It was necessary," the man who gave her water said.

"Where are you taking me? Where is my father?" Sienna's dry throat gasped.

"Shh. It is okay, my dear. You will see your father again, provided he does what is right," the man tried to comfort her, "That shouldn't be too difficult, he *does* love Mexico, doesn't he?"

"Yes, of course! My father works for Mexico. He is an ambassador."

"He doesn't work for Mexico yet, but he will!" the man in the delivery uniform shouted.

The man with the water turned to face the delivery man, like a coiled snake, his arm lashed out and smacked the man in the face, "Silence!" His snarl relinquished as he once more turned to Sienna, "Forgive Paco, he is a principled man, just not as refined or as schooled as say your father and me. He does not understand decorum. Suffice it to say, we are soldiers for Mexico, your father is in trouble, we felt it best to keep you safe."

Numb from hours of torture and fear, the only response Sienna could offer was silence. Her brown eyes had glazed and darkened far beyond what any five-year-old should. Gone was the vibrant, playful sparkle that met her father each day. In its place was a blank stare that allowed the conversation to cease. Her own quagmire of thoughts was more soothing to her than the twisted words from this horrible man. Shifting her gaze to the brown and beige countryside that flowed by the window, she drifted into a trance, filled with visions of her father's open arms reaching out to her.

Tommy Haskins wiped the stream of sweat from his bow. His heart raced as he questioned how he had gotten himself into this situation. Things were going so well. He had just passed his Staff Sergeant's test; he had an incredible fiancé at home, everything he could ask for at his young age. Then the tip. The can't lose odds on the Final Four winner. The can't lose odds that lost and led to the jeweler's phone calls demanding payment, the bank threatening to repossess his fiancé's Mustang, his application for off-base housing denied. Then the mysterious phone call. One simple task and his financial woes would be instantly resolved. His fiancé would never know what he had done. His fiancé's parents, who hated the fact that their daughter was marrying a marine instead of one of those lawyers she had gone to school with, would never know.

He looked over his shoulder to ensure that he was alone. As he shuffled into the cargo bay, he tried to justify what he was about to do. It's not like he was handing the weapons over to terrorists. These were U.S. military personnel. He was probably helping a covert ops team that had to acquire their gear off the books. Probably ordered by the president himself. He was doing his duty as a patriot.

The self-talk didn't seem to relieve the jagged pit that had formed in his stomach. He knew deep down that what he was doing was wrong. Flipping through the dossier he was holding; he found the crate that had been requested. The latest in long-distance firepower sent over on the military transport from AIR, Inc. in Great Britain, one of the foremost defense contractors specializing in sniper and sniper-rocket conversion rifles. The case was sealed in an air and watertight container. His job was to see that the four by 6-foot crate found its way into the waters just inside the Intracoastal Waterway. He looked at his watch; they were due to dock at the Sunny Point Depot north of Southport in forty-minutes. If he waited any longer, the tugs would be hooked up, and lights along with dozens of eyes would be focused on his vessel. He had to act now.

Slipping the tongue of the dolly under the case, he pulled back and scooted down the dark alley of the cargo hold. With each step, the wheels of the dolly squeaked, each squeak sending chills down soon-to-be Staff Sergeant Haskins' spine. Fortunately, the heist couldn't have been planned on a more perfect night. The early spring storm brought howling wind and rough surf slamming against the side of the boat, providing some degree of comfort.

The overloaded vessel that was running from the Navy yards in Virginia to the weapons storage depot in North Carolina was breaking countless regulations to achieve efficiency – the Navy was spread thin with fleets strewn throughout the oceans of the Middle East and Indian-Asian coastlines. The likelihood of a singularly lost item could blow under the radar, with officials not wanting to put their signatures for the vessel's condition on the line. Haskins just had to make sure he wasn't caught.

Responsible for the placement of the hold items, Haskins had ensured that the case was in close proximity to the outside and easy access to the edge. Checking his watch, he knew his friend Ensign Bryan would make his walk-by in less than a minute. Tugging hard, Haskins fought the swells and brought the case to the exposed deck. Knowing at this stage it was do or die, he didn't hesitate in plowing forward, ramming the case to the rail. Bending down, Haskins caught the lower edge of the case with his fingertips and heaved the container off the side and into the frothing convergence of the Atlantic, the Intra-coastal Waterway and the emptying Cape Fear River.

Without taking the time to watch his handiwork splashdown, he spun towards the hold. His heart stopped as Ensign Bryan was marching towards him, the beam from his flashlight cutting through the diagonal rain.

"Haskins! What the hell are you doing?" Bryan called sharply, "Having a smoke without me?"

Awash of relief fell over Haskins. He had thought for sure they had seen his task, "Don't worry, bud. I'm not breaking without you," Haskins breathed deep and looking at his hand attached to the hand truck, "Some joker didn't latch this down, the storm shook it loose, and I had to chase down the deck. Damn thing nearly went overboard."

"Well, put it away. Last break before we dock, the tugs'll be here in fifteen."

Disappearing into the hold, Haskins leaned against the nearest stack of crates. His entire body trembled, and he felt sick. He hoped he had done the right thing. If not, he hoped he would never find out.

Tug Gaskill sat in a dark warehouse in an old industrial district that had fallen derelict years past when I-40 had been stretched to the coast. The crate he used as a seat, like the others littering the warehouse, had been liberated from the U.S. military. It never ceased to amaze him how easy it was to stock his coffers when he needed to at the disposal of the U.S. government.

The team he had assembling in front of him was one the best he had ever created. The fall-out from the wars in the Middle East had created a large pool of candidates who came back to lost jobs, crumbled marriages, and other misfortunes that had fallen during the course of their serving the country. Tug put their unique services to use, paid them well, and offered a little retribution to the ingrates that made up the citizen of the country they had all served.

"Fellas," Tug called his crew to attention, "Some of you know me, others have come with tremendous recommendations. Most of you have reasons to be… disgruntled with this great country of ours. I don't blame you. I felt that way once before as well. What I have learned since my days in the uniform is that our country is still great. It is just led by idiots. They are not all our enemies, they need our help in making the decisions they are too scared to make themselves. Our job is to help them along. We have the chance to make a difference. Make this country great like it once was, like we know what it can be. George, you grew up in Texas. What is your town like now?"

"That town is gone. It belongs to the Mexicans now. Illegals have destroyed the place!" George shouted.

"Bill, how about you? Is San Diego the way you remember it when you were a kid?"

"Hell no! Those bleeding-heart liberals are letting anybody come across the border and get free health care, put their kids in our schools, everything. There might as well not be a border."

"That's the problem we intend to fix," Tug said flatly, turning his attention to the screen behind him. Projecting off of a laptop, an image of the United States-Mexican border displayed. "Fellas, we are going to start a war. That war will close that border forever!"

Alberto Gutierrez was practically floating in orbit. All morning long, the accolades of his group's efforts to secure the free trade agreement and the prospect of what it would mean to the people of Mexico flowed non-stop. He beamed as he strode through the halls of the Manhattan embassy en route to his office. Staffers and appointees to the Mexican President Lopez stopped him to shake his hand and congratulate him on the victory. He was notified that President Lopez himself would call this morning.

Arriving at his office, he motioned his aide to have a seat on the couch and plopped into his luxurious leather seat behind his desk. Before he could even pick up the dossier and the updated schedule for his speech, the phone rang. Beaming, he expected the voice of President Lopez.

"Ambassador Gutierrez…"

"Senor Gutierrez, you have thirty seconds to understand the situation, so do not speak until asked," the voice snapped, dropping the jovial expression immediately from the ambassador's visage, "We have someone precious to you."

From what seemed like in a cave, a very shaky, frightened Sienna called out, "Daddy!"

"Do not speak! I know you have questions, and I know you do not want your little girl harmed. You cannot allow the signing of the Free Trade Agreement. If you do, your darling daughter will die. We have operatives within every branch of the military and policia, if we hear that you have contacted any of them, she will die," the cold, even voice demanded, "If you understand, simply say 'yes'. If you comply, we will contact you with assurance that Sienna will be delivered back home."

The ambassador was nearly bursting with anger, fear, and worry, but managed to a very calm response, "Yes."

The phone went dead instantly. Gutierrez stared at it blankly, wishing that the conversation had not really taken place. His aide across the room was the only reason that his emotions weren't unleashed on the inanimate object on his desk. Knowing that his demeanor had abruptly changed, he could feel the loss of color in his cheeks. He looked over to Cortez.

"What is it, sir? What's wrong?" the aide asked.

"The Agreement. It isn't ready," the ambassador lied and switched his gaze to the window. Somewhere outside of the embassy in that grey world was his daughter.

"What do you mean it isn't ready? All of the pieces are in place, both sides have agreed…"

"It's not ready!" Gutierrez slammed his fist on the desk as he returned his eyes to Cortez, "There are some elements we had conceded that after further review, must be worked out."

"Forgive me, sir, but what?" Cortez stammered, his furrowed brows emphasizing his confusion.

"The taxation structure will cost our country millions. We can't afford that. The Americans can withstand the hit. If we could just get them to grandfather in a safety timeline to allow us to get on our feet and then withdraw the clause, it would speed our turn around," Gutierrez said half-heartedly.

"The committee has been through that. We agreed to the terms. An evolutionary turn in our economy," Cortez protested.

"Slow growth for us while the U.S. takes advantage," Gutierrez snapped, and realizing that his actions were not sensible. If he were in his aide's shoes, he would be feeling the same. These arguments had been born out, and the ambassador had always been in favor of the quickest solution to get the U.S. on board. This abrupt change will raise some serious concerns. Calming his voice, he continued, "All I'm asking for is a delay. I think we should run this through the committee one last time, to see if we can barter for leniency."

Exasperated and confused with his boss' request, Cortez shrugged his shoulders and agreed to push the program back to the committee one last time. "So, what do I tell the press?"

Gutierrez sat thoughtfully for a moment, "Nothing just yet. Let me make a few calls, and then we will see what kind of timeline we can produce. I'd rather come to them with a make-up date than empty unknowns."

The ambassador watched his aide shake his head and leave the office with the file in hand that Gutierrez knew would change the lives of all Mexicans forever. As soon as the office door closed behind Cortez, Gutierrez frantically stabbed at the numbers on his phone. The line rang and rang and rang until his wife's voice could be heard on the answering machine with Sienna chiming in in the background. Dialing one of his security detail, he dispatched his most trusted man to discretely run to the house and visually inspect the site. In the meantime, he prepared for the political fallout that was sure to come. Thirteen years as the Mexican Ambassador to the U.S. Likely, this would be his last.

Most of all, he twirled the picture of Sienna on his desk. Her perky brown eyes beaming at the camera while Minnie Mouse hugged her. The photo was taken just a month ago. He prayed he would see his little girl again.

Three

In a blur, the low figure crept past the scope. Sergeant Diego Martin carefully adjusted his settings. Soon, just over the shoulder of the steel silhouette target, he saw it. A reddish-tan wolf twenty-five yards past his target. Dialing in, Martin held his breath. Gently, he squeezed his finger on the trigger, sending the shot ringing through the desert commune. Following his shot through his long-range scope, Martin saw the oblivious creature buckle as his shot hit home, sending the wolf tumbling into the dust, a meal for the scorpions and vultures.

"You missed Martin! And here you were supposed to be the big shot sniper!" Lance Corporal Guerrero stared out on the makeshift range.

"Did I?" Martin handed his field binoculars to the range instructor, "Look on the ground twenty-one hundred meters."

Guerrero snatched the field glasses and panned his view towards the target and then further downrange. Sure enough, covered in dust, there was the carcass of a dead animal. A vulture had already landed and was taking stock at his lunch. "Not bad. I missed judged. Definitely on the outer range of the sniper rifle. Good kill soldier!"

Handing the binoculars back to the sniper who was readying himself to attack the posted targets once more, Guerrero's attention pulled away from his men and to the cloud of dust approaching on the compound on the one road in. They didn't have many visitors in the box canyon. Chewing on the stub of his cigar, he strode toward the crude oval parking area at the end of the road. Two Range Rover SUVs were followed by a customized Hummer and two more Range Rovers.

Coming to an abrupt stop, men jumped out of each of the lead and trailing Rovers and moved to flank the passenger doors of the Hummer. One of the men opened the passenger door of the Hummer while the other men stood with semi-automatic weapons to the ready. A man dressed from head to toe in a tailored white suit, white shirt, and tie stepped out. His head was covered with a white brimmed hat, and he removed his gold-toned sunglasses as Guerrero moved closer.

"Lance Corporal Guerrero?" the man asked.

"Yessir…"

"My name is Tiberon La Costa. We have a mutual friend in Colonel Reyes. I was told that you were a savvy man who loved his country and could make things happen."

"I suppose. What is this about?" Guerrero asked, his tone drenched in wary suspicion. His eyes flitted from each heavily armed sentry and then back to the man speaking. In the reflection of the Hummer's windows, he could see his own men taking sniper positions to his flank.

"Please, I know this must seem like an intrusion," La Costa held his hands up in front of him, "I do not normally become involved this closely in these matters, but this is a special instance. I was asked to seek you out and offer my services."

"Services for what? The Mexican Army supports all of our needs."

"Not what I have to provide, I assure you," La Costa grinned.

"I will call Reyes and see what this is all about!" Guerrero snapped, tiring of the cryptic conversation.

"No need...," La Costa pointed in the air. In the distance, a black dot approached, and soon, the American-made Apache Helicopter came into view, "Ah, there is Colonel Reyes now."

The air surrounding the helipad stirred in a cloud of dust as the helicopter set down. In moments, the rotors slowed, and several men climbed out of the machine, Colonel Reyes in the center of them. Seeing the crowd near the SUVs, he strode toward them.

Guerrero met Reyes as he approached, "Sir, what is this man doing here? He says he is connected to you."

"He is Sergeant. I need you to send any men who are not loyal on leave immediately and then join me in the command post," Reyes kept walking toward La Costa.

"Sir, they are all loyal," Guerrero called from behind his superior.

"We'll soon see," Reyes smiled as he reached La Costa. The two men exchanged a brief hug, each slapping the other heartily on the back, "These are important times, my friend."

"Indeed, they are. Are you sure you have the right personnel for this?" La Costa asked.

"I do. Perhaps a demonstration?" Reyes asked with raised eyebrows.

La Costa nodded as they led him toward the firing range. Reyes turned to Guerrero, "Who is last in the regiment testing battery?"

"Private Jolla, he is still indecisive in the live-fire exercises," the sergeant replied.

"Send him to manually reset the range targets and assemble your squad on the line."

Guerrero signaled his men to take position at the firing line and instructed his youngest cadet to reset the steel targets downrange. As the Private Jolla reached the third steel silhouette, Reyes ordered his sergeant, "Command them to take him out."

"Excuse me, sir?" Guerrero looked at his superior in bewilderment.

"Take him out, sergeant!"

"Men, Jolla is your objective, fire at will!" Guerrero commanded.

After a moment of hesitation, an erratic array of shots rang through the canyon. The young private's back peppered with dozens of shots from the line, launching him forward into the dirt. "Cease fire!" Guerrero cried.

Colonel Reyes motioned the men who exited the Apache with him toward the line. One by one, they inspected the weapons of the squad. When they finished, they pulled two from the ranks. In escort, they brought them to the viewing deck. "Full loads, sir," one of Reyes' men called out.

Guerrero grew pale and in understanding the Colonel's intent, unleashed on the two men, "You disobeyed a direct order! You are unfit for this unit if you cannot follow commands."

"But Jolla...," one of the men stammered. He was cut off quickly as Guerrero struck the soldier in the face with a gloved hand.

"Silence! You have demonstrated your inability already, do not insult me further by opening your pathetic mouth!" Guerrero snarled, "Perhaps it should have been the both of you out there instead of Jolla!"

Pleased with his test, Reyes turned to La Costa, "Let's get out of this heat and discuss what I have brought you out to this desert for."

Pausing, the colonel turned to Guerrero, "Sergeant, take the clips out of their guns and put them in the simulator. This could be a splendid exercise for the squad."

"Yessir."

"And, Sergeant…don't ever hesitate with one of my orders again."

Senator Johnson stood in the lobby, shaking hands with delegates from all three countries represented. Canada's Minister of Commerce and Foreign Trade Jack DuPont joined him. "Rick, good to see you. So, we're going to get this done."

"Looks like it, Jack. We've had our difficulties. I think President Marshall's support helped us push it through to the Senate vote. Still have some work to do there, it is a heady issue. Senator Small is trying to ride a platform to derail any agreements," Senator Johnson replied.

"There is some similar sentiment in our parliament, but I think if the U. S. goes with it, so will we," DuPont conceded, "What do you suppose Small is trying to gain?"

"I don't know for sure. He had been quiet, going with the flow until recently. He seems to catch any publicity he can at the moment. I suppose this as big a stage as any. He's trying to pass the Trade Agreement off as unpatriotic," Johnson shrugged, and then looking past the crowd, he perked up, "Hey Jack, here's someone I want you to meet. Sean, over here!" Sean and Miranda wriggled their way through the crowd to the Senator.

"Commerce Minister DuPont, Sean Kendall, and Miranda Shaw," Johnson introduced the two, "Sean saved my life – *twice,* so I figured I better bring him aboard my staff. Miranda is a world-class biologist. She specializes in whales off our coasts."

"It is a pleasure," DuPont extended his hand to the two, "Saved his life, are you in law enforcement?"

"No, sir, just in the right place at the right time," Sean replied humbly, his cheeks flushing with the accolade.

"And Ms. Shaw, perhaps we could use your hand in protecting the Belugas in the waters between our borders. They seem in a constant battle between our government's industrial trespasses."

"I have read a lot about it. They are extremely endangered, and their habitat is threatened by manufacturing plants along both coasts. I'd love to come visit and assess the situation for myself," Miranda smiled.

Wilkins found Secretary Lamarillo weaving through the crowd, a large contingent surrounding him. "There is our host, is everyone ready to go?"

The seas parted as Lamarillo's men made their way toward the waiting line of dark-tinted Cadillac SUVs in the cobblestone drive. "He's quite popular," Sean mentioned as he watched the adoration expressed by the hotel staff as the Mexican dignitary walked by.

"He is, quite. Senator and Minister, would you join the secretary in his car? The rest of you can follow in the next vehicle, yes?" Silverio had snaked through the crowd to meet the group. Holding his hand out to direct the men to join Lamarillo's group, he waved to Sean and Miranda to follow him, "You two can ride with me!"

Following the beaming government staffer, Miranda grabbed Sean's hand, and they climbed into the backseat of the leather-clad vehicle. One by one, the shining trucks pulled out of the cobblestone drive and weaved their way to the palace-like building for the fiesta. "Your rooms are pleasant?" Silverio asked his riders.

"Oh, they're magnificent! I think I could live on one of the balconies alone," Miranda smiled.

"Good. We like our guests to be comfortable. I think the work that your senator is doing will improve the lives of millions of people. Good, hard-working people," Silverio said, "He is a good man, Senator Johnson, isn't he?"

"He is," Sean agreed, "Rick is one of the most honest, down-to-earth men I have ever met, especially in politics."

Silverio laughed, "Politics can be very corrupt here. It can be difficult to know who to trust."

"You trust Lamarillo?" Sean asked.

"Yes. Yes, I do. He is the example of what typifies all that is good in Mexico. Family first, take care of people. He would make a good president," Silverio replied, "In fact, his family is coming tonight. He brings them whenever he can."

'That's great. It is always refreshing to see the human side in our politicians," Miranda said.

As the truck turned the corner to the Opera House, the staffer exclaimed, "Uh oh!"

Looking over the driver's shoulder, Sean saw what Silverio was concerned about, a vast throng of protesters were pushing their way to obstruct the entrance to the opera house, "I guess not everybody is happy with the Trade Conference."

"There is always resistance to things that are new," Silverio agreed, "There are many in the government that oppose Lamarillo. They fear that he will take Mexico out of the hands of the corrupt."

"These look like regular citizens, why would they oppose that?" Sean asked.

"The corruption runs deep. You might be surprised how many people depend on illegal trade. Some fishermen do not catch fish. Policemen that do not apprehend criminals. Politicians who look the other way. And a closed border...a proper border would destroy a prevalent business in trafficking the less fortunate to your country," Silverio responded.

The truck pulled to a stop and waited for security personnel to push the crowd back and clear the entrance to the opera house. The clash was brief, though escalated briefly as some in the crowd hurled bottles as the security staff. The effort to secure order was almost brutal as the security detail was supplemented with the *policia,* and the protesters were pinned to the ground before being loaded into several vans that were quickly whisked away. When control was maintained, the doors to the SUVs opened, and the Fiesta goers meandered inside.

Silverio led Sean and Miranda to a large table upfront, seating them alongside Senator Johnson and Wilkins. Secretary Lamarillo stood up and approached the two, "I am very sorry you had to witness that disturbance. There is an element throughout Mexico very resistant to change."

"I think that is what makes our countries great, our citizens can voice their concerns publicly without fear of reprisal," Senator Johnson added, trying to relieve Lamarillo of his embarrassment.

"Provided they do not resort to physical disobedience," Lamarillo agreed and swinging to a more upbeat tone, "Come, I would like you to meet my wife, Carissa. The most important thing in my life."

Secretary Lamarillo held out his hand for his wife to join them. Soon the brief, but violent entry into the Opera House was forgotten, and they were consumed by festive music, rounds of tequila, and traditional Mexican fare.

The SUV that Tug drove bounced along the washboard dirt road. The ranch that the drive led to had been long abandoned. Tug's recon had told him of an enormous barn that though rickety, would work well to conceal most of the trucks that were making their way. Situated mere miles from the Mexican border, the forgotten New Mexico ranch was going to make a suitable staging area for their plans.

Two more trucks came to a stop behind Tug's SUV. Hopping out of their vehicles, the men instantly began to search the few remaining outbuildings on the ranch as well as the giant barn for any vagrants or other unwanted guests. Door by door, the men kicked their way through, their barrel-mounted lights of their assault rifles illuminating each crevice of the buildings.

The outbuildings secure, the team tackled the barn. Upon entry, there were signs of previous inhabitants – old bean cans, discarded water bottles, and tattered clothing littered a corner of the rickety barn. One of the scouts climbed the ladder leading to a loft, carefully scaling over sections where the rungs had rotted away and fallen to the floor. As the mercenary peered over the edge, he found several men and women huddling in a corner. Hearing the team's arrival, they stowed away in the loft, hoping to avoid detection.

Training his light and muzzle of his weapon at the group, the mercenary called in his find, "Tug, this is Scott. I got a group of wetbacks here in the loft. What would you like me to do with them?"

"Bring 'em down. I'll send Byron over to corral them at the base of the ladder."

"Roger that," Scott confirmed and motioned with his weapon for the group of immigrants to make their way down the ladder, "Let's go amigos. Andale!"

Frightened, one by one, the group of immigrants silently descended the ladder and were met by another armed man at its base. When the last one reached the floor of the barn, Scott followed, "Barn is secure."

The main doors were drug open, and the SUV and two pick-ups were driven inside. Tug hopped out of the SUV and surveyed the situation.

"What do you want us to do, boss?" Byron asked, watching Tug's eyes move from man to woman to child, eleven in all, three of them children.

"Wrong place, wrong time," Tug sighed as he shook his head, "Take them to one of the outbuildings. They are collateral that need to be silenced."

Reluctantly, the two men guided the group immigrants out the barn and into one of the dilapidated shacks beyond the barn. Grateful for the silencer, the shots would not be heard, and the brief round of screams would not travel to unwanted ears. As the rest of his men assembled, he had four branch out to the quadrants of the property to maintain a secure perimeter. He posted one man in the loft of the barn in a sniper position that afforded a one-hundred- and eighty-degree view of the north side of the ranch, where any traffic would come on the rutted road.

Over the radio, the sniper reported a dust trail heading in on the road. Climbing to the loft himself, Tug trained his field glasses towards the long, winding drive, "It's our first shipment. There should be three more, keep a lookout, and advise when you see more traffic. I don't want to be blindsided by the Border Patrol or some yokel sheriff poking his nose around."

Leaving his man to keep an eye on the road, Tug descended the ladder and waved a man to open the barn doors once more to allow the freight truck to enter. Rolling up the doors, his crew began pulling cases out of the container and stacking them in sections as their leader had instructed. Tug was as competent a leader as he was ruthless. Leaving beyond a promising career in Special Forces, he abandoned the military and became one of the most feared rogue mercenaries. His political views and lust for money opened him up to a world of kill for money enterprise.

Surveying the scene below, he watched as his men unloaded the Barrett sniper rifles, the Steyhr assault rifle-convertible grenade launchers, the Tomahawk cruise missiles. All distinct weapons known world-wide as crucial parts of the U.S. arsenal – each an integral part of selling the statement that they were tasked with making.

Four

Sean opened a single, tentative eye. He feared the pains of the previous evening's tequila-infused elbow-rubbing, dancing and small-talking would have on his body. The stream of light shooting through the slits in the shutters urged him out of slumber. He eyed the empty liter bottle of water on the nightstand - a good sign that he had taken the most basic of preventative measures. Resigning to complete the task of getting the day started, he kicked off the single sheet and rolled his legs off the side of the bed.

Sitting straight, his mind slowly worked through his body, starting with his head and traveling to his toes, ensuring that no residual effects were present. Pleased, he was surprised that except for a dry mouth, he had escaped any maladies potentiated by the reception.

Crossing the room to pull another water bottle from the fridge, he found the adjoining door to Miranda's room wide open. Unable to resist, he paused in the doorway. Across the room, in her own bed, the auburn-haired marine biologist that had stolen his

Looking straight into her luminous eyes, Sean leaned forward to kiss her, pressing softly against her lips as she wrapped her hands around his neck. The touch, mixed with the warmth and comfort. A mix he had missed while they were apart.

Miranda grabbed his hand, pulling him off of the couch, "Come on, we have more turtles to save." Pausing at their adjoining door, she added, "*After* we brush our teeth. Tequila – not so good the next day."

Sean could barely hear the knock on the door over the Miranda's blow dryer. Figuring it was Wilkins coming to notify him of a change in the itinerary, he ambled across the room. As he looked through the peephole, he was surprised to see the grinning face of his friend Adam Raines standing in the threshold.

Grinning, he swung the door open, "What are *you* doing here?"

Adam's face washed into a look of mock offense, "Well, that's a fine way to be greeted after flying all the way here on a red-eye. I expected you to be a better host, Mr. Kendall."

Sean had expected some sort of sarcastic greeting from the man in his doorway. Adam Raines was known for his dry, sarcastic sense of humor – a feature that helped to disarm the Fish and Wildlife Officer's imposing physique – at six-five and a well-proportioned 250 pounds, his affable nature, red-hair, and relentless grin made him appear not as threatening. As Sean's best friend, the two were like brothers. Sean knew Adam to be fiercely loyal, someone reliable when the need arose.

Ignoring his friend, he peered around the lumbering man to the much more demure, Laura Raines, "Ah, now *there* is a welcome visitor." Smiling, Sean reached out his arms and hugged the slight brunette.

Beckoning the two in, Sean re-asked his question, "Seriously, what *are* you guys doing here? I didn't think the big lug ever left the northwest."

"He won't for *me*," Laura chided.

"Aw c'mon now. When I was in Spec Ops, I had landed in nearly every corner of the globe. I just found the northwest to be the best. And with you, honey, I have everything I need there," Adam grinned and poked at his wife, "The good Senator sent us an invitation. Figured I might be able to keep you out of trouble."

"*You* keep *me* out of trouble? Are you sure the invite was meant for you?" Sean asked.

"That's what I told him. But he insisted on coming with me anyway," Laura sighed.

"So, Johnson's man Wilkins called and said the senator wanted to find a way to thank me for helping him in Seattle. He thought having a little fun in the sun would be a good way to repay the debt, and we couldn't disagree," Adam filled in his friend, "We thought it would be more fun to surprise you."

"I'm surprised," Sean admitted, "Though I'm not sure how much I'll be able to hang with you guys, the conference schedule is pretty jam-packed."

"Wilkins thought you would say that, so he has us booked on an excursion today. Your day off for good behavior. He said today was a bunch of good feely elbow-rubbing stuff, so you have a little time to play," Adam said.

The adjoining room door creaked open, and a voice called out, "Sean, who are you talking to?"

"Well, Ms. Shaw. An adjoining door…?" Adam raised a disapproving, playful eyebrow.

"Adam Raines? Oh, my goodness…what in the world are *you* doing here?"

A quizzical expression drew on Adam's face, "I see you two have the same manners. Laura, will you teach these two ingrates how to greet guests?"

"Laura? Hold on…I'll be over in a moment."

Adam shot his friend a grin.

Laura punched her husband in the arm, "Leave them alone, Adam, they've been through a lot."

"So, what's this excursion you mentioned?" Sean asked.

"All set up through a Lamarillo, somebody or other…," Adam shrugged, "Supposed to meet down in the lobby at ten."

The big wildlife officer pushed through open the sliding glass door, "Man, this place is nice. Johnson sure set us up well."

"Yeah, great view. We could throw a heck of a party out on that deck," Sean agreed, "Are you guys staying here?"

"Yep. Right down the hall, so we can keep an eye on you kids."

"I heard that!" Miranda called from the next room.

"What is it with women and their bionic ears? Anyway, we stowed our stuff, hopped into Mexicali clothes, and beat on your door."

"Hi, guys! Welcome to Mazatlán," Miranda called, arms outstretched to hug the two newcomers, "I can't believe you're here!"

"Don't mind him," Laura sighed, "He's even more obnoxious on vacation."

"So, what's this mysterious excursion I overheard you talking about?" Miranda asked.

"I guess we get to go to a Tequila factory that some friend of Lamarillo's owns, he's the guy Johnson's working with, right? Then we stop at his ranch and have authentic Mexican lunch, shoot some skeet, the ladies get to ride horses…"

"Sounds great!" Miranda said excitedly, "If we're leaving at ten, we still have time for breakfast. Clarissa was telling me about this great spot right down the road…"

President Marshall sat in the blue room across from his Chief of Staff and the Secretary of State. Fingers clasped together, he held them under his chin, taking in the latest poll on the North American Trade Alliance. The numbers were so evenly split on almost every point, he knew any misstep could spoil the balance, and his hopes for retaining office would crumble away. For a moment, he wondered how an entire administration could be hinged on a single resolution. He had successfully avoided a recession - if barely, the crises in the Middle East and Asia were quelled recent breakthroughs in sustainable bio-derived fuels prevented having to tap into the ANWAR province's oil reserves…though the last four years had been tenuous, he felt that his administration had done an admirable job.

Finally, he pulled his hands away from his chin and spoke, "The initial push in the Senate was pulled back for revision, led by Small?"

"Yessir, the committee worked around the clock to tweak some details that were hanging it up – removing the context that either the Mexican or Canadian governments could administer punishment for conservation violations, flattening out the taxes that could be charged across the borders and removing completely any tariffs between the nations," Henry Richards, the president's chief of staff and confidant since entering politics, said, "About Small, sir. It would seem he is serious about opposing you in the next election. He seems hell-bent to take any resolution you recommend and running it through the meat grinder."

"That's politics," Marshall shrugged, "Like the free market, competition makes us all work a little harder."

"I wish we could have delayed this bill until after the election," Richards started before the president cut him off.

"I wish I were a little more handsome, but that won't help me look any better," Marshall laughed, "We need to maintain focus on what we can control. This treaty resolves a lot of issues that have plagued our country for decades – illegal immigration, inequitable trade practices, worthless environmental agreements. We just need to make sure that all three nations maintain accountability."

"Yessir."

"I agree with the president Henry," Katherine McAdams, the Secretary of State, nodded, "I have been working closely with both Canada and Mexico. They seem to echo our concerns, and from the top down, they want to see this accord be a success. Senator Johnson's team has a pretty good grasp of what is at stake and has created a designated task force to help see it through. Canada and Mexico are establishing similar working groups, and that should provide enough transparency to make sure we are fulfilling our obligations. The press is the press. We all know how ugly it gets the closer we are to election season. I'm not sure we had much of a choice to go through with this, it is more about what we do with it once the accord is signed."

"Most polls are calling the administration centrist. At the end of the day, most of America is closer to the center than either of the polls. I don't see that as a bad thing. Let the far-left and the far-right squabble. We have to make decisions that are on par with the average American," President Marshall tried to calm is number one man.

"Where the "average" citizen is concerned, is how much we can trust Mexico. Everyone knows what is in it for them —some hope for financial stability, but among the corruption of the power base and depravity of the masses, how long before they bring us down?" Richards warned.

Senator Johnson followed Wilkins into the conference room. Set up on the top floor of the recently finished executive tour adjacent to the Golden Zone Convention Center, the hall offered a commanding view of the Pacific Ocean. Seeing Secretary of Commerce Lamarillo and his staff standing near a lavish spread of pastries and fresh fruit.

Extending his hand, the senator greeted the Mexican dignitary, "Thank you for your hospitality last night. The fiesta was wonderful, and it was a pleasure to experience the culture of Mexico."

"Tell me," Lamarillo put his hand on Johnson's arm and looked at with a serious expression on his face, "The tequila we sampled last night, it was far better than you expected, yes?"

The senator smiled warmly, "Indeed. I was very impressed. I don't mind telling you, back home, the mere thought of drinking tequila makes my stomach churn. What we drank last night was excellent."

"People are often surprised. Good tequila is like vodka. There is a broad range of quality from exceptional to well…the swill we send to the U.S. distributors," Lamarillo explained, "A good example of what our accord can do for us. There are quality products that do not seem to make it north of the border. With your help, Senator Johnson, the good people of Mexico, the hard workers can finally be rewarded for their efforts, and in turn, we can perhaps stop spilling our less desirable inhabitants into your country's lap."

Lifting the coffee cup Wilkins had slipped to him, Johnson smiled, "I'll drink to that Mr. Secretary."

"Your congress and senate have passed the agreement?"

"Yes. We implemented the changes that you and I had discussed. It passed, and with the strong blessing of President Marshall. And your legislature?"

"It has been approved. As a symbol of goodwill, our ambassador to the U.S. will announce our passage in a press conference this morning. We felt an international stage would cement our feelings towards the accord and our greatest ally, the United States."

Two gleaming topless Humvees pulled to a stop under the arched adobe entrance to the Royal Villas hotel. A grinning Silverio pushed his sunglasses to the top of his head, "You guys are punctual. I like that."

Hopping out of the lead truck, he helped Miranda and Laura climb aboard and nodded to Sean and Adam to take the one behind. "We have one more guest, Ms. Carissa will be joining us. We tried to get the Canadian's wife to come, but she had prior commitments," the aide said, and then pointing to the driver of the second Hummer he called out, "Amigos, this is my cousin Freddy. Freddy, our good friends from America. Now, I'll be right back!"

In a flash, Silverio had disappeared into the hotel. Within minutes he had returned with a stunningly attired Carissa Lamarillo. Smiling to Miranda and Laura, the Secretary's wife smoothed out her delicate linen garments, "We may be trouncing through some rough country, but a lady can still dress nice!"

Miranda and Laura laughed as the big SUV wheeled onto the street and raced off for the coastal mountain range. The mood sobered as the view outside of the Humvee quickly transitioned from elegant hotels and condos alongside the coast to primitive settlements of lean-to buildings, concrete hovels lacking windows or doors, and other dwellings pieced together with a wide array of miscellaneous hardware fragments. Gone were the lush lawns lining swimming pools, the rows of towering palm trees swaying with the Pacific breeze; in their stead lie miles of dust-covered land, sprinkled with the occasional saguaro cactus. Instead of tourists being pampered by cordial Mexican hospitality workers, children played soccer in front of ramshackle schools, kicking up dust as they chased after a soccer ball.

Miranda almost winced as she watched a bus pass from one of the rustic towns. Passengers heading towards the coast were dressed in their hotel attire, ready to assist the American, European tourists as well as the Mexican upper class – or had some connection with one of the many vice cartels that plagued the region. As well as she had been treated, having seen where many of the workers lived filled Miranda with pangs of guilt.

Relief washed over the biologist as the big SUV sped past the outlying region near the coast and began climbing into the hilly country of nearby Chihillo. The seemingly endless miles of dust and dirt, towns that by American standards would equal the lows of poverty, moved to terrain increasing in vegetation and held no further examples of the profound separation that the country held between the "haves" and the "have-nots".

As the tandem of trucks ascended the hills, they came upon a switchback that paralleled the coastline, many miles below them. Looming on the ridge, was a large stucco building appearing almost as a Mediterranean castle overseeing the land to the west. A long line of fencing stretched in all directions as far as the eye could see around the building. Veering off of the paved road, the SUVs turned toward a large iron gate that separated the long line of fencing. Silverio leaned out and spoke into a box that was attached to a post along the drive. Within moments, the massive iron gates pulled inward to allow the trucks to make their way into the estate. The dirt drive transitioned into a cobblestone path, curving around a fountain and coming to an end in front at the entry of the stucco building.

Piling out, the road-weary passengers stretched their legs, Sean spun on his axis to take in the view. The landscape before him was a fascinating picture, almost as though it was a photograph from a National Geographic or yellowing photos from a past era. Saguaro and sage dotted hills flowed into the valley and, ultimately, out to the sea, a mere streak of blue separated from the sky by slight variations in shade.

A pair of enormous wooden doors opened to the building. Two women dressed in white linens welcomed the visitors. Silverio kissed each greeter on the cheek and led the way through the arched-ceiling halls. Barren, except for occasional alcoves cut into the adobe walls, the parade of footsteps echoed as the troop moved forward. Antique tequila bottles filled the nooks, showing the visitors the progression from the 1800s to those that are currently stocked in the local taverns.

As the hallway spilled into the main room of the building, two men greeted the group. One was introduced as Silverio's cousin Frederico and the other, his assistant Carlos. Both men hugged Silverio and then turned their attention to Mrs. Lamarillo before finally addressing the rest of the group.

"Welcome to Hacienda Tioga Tequila factory. I believe we have some of the best spirits in all of Mexico," the man beamed, he wore a khaki suit, draped over a white shirt, open to the middle of his stomach, "You like tequila?"

The expression on Miranda's face gave her thoughts on the distilled agave drink away. Frederico laughed while raising a discerning eyebrow, "Your experience with tequila is with Jose Cuervo, yes?"

Miranda nodded her head, "I can manage it in Margaritas, but…"

With his hands up, the proprietor smiled, "I cannot drink that stuff either, *amiga*. Today, you taste *real* tequila." Walking over to a cask in the middle of the room, he took several glasses from a nearby tray and poured a quarter ounce from the tap. Holding the liquid up for the group, he swirled it around.

"It's clear!" Adam exclaimed.

Laura rolled her eyes as she threw sideways glance at him for blurting out the obvious. One of the things she loved about her husband is that he always acted the part of an overgrown kid. Seeing the exchange, Sean laughed at the two.

"As I say to visitors in my country – if it is yellow in Mexico, do not drink it, my friends," the group laughed as Frederico nodded for Carlos to begin handing out small glasses, "Good tequila, using the best quality blue agave plants, spring water and careful, patient distilling techniques delivers *real* tequila. Please, try it."

One by one, the group, including Silverio and their host drew back a sip of the clear liquid. Laura and Miranda visibly winced as they swallowed their drinks. Each of their expressions were of surprise when they swallowed.

"That wasn't bad at all," Miranda conceded.

"It was actually pretty smooth. It doesn't even have that funny tequila smell," Laura agreed.

"*Mi amigos,* you have tested real tequila," turning to the American ladies, Frederico asked, "You like?"

Miranda shrugged as she admitted, "I probably wouldn't sit and drink a glass full, but it doesn't offend me the way the stuff I am used to does."

"I have a solution for the ladies," Frederico snapped his fingers, "Carlos..."

Moments later, his assistant returned with two glasses of orange-colored liquid. "Please, try...," Carlos requested.

Miranda and Laura shot each other curious glances and placed the glasses to their lips. Miranda was surprised. The beverage had a citrus flavor and no real trace of alcohol in its palate. Hoisting the glass in the air, "Now this, I can drink!"

Laughing, Frederico replied, "Infused tequila. Aficionados would be offended, but I understand not everyone, especially the ladies, appreciate sipping liquors. I created the citrus-infused tequila when I had a batch of the Hacienda Reserve not meet my expectations. I am glad you like it. Now please, refill your glasses, and I will show you the process."

Room by room, Frederico, who insisted the group call him "Freddy", the tour showed the visitors the entire process of preparing tequila, from the plant to the bottle. The group tried several variations of tequilas, designated as blue, white, black, and reserve. As they concluded, Freddy insisted that each could choose their favorite, and Carlos would package bottles for their return trip.

Freddy led the crew to a veranda facing the hillside. Smells of barbecued meats filled the air. A smoker was releasing delicious smells into the air, while a man was busily carving avocados on a large butcher block next to it. Piles of chopped tomatoes, onions, and cilantro filled a large bowl. A few feet away, a tiny woman was busily rolling out tortillas and placing them on a large wooden plank before inserting them into a wood-fired oven.

"Man, *that* smells good!" Adam grinned, conspicuously in the air.

Sean silently nodded in agreement as he stared at the rustic landscape behind the estate. Two giant buzzards circled the hill, casting shadows over the terrain as they drifted in the warm currents. A hand slid around his waist, and Miranda's lips brushed his cheek softly as she pulled him tight.

"This is fun," she smiled.

"Yeah, it is. A nice surprise since I thought I would be working today."

"Rick is a good man, and he thinks you are deserving of a break once in a while."

"Yeah. I never thought I would enjoy working with a politician, but I think he has his head dialed right. A rarity, I presume," Sean admitted and then grabbing her waist, he spun her to face him, "It's nice to have you here with me."

Miranda grinned, "Are you kidding? Orange tequila, the tropics, all those turtles to save…."

"Alright, you two, break it up. This is a family show, for Pete's sake," Adam groaned.

Before the two could retort, Laura grabbed her husband and spun him to face her, planting a kiss on his lips. Sean quipped, "Finally, we found a way to shut him up."

"*Amigos, cervezas?*" Carlos asked, and tossed Dos Equis at the Americans and Silverio, "Come with me, you shoot guns with me now."

"Beer, guns…count me in!" Adam grinned before taking a swig of beer.

"Tell me, Sean, is he always like this?" Silverio asked.

"Since I met him at least. Not sure how Laura puts up with it," Sean laughed, taking a jab in the arm from his big friend. Led to the side of the veranda, a row of shotguns stood in a rack. Attached to the railing, a trap shooter was armed and ready with several dozen clay discs. Setting their beers down, the men were quickly filling the air with well-aimed shotgun blasts.

The girls filled their time fielding endless questions toward one another about life in their opposing cultures while they sipped frozen margaritas. Carissa Lamarillo was thoughtful, candid, and well-spoken. Her husband had been a powerful businessman in Mexico City, dealing with interests in Western Europe, Canada, and the United States. His success brought him into the view of Mexico's powerful politicians when the then minority party was poised to make a comeback, fitting their policies around the needs of the people. Her husband's main goals were to make Mexico an attractive and viable country for all Mexicans. He was offended and embarrassed by the stream of emigrants that illegally made their way into the U.S. She admitted that though her family was wealthy, they had always tried to give back in ways to make her people more prosperous themselves.

Her husband had worked with her father on several occasions, and that is how the two met when Carissa was seventeen. By nineteen, the two were married, and her husband's career took off. Miranda spoke carefully about her meeting Sean, avoiding entirely anything to do with her cousins – a subject that she still found too painful to engage.

Fortunately, the call for lunch came, and Miranda did not have to supply too much detail on their courtship. The spread before them was fit for an Aztec king. Mounds of pulled pork, freshly caught tilapia, fresh from the oven tortillas, and bowl after bowl of Mexican delicacy were placed in front of them. As

Miranda thought she had filled her stomach with all that it could hold, the serving of flan was delivered to the table. Her lust for quality flan overcame her desire to push away from the table and accepted a healthy portion of the custard-like treat.

Alberto Gutierrez stood nervously at the podium. The crowd of reporters, countless video camera lenses, and rows of microphones strung in front of him felt like having thousands of lie-detectors focusing on his every word. He was quite sure that with a single sentence, his political career was over. As far as his superiors were concerned, the deal with the U.S. and Canada was done. This should be the announcement to declare Mexico's signing of the accord. Beads of sweat sprouted onto his forehead, forcing him to dab at them nervously with a handkerchief.

Given the go sign, Gutierrez paused. For a moment, he truly did not what to say. He knew what was right. He also knew the real likelihood that he might never see Sienna again regardless of what words he spoke. Yet, doing what he was told seemed like his only choice. Looking into the cameras, the faces of the reporters, most of which he had known for more than a decade, was like looking into the eyes of all the people of Mexico.

"I know that right now in Mazatlan, some great people from Canada, the United States of America and Mexico are working together. Working to make all three countries a better place to live for all of their people. The strides we have made in the North American Ecological Alliance – an accord that affects much more than just improvements for the environment, but key agreements on trade law and immigration as well. It is because of the very importance of this accord that…that I must inform you that we are continuing to review the package and look forward to a complete resolution very soon. Thank you all, I will not be fielding questions at this time," Gutierrez quickly spun from the podium and away from the throng of reporters in the United Nations press room as the audience exploded into a roar of surprise followed by a torrent of questions. Avoiding eye contact with his staff and his superiors, the ambassador darted down the hall for his waiting car to return to his office. He prayed his phone would ring, and a voice would tell him of his daughter's safe return. Heartbroken, but not surprised, that call did not come.

The meeting broke to watch the telecast on the large flat panel television on the wall of the conference room. Secretary of Commerce Lamarillo, beamed with pride, exchanging smiles with Senator Johnson and Trade Secretary DuPont. As the words left Ambassador Gutierrez' lips and reached the speakers in the conference room, Lamarillo and his team erupted into a furor. Senator Johnson and DuPont sat quietly back in their seats, disappointed in the delay, as well as sympathetic for the blind-sided Lamarillo.

"*Senors, mi amigos*, I express my deepest apologies. This is not what I was informed would happen," the proud Mexican looked sullen on is side of the boardroom table.

"Secretary Lamarillo, this minor setback should not defeat us. We can still accomplish many great things at this week's conference. I think we all in this room feel very good about the progress we have made. If our governments choose to move forward a bit more cautiously, we will learn to maneuver within our constraints," Senator Johnson declared, trying to put the Mexican dignitary at ease. To Johnson's own desired end, he wanted to see his time in Mexico lead to components of positive change, even if the full NAEA was not yet ready to be signed.

With the Canadian Minister of Commerce's agreement, the newscast was turned off, and the representatives from the three countries pressed in their dialogue. This time, contingencies for tearing the package apart into several segments for easier passage were noted.

The smell of gun powder on their fingertips and tequila on their breath, the four *gringos* thanked their hosts for the day's hospitality. Walking to the waiting Humvees, Adam clapped Sean on the shoulder, "Boy, you did some nice shooting. Those clay pigeons didn't stand a chance. Are you sure you won't start hunting with me?"

While his friend was an avid hunter and he couldn't help but admit he frequently enjoyed the spoils from Adam's excursions, Sean struggled with the concept of pulling the trigger on an unsuspecting animal. Adam had hoped he could turn his friend into a hunting partner as Sean possessed excellent tracking skills to go with being a crack shot. "No. You kill 'em. I'll eat 'em," Sean grinned and taking Miranda's hand to help her into one of the SUVs, "You didn't do so bad yourself. I hope you never get angry with me with a weapon in your hand."

Flashing back a wry smile, Miranda retorted, "Then I guess you had better just treat me right."

After helping the other two ladies into the truck, Sean joined Adam and Silverio in the second Humvee. The men enjoyed open air as the top was taken down while the women returned to the resort area in air-conditioned comfort. In unison, the two trucks snaked down the driveway toward the massive iron gates. As they waited for their turn, a glint of reflected light caught Sean's eye further down the rough road leading to the highway.

Darting forward, the two trucks bounced their way toward the paved road. As they made their way around a sharp bend flanked by a larger boulder on one side and a ravine to accommodate the area's frequent flash floods, they met another vehicle. An old Toyota pick-up truck sat in the middle of the road, barring room for a second vehicle. "Hold on, guys!" Silverio called as he stood on the brakes, sliding to a stop just short of the Humvee in front of him.

Instantly, the layer of tequila-induced cloud that had pleasantly filled his mind from the tour instantly fled him. His instincts flushed the mind-numbing toxins from his body, screaming to him that something was wrong. As the driver of the pick-up opened his door, Sean noticed between the row of lights bar that lined the roll bar. A large semi-automatic rifle was pointed in their direction.

At first, the driver seemed apologetic, speaking rapidly in thick, colloquial Spanish. His head, low under the wide brim of his straw hat, hid his eyes. Quickly, he lifted a hand from under his poncho, revealing a sawed-off shotgun, pointing it directly at the driver of the girls Humvee. Two more men with handkerchiefs tied around their faces jumped from the passenger doors of the Toyota and raised an AK-47 in the air. He made his way quickly to the other passenger side of the Humvee, preventing any acts of heroism.

"Banditos," Silverio cursed in a low whisper, "*Amigos*, slide your wallets under the seat. Take out a small bit of cash for them to take; they may let us go."

As Sean watched the men close in on the vehicles, a shadow to the side of the road told him the men had positioned a man in the ravine to cover the flank of their SUV. Reaching into his pocket, he felt a couple of unused shells. Glancing to Adam, he led his eyes to the shotguns wedged beside the driver's seat and slowly opened his hand to reveal the two shells.

Surveying the scene, Sean tried to devise a plan that would separate the gunmen or liberate a weapon. Most of all, he wanted to get the attention of the robbers on the men's SUV and the lead vehicle the ladies were in. As the shadow in Sean's peripheral vision closed in, Adam's voice broke the uncomfortable silence that fell on the hillside as the gunmen surrounded the tandem of vehicles.

"So, you're a *bandito*," even in the intense moments of several gun barrels pointed at them, Adam's voice rang with its usual sarcasm, "You want some money, huh? *Pesos* okay? Not worth much, but I cashed in all of my American money."

"Just shut up and hand over your wallets, *gringos*. All of it, credit cards…and your shiny watch too!" the man right next to Adam snarled as he eyed Sean's wristwatch.

"Alright, alright. Take it easy," Sean hastily ripped at his watch, and as though he were intensely nervous, dropped it to the floor of the SUV, "Aw man…." Bending to the floor, he arched his back to try and hide his yanking one of the shotguns from its berth.

"So, this pay better than hopping over the fence and picking lettuce?" Adam chided the man, trying to occupy his attention. As the man began to deliver a hasty retort, Adam suddenly lunged across the doorsill, grabbing the barrel of the gun pointed at him. The strong wildlife officer pulled easily pulled the weapon free into his possession.

"Hey!" the man closing in behind Sean yelled as he raised his automatic rifle. Before the man could get a precise aim, Adam released three rounds from the semi-automatic he liberated into the man's chest, sending him collapsing to the ground. By the time the man who had lost his weapon could pull a sidearm from its holster,

Sean had slid a shell into the chamber of Silverio's shotgun and rose to send a load of birdshot in his direction. Most of the tiny pellets caught the bandit in the head and neck, sending him backward, reeling in pain.

From the other side of the vehicle, frantic shouts and a volley of bullets from the Toyota rang through the air. As the first gunman found his way to the second Humvee to confront Sean, Adam had rolled out of the vehicle and was positioned to drop him with a spray from the semi-automatic, knocking him backward onto the dusty road. Rolling out of the SUV and to the side of the road, Sean yelled for Silverio to reverse the Humvee backward towards the gate. The spinning wheels filled the area with thick dust, depleting visibility. Sean used the diversion to hop free from the vehicle, pumping the shotgun to load his last shell.

Wild shouts in Spanish could be heard over the growling engine, following the closest voice, Sean stepped carefully forward. As the dust settled, the man who had first approached from the Toyota stood face to face with Sean. The barrel of the shotgun aimed right at his chest. The man's weapon pointed harmlessly where the SUV once stood.

The gunman in the Toyota swung his rifle to get a bead on Sean. Before he could line up a shot, a spray of bullets took out the two off-road lights nearest him, freezing him in place. The gunfire made the man facing Sean raise his gun upward, forcing Sean to pull the trigger and blow the man to the ground.

"Don't do it, amigo!" Adam warned, leveling his sights on the man's body. Waving his hand wildly, he urged the man driving the lead Humvee to back the girls out of harm's way. Dropping his gun to the ground, the man in the back of the Toyota sat on the wheel well, allowing Sean to reach over and, with one arm, pull the man by his neck to the ground. Kneeling on the captured would-be bandit, Sean waited for help to arrive.

The wait didn't take long as a dune buggy roared down the hill from the estate grounds. Frederico and the man who had worked the skeet range drove at break-neck speed across the wild terrain. Skidding to a stop, the two men jumped out, both heavily armed.

Observing the situation, Frederico spit and shoved a toothpick back in his mouth. Sean wondered how he kept from choking on it as he rode in the buggy. Calmly, the tequila purveyor's eyes swept across the pair of dead bodies in the road, their bodies riddled with birdshot. He smiled as he saw Sean patiently sitting atop one of the bad guys.

Cautiously, Adam peered into the ravine for the first bandit Sean foiled, but the man was nowhere to be seen. "We lost one! Should be easy to find, he was peppered pretty good with Sean's shotgun blast."

"If his wounds do not take care of him, perhaps the desert will, if not the desert, we will send Jave in the buggy to find him. If Jave finds him, he will wish he was already dead," Frederico declared. Motioning, he had his range master retrieve the man that Sean had apprehended, "We have called the *policia*. Come, I'll call the Humvee back, and we will retreat to the hacienda."

Silverio's HUMVEE bounced along the drive to a stop in front of the group. Taking some duct tape from a toolbox in the rear, Jave went to work, binding the bandit's hands and kicked him step by step to the Humvee. "I guess today's skeet was good practice for you two," Frederico scoffed to Sean and Adam, "But you two are loco. You need to be very careful. Men like this will not hesitate to kill you and the women if you make a mistake."

Sandwiching the man between Sean and Adam, Frederico hopped in the passenger seat near his cousin and leveled an Israeli Arms Desert Eagle handgun at the duct-tape hostage. In front of them, the Dune Buggy roared to life and defied gravity by negotiating down and over the drainage ravine before tearing through the barren countryside.

In the hacienda, they found three very shaken women. Miranda being the least affected, tried to console a distraught Carissa. As Frederico steadied his sidearm at the bound outlaw while nudging him, a look of disgust washed over Carissa's face. Launching out of her seat, she crossed the room and delivered a fluid, open-handed blow to the man's face. A stream of words left her mouth so quickly that had the words she used been taught to Sean in college, they were coming with such speed and fury he could not have been able to keep up in translation.

Realizing her outburst was on display, the usually demure and polite woman pulled back. Blushing, she turned to her new American friends and apologized. "This...this cretin is exactly what my husband and I would like to fix. Return my country to one of grace and pride, not one of vandals and thieves!" the Commerce Secretary's wife pleaded.

"Every country has their bad seeds, Carissa," Miranda comforted.

"Thank God for Sean and Adam. You are courageous men," Carissa sighed.

"Foolish men," Miranda said sternly.

Adam had already flung his arm around his wife. He had hoped from her position in the lead Humvee, that she had need seen the men get shot. She sat very numbly on the bench inside the hacienda entry. Leaning in, she accepted her husband's comfort.

"The *policia* will be here soon. The gate is locked, and you are all safe here," Silverio declared, "Can we get anybody anything while we wait?"

"You know, some of that fine tequila sounds great right now," Adam grinned. As much as he can take just about anything in stride, his nerves were shot. He had been in skirmishes when he was in Special Forces, but he never had his wife in the line of fire.

Sean rolled his eyes. He had wanted his mind sharp in case more trouble was on its way, never mind for the discussion he was going to have with the Mexican police about his killing a man in their country.

Five

Slamming his empty highball glass on his desk, Ambassador Gutierrez stared at his daughter's photograph. Her smile balanced by two pigtails strung with pale blue ribbons. He loved his country. But he loved Sienna even more. Since her mother died, she was the most important thing to him. He had hoped to create a better Mexico for his daughter. Now all he hoped for was to see his daughter again.

He had been ignoring his phone all day, which was ringing off the hook. His assistants continued to try and get time with him, but he sat behind his mahogany desk, waiting. Waiting for the call that had no number on the caller ID. The same one that told him they had ripped his daughter from their home. He had done what they wanted. He shot Mexico's future and his career in the foot. Where was his little girl? Spinning his chair around to look upon the streets of New York City. All of those people glibly going about their daily lives like a bunch of ants. All while his life was being torn apart.

The phone on his desk rang out. Despite the hundreds of times it had earlier in the day, he whipped around, staring desperately at the display. No number, just the word "Mexico".

Snatching the phone from its cradle, he answered it. "Where is she? How do I get her back?"

"Relax, Senor Gutierrez. We have a long road ahead of us. That was merely the first step," the voice declared in a mock soothing tone.

"What the hell do you mean? I have done exactly what you have asked!" growled the ambassador.

"You did very well," the voice cooed, "But, we can't have you burning any bridges. There is a part of the accord that discusses corporate buy-outs. Under the current structure, American and Canadian investment groups could run roughshod over our interests while Mexican businesses cannot match their power. You caught it. It can be easily tweaked. You go from goat to hero and are trusted once again."

"I get Sienna back?"

"If you remain compliant. Call Secretary Lamarillo with your discovery and tell him the accord can be signed as early as tomorrow. Your name will resonate well throughout Mexico City and the mockery of a conference in Mazatlan."

"When…"

"When we are finished. Do your job, you will hear from us."

The line fell silent. On his desk, Gutierrez pulled up the electronic file of the accord. Scrolling through the section on corporate law and stock buy-outs, he noted the clause that was referenced on the phone. He did not see that clause in there before. Lamarillo's team would not have allowed that to pass.

Pressing a button on his phone, he buzzed for his assistant. In moments, the door opened, and Cortez walked in.

"Sir, Secretary Lamarillo and everyone on his team have been calling nonstop for an explanation. Even President Lopez called for you…" the exasperated assistant gasped.

"Something was bugging me about the final draft. I found it in the corporate agreements," Gutierrez filled his assistant in asked him to get Lamarillo on the phone immediately.

In Senator Small's Washington, D.C. office, the mood was jubilant. Harold Billings, an energy tycoon and avid financial backer to Small, joined him in his toast to the news of the NAEA news.

"Mexico. Last thing we need is to open up *that* floodgate. I say build a wall so damn big it'll keep that dung pile where it belongs," Billings barked behind his cigar, "Line up the U.S. army tanks down there and shoot anything that even looks to the north."

"Well, you might still get your tanks. This is a nice bit of news, though. It shoots Marshall, and all of his damned liberal cronies square in the chest," Small declared.

"I can't believe they were backing that bunch of garbage. Who cares if they can't wipe their own noses, why do we have to spend American money to fix every broken dump in the world? Damned bleeding hearts. That's why we need you to oust him. It's time we get one of the good ol' boys back in the White House!" Billings clapped the senator on the back, "'Course, provided you pay attention to those who put you there."

"Harold, you and I both know I am the only one who can defeat Marshall. No one else has the guts to do what it takes to get it done. He's too damned goody two-shoed. We need to pull the rug from under his feet," Small replied confidently, "By the time we get done with him, the country will be begging for a change."

The ride back from the tequila factory had been uneventful. Though with a full police escort, it would have taken a military strike to get to them. The conference center was buzzing with news media and federales. Lamarillo demanded that a wide gap be pushed into the crowd to allow the returning group to get into the lobby unmolested. The Commerce Secretary was the first to greet them. He hugged his wife and looked over the group as if to see for himself that were unharmed.

Senator Johnson was also eager to assess that the crew was indeed unmarred by the incident. "Back at your old tricks, eh Kendall?"

"Yes, sir. Not sure if I find trouble or it finds me," Sean replied glumly.

"Nonsense. I understand you were very heroic. Without you and Adam, who knows what would have happened. Unfortunately, this kind of thing happens all too common when you are off the beaten path in my country. From now on, I will have a security detail with all of you when you depart the conference center," Lamarillo declared.

Sean started to object but thought better of it. For most of the remainder of the trip, he would be beside Senator Johnson at the conference. He was sure that he would be able to concentrate better, knowing that Miranda and his friends would be safe. He was also starting to realize that the convention itself had brought with it a lot of attention for the citizens of Mexico – both for and against a stronger North American alliance.

The Commerce Secretary excused himself and saw his wife to their room. Senator Johnson invited Sean to join him for a cocktail in his suite. Adam said that he and Laura would take Miranda with them to the poolside cantina to watch the stars.

As the door shut and the senator handed Sean a glass of port, he motioned to the massive veranda. The ocean-front deck was so large, he felt it very unlikely that their conversation would be compromised. Earshot from any probable advantage was too far away. "It sounds like we both had quite a day," Johnson said. He proceeded to fill Sean in on the ups and downs of the NAEA accord had been through that day.

"So, a small delay…that's not so bad," Sean said, taking a sip from his port glass. His shifted outward as though he were in deep thought, "But I thought I had read the final draft. I don't remember seeing anything that seemed so one-sided in any part of it…don't get me wrong, once the business section drifted into legalese minutia, I would confess my attention waned a bit."

"No, Wilkins and I both said the same thing. Oddly, the entire room seemed to agree the catch caught them off guard."

Sean tossed a quizzical glance the senator's way, "It seems a little fishy to me. Like someone trying to discredit the process."

"That's my thought exactly. I suggest we stay on our toes this week. Frankly, the deception could come from any one of the three countries. None of these plans are perfect, they won't make everyone happy, but they do address the needs of most and provide the right mix of sustainability for all three nations," Johnson conceded.

"What would you like me to do?"

"Since you are here as part of my lobby support, you are kind of a wild card. Wilkins and I can remain intensely focused on the details. Your position may allow for a little more flexibility to maintain a higher-level view of all three delegations. Do what you do – build relationships, mill around."

"And keep my nose clean while doing so," Sean added.

Lifting his glass, the senator motioned that they understood each other.

Sean found the crew in the cantina seeming no worse for the experience they had endured earlier in the day. Declining a drink, he declared that he would turn in for the evening so that he could function well in his official role as the conference continued. Despite the groans and condemnation from Adam, Sean held steadfast to his decision. Before he could pull away from the table, a waitress showed up with four shot glasses filled with clear liquid.

"One shot?" Adam grinned, his attempt to appear innocent failing miserably as it washed with wickedness.

Pausing, Sean looked at each of the faces peering up at him. Silently, he liberated the glass from the tray and held it up. Each of his colleagues followed in suit. "Salut!"

One by one, the glasses were pounded on the table in front of them. "You all have fun. I will see you tomorrow sometime after three, when the main meetings adjourn for the day."

Miranda smiled at Adam and Laura, "Thank you for letting me be the third wheel."

"You are always welcome. Tomorrow we are snorkeling with sea turtles!" Laura exclaimed. Sean had noticed that Laura's speech and smile were a little different than usual. After the stressful day, he surmised that tequila had afforded her a form of therapy.

"I *do* love turtles. In fact, I think I will turn in as well so that I am ready to tackle the deep blue," Miranda flashed the couple a wry smile and turned to Sean, "Walk me to my room?"

Waving goodnight to his friends, Sean linked his arm with Miranda's and walked her towards the elevators. Outside of the tavern, the hotel was silent other than babbling of the Koi stream that snaked through the lobby. The warm tropical air mixed with the more refreshing ocean breezes that night time beckoned, filling the foyer with floral essence from the colorful plants and flowers which lined the stream. To Sean, the setting felt so peaceful, in sharp contrast to the events of the day and continuous protests and demonstrations in the streets surrounding the Conference Center.

As the elevator bell announced the arrival of the car, Sean gently led Miranda inside. Just as the doors closed, Miranda's arm slipped free from Sean's, her hand glided around his back and pulled their bodies close. Looking up at him, she smiled.

The brief moment shattered by the doors opening to their floor. Miranda kept her arm slung around Sean's waist. Outside of her door, she grabbed his shirt gently, pulling his face to hers. "Stay with me for a while tonight?" her blue eyes bright and yet appearing fatigued, "I don't think I want to be alone."

Silently, Sean slipped her key into the lock and pushed the door open. He was exhausted and knew his mind and body were requiring rest. The next day was jam-packed with meetings covering partnership agreements with dignitaries from both Mexico and Canada, yet he felt like the process of healing their relationship was developing so well in this neutral locale, he couldn't resist.

"I'm going to clean up a bit. Open the doors to the balcony for me?" Miranda called as she disappeared into the bedroom.

Heaving the large wooden shutters that closed of the wall of glass overlooking the Pacific aside, Sean found the lock for the massive sliding glass doors and opened the room to the symphony of waves breaking against the shore. Looking out at the mighty ocean, an activity he found immensely therapeutic, the day's events flashed through his mind. Numb to most of the memories, what bothered and intrigued him the most was his new-found ability to shrug off the killing. He was becoming desensitized to violence and death – a loss of emotion that frightened him. Not that he had time to think about his actions, if he didn't pull the trigger, either his friends or himself would have been the ones to die. Still…

He jumped slightly as arms reached around him and pulled him slightly backward. "You're a little jumpy," Miranda chuckled.

"Yeah, a little, I guess," Sean admitted, shrugging his shoulders.

"Watching you today…I realized what it must have been like for you when you were fighting Jeb," Miranda spoke of her cousin that Sean had killed when he uncovered their involvement in a plot to attack a WTO convention, "You had no choice. You had to either fight or allow others to be harmed."

"I'm sorry it came down…."

Spinning him around to face her, she placed a finger firmly to his lips, "It wasn't your fault. I see it in you. I saw it in you today. Your eyes held a look of desperation and concern for us, not of anger or menace. You are a great man, and *I* am the one who is sorry for taking my family's misguided acts out on you. Jeb's death wasn't your fault. It was his. It was my uncle's and grandfather's. They created the hatred in him. A hatred that would have killed a lot of innocent people if you hadn't stopped him." Slowly tears began to well up in her eyes, dancing in the moonlight as they worked their way down her cheeks.

Angrily wiping them away, Miranda stared up at Sean, "I'm not crying for them. I'm crying for how I treated you."

Unable to string enough words together that he felt were reasonable, he hugged her tightly in silence. The thick Mexican air seemed to hang even heavier on Sean's shoulders. The weight of the day, the emotional load of the conversation, and overall fatigue from the day pressed down on him. The moment was lifted as Miranda looked up at him and pushed her lips to his. Salt from the tears that migrated down her face met his tongue, stinging him with the tangible taste of emotion. Silently and without conscious effort, they sunk on the chaise lounges overlooking the beach, watching and listening to the surf roll in. A position they would find themselves in when the sun rose the next day.

The moon hung high in the air above the decrepit farm. Shards of light stabbed through holes in the sagging roof of the barn the mercenary team had settled in. Tug had wished clouds would move in to further conceal their movements. To him, the mile and a half to the border might as well be lit up with lights from a football stadium. Chuckling, he almost pictured booth announcers giving the play-by-play of his team's assault along the Rio Grande. The light thought was fleeting as he snapped his focus on getting his team geared up. They would need to move fast. Border Patrols would be scouring the area, and once the attack commenced, the open terrain would leave them sitting ducks.

In a single motion, he flagged the lead team to head out. Separating into small groups, they fanned out, each heading south, but with a slight deviation on the latitudinal plane. The hope was that moving out in small sections, they would not be picked out on satellite as such an overt anomaly.

In concert, two-man Chenoweth Desert Patrol Vehicles rocketed out of the cover of the barn. Each of the open cockpit four-wheel-drive vehicles was outfitted with either an MK-19 grenade launcher or an M2 .50 caliber machine gun. Both options were capable of handling any obstacle that crossed their path – rogue smugglers from Mexico hauling either their human or narcotic contraband, and overzealous Minutemen or Border Patrol agents trying to exert futile control over the region's fragile southern border.

From his command position, Tug Gaskill could track his troops' movements as they roamed in their alternating southwesterly or southeasterly routes. When the Chenoweths reached their halfway point to the target, Tug released the trucks. Three personnel carriers and three cargo trucks, each towing a variety of black market or refurbished Howitzer artillery guns, followed the path of the Chenoweths. Snatching the handle of his specialized field laptop, he jumped into the driver's seat of his own Desert Patrol Vehicle. Before he could start the engine, his southeast team reported traffic. A group of travelers fifty strong were making their way across the rolling pastureland.

"What do you want us to do, boss?" the mercenary in the lead vehicle called out, his voice sounding irritated by the delay to the objective.

"Who are they? Minutemen? Immigrants?" Tug asked, realizing that the answer didn't matter, his response would be the same regardless.

"Looks like immigrants. Probably dumped over the border from their coyotes and left on their own."

"Take care of them. What is a war without a few casualties?"

"Roger that."

Glancing at his computer screen, the field map showed the lead triangle on the left come to a stop. Moments later, the subsequent triangles fell into line. In moments, muffled gunfire roared to life throughout the range. Tug wasn't concerned about the fallout from the noise. A group this big had likely already been picked up by an unmanned drone and the Border Patrol alerted.

Whether they had the manpower to respond was another question entirely.

As quickly as the gunfire began, it ceased. His headpiece came to life, "We got a runner!"

The triangle on the laptop moved quickly to the east, once more coming to an abrupt halt. A single gunshot from a high-powered M2 .50 echoed across the pasture, signaling an end to the delay.

"Sir, the range is clear."

"Move out. Team 2, update?" Tug called to the Chenoweths that had snaked to the southwest.

"Team 2 is in position at the objective. Waiting for the toys to catch up," a voice crackled across the secure frequency.

"What does the playing field look like?" Tug asked as his vehicle roared to life.

"Clear skies and good turf. The end zone is unblocked."

"Good. Toys and Team One should be there in minutes. Get set up. We're about to kick off."

Six

Usually, Senator Small would have groaned when his alarm clock beckoned him at such an early hour. The bright blue LCD screen told him it was three o'clock. He didn't mind his slumber being interrupted this morning. Instead, he jumped out of bed like a child ready for the first day of school. Rushing through his routine, he quickly dressed and headed for the front door. His beeping cellphone told him that his assistant Jerry Rhinehart was already parked outside.

Swinging open the door to his Georgetown brownstone, he saw the Lincoln Sedan idling out in front. Rhinehart jumped out of the car and opened the door for the Senator.

"Good morning, sir!" Rhinehart beamed.

Small rolled his eyes. It didn't matter what time of day it was, his assistant was always gleaming. As he ducked his head to get into the car, he thought to himself how strange it was that such an eternally, frankly annoyingly happy individual could also be so pessimistic – a trait that Small had learned to capitalize on. His aide was always playing the role of the devil's advocate, poking holes in nearly every plan that Small intended to act. Often,

Rhinehart's concerns revealed serious undesired consequences allowing the senator to change direction or fix issues before they were too far along to be recalled.

"Coffee, sir?" A piping hot cup of Starbucks was held up for the Small to grab. The busy, twenty-four hour a day city of Washington D.C. provided easy access to caffeine around the clock.

Accepting the coffee, the senator brought the cup to his lips. As Rhinehart negotiated the lightly traveled streets, Small wondered about the reactions to the morning's plan. He wasn't nervous. He was far removed from any trail that could even remotely implicate him. He just truly did not know how the nation would react. Models showing public reaction as a mere police action to embarking into a full-blown war were conceived. Either way, the result was increased tensions. Selfishly, the senator had hoped for the latter scenario. His investments in the military complex were great, and as much as conflict in the Middle East had helped to spur on defense spending, having an enemy right in your backyard would bring tremendous increases in weapons development and deployment. Ultimately, it was the bad blood that he needed to be the outcome.

Small knew the President's backing of the North American Free Trade Alliance and the current commerce and conservation agreements on the table between the three countries would create an enormous groundswell of distaste for the current "soft" politicians. America would finally be ready for someone fit to close the doors to the flood of worthless immigrants, the ridiculous outpouring of hard-earned American money handed out to one pathetic country after another. Small wanted to return America to the greatness it once was - a superpower that took care of itself first.

As he raised his cup higher, he realized that he had already drained his Venti latte. His mind consumed with the thoughts of knocking Marshall off his perch, that he had barely been aware enough to enjoy his morning ration of caffeine. He was pleased that Rhinehart had pulled into a loading dock and was already on his cell phone, presumably with someone on the other side of the large steel door that rose just long enough to allow the Lincoln to slip underneath.

Rhinehart pulled the car to a stop next to a small row of other vehicles. The room was dark, with underpowered lights lining the walls, offering enough visibility to see where you were going without running into something, but little more. Even before Small could heave the heavy door open, a well-built man in a turtle neck was there to greet him.

"Senator, right this way, we are ready to begin," the man said softly, his calm voice belying his intimidating physique, "We will have you back in the District before you are missed."

Following the man, Rhinehart and Small were led up the stairs flanking one side of the warehouse. Rhinehart flipped quickly through a file folder and leaned in to whisper to Small, "Former Major Thomas Krause. Been sympathetic to the cause since his work with a CIA operative that clued him in."

The former major was greeted at the top of the stairs by another athletic figure who, in the dim light, was even more menacing as he held an M-4 assault rifle in his hand.

"Senator Small and his aide Jerry Rhinehart," Krause said simply.

The man with the assault weapon turned without a word to punch a set of numbers into a digital keypad, allowing the heavy steel door to open wide. With a hand on the knob, the sentry returned his gaze to the warehouse. As Small took a glance behind him, he found a similar sentry at all four corners of the warehouse.

In another dimly lit room, the Senator's eyes adjusted to a half-dozen brilliant flat panel screens lining the far wall. Standing with arms crossed were several gentlemen, each keenly attentive to the screens on the wall. One display was a map with an overlay of digital symbols revealing the mercenary group, the intended target, and any encroaching threats. Already splashed on the screen were several red 'x's displaying the unfortunate group of migrants who had wandered into the kill zone. The other subsequent screens were amazingly crisp and detailed live satellite videos of the area, one panned wide, the others focusing on either the assault team or the target. Each screen, despite the green hue from the cameras being in "night" mode, gave a clear view of the scene along the southern U.S. border.

One of the men took their eyes off of the screen to greet the Senator, "Welcome Senator. The group is engaged and closing in on the target zone."

"How did you get the satellite feed without attracting attention?" Small asked the man.

Former General Chambers gave a slight smile and nodded his head towards a man in a dark blue suit, beaming jubilantly in front of the screens, "That man there is Roger Jones. He is the lead engineer on the latest satellite just sent to orbit last week. He has this logged as programming time. It isn't officially supposed to be online until later in the month. There will be no trace of the feeds. We were lucky to find he was sympathetic to our cause."

The general himself had only aligned with the "cause" little more than a year ago. He was the scapegoat over a failed execution in the Middle East conflict by the former administration. He, like many others, felt like America's preoccupation with the rest of the world's concerns were driving the great nation into long term peril. He and the Senator had aligned on many issues and, in doing so, realized they were of similar mind.

"Where are we at?" Small asked, and eyeing the screen with the overlay was pointed without trying to seem too nervous, "What's with the kills?"

"Gaskill reports his team running into a band of migrants. They used suppressive fire. Ultimately, it will only add to the desired outcome. A good thing," the former general said, his eyes squarely on the three screens dominating the room.

"Border patrol?" the senator asked.

"None so far. The drones will make a fly-by at some point. They may pick up activity. Tug has a plan to minimize any impact on the mission. Of actual patrols, if we pull back on the map to the right, there is what looks to be a single patrol vehicle heading their direction. Once the fireworks start, we calculate he will be on the scene within fifteen minutes and birds in the air shortly after. We chose this location specifically because of its lack of adequate coverage," Chambers relayed to the senator, the politician's concerns revealing themselves despite his attempts to conceal them.

Small turned his attention on the overlay screen. All of the green triangles stopped in a jagged line approximately two hundred yards from the border. All of the vehicles with their discrete GPS signals electronically coded to only be picked up by Chambers' small group at the warehouse showed that they had reached the target and were preparing to commence the mission.

While small arms and dumb artillery would not show on the overlay, activity on the satellite feed caught the senator's eye. Streaks filled the sky as men worked the Howitzers. Soon the overlay lit up with color-coded displays marking the path of the

GPS guided smart missiles. The attack was on. In a few hours, reports of a border skirmish between the U.S. and Mexican militaries would be carried over the airwaves.

Tug's men had acted with precision. The first launches of artillery from the Howitzers had almost been simultaneous. The sundry of missiles that they had unloaded and aimed for the unsuspecting town of Camello were delivered across the border immediately after. Tug himself had manned one of the six Dragon's Eye missiles that they had absconded with from the Sunny Point Munitions Depot. Each of the GPS-guided munitions launched with the specs detailed in the master plan for the assault.

Unlike the missions Tug ran while a member of the U.S. Special Forces, precision was less critical. He had no one on the other side to relay positive hits and kills. Moreover, it didn't really matter. This one-sided battle was more for effect. The emotional turmoil that would result from the attack was his backer's true litmus for success. Nonetheless, he still began to receive feedback over his sat-com stuck in his right ear. The Camello police station, town hall, and bus depot were all destroyed within the first three minutes of firing. Any other damage and casualties would be gravy from here on out. With that in mind, Tug urged his men to empty their stock of firepower as quickly as possible and prepare for pull out.

He watched as his team emptied their supply of deafening bombs through the noisy Howitzers. He tracked the final flames of the last Dragon's Eye as it rocketed through the sky. When the major munitions depleted, he signaled for the crew to set the charges for the gear and take their Desert Assault Vehicles to their respective Exfil locations.

Before the charges could be set, the flashing blue and red lights of a Border Patrol Chevrolet Tahoe appeared on the horizon. Without even a second thought, Tug grabbed a Stinger missile from its case, flipped the sight down to his right eye, and pulled the trigger. In seconds, the SUV was launched in the air, engulfed in flames.

Press Secretary Judith Myers was hopeful with the morning's first press briefing. She had prepped President Marshall on the advances made at the conference in Mazatlán. The wins had outnumbered the concessions that his delegation, led by Senator Johnson, had had to make. The news of the conference had spurred decent gains in the economic sector, and members of both parties had reason to be hopeful – the democrats with the environmental implications and the republicans with the benefits to the business sector.

She was already focusing on the afternoon's session, set to cover the upgrade to the educational system. When the report crossed her desk, she had to sit back. At first, she thought that it was in error. Maybe a skirmish between the Minutemen and some illegal border crossings, but the city of Camello sustaining substantial damage from an artillery attack. That was insane. She reserved hope that the root cause, when uncovered, would lead to drug cartel actions. Yet in black in white, it stated that the unprovoked attack launched from the American side of the border.

Pushing away from her desk, she ran towards the Situation Room. By the time she had arrived, the president was met by a throng of his advisors. She could overhear Chief of Staff Chambers informing President Marshall of the Mexican President's Lopez' urgent requests to receive his phone call. Even as she walked, she began sketching out a statement for his morning address on her electronic notepad.

Catching the president's eye, Myers cast her concerned glance, "I see you've heard…"

Managing a weak smile breaking the countenance he wore, "I *am* the president. I hear things."

Appreciating Marshall's attempt to bring levity to the dire news encouraged Myers to lend her hand to help diffuse the morning's media, "I have already begun drafting a statement. I wanted to review the fine points with you and then send it quickly to the staff writers to clean up before eight."

"Have Rebecca proof it if you would. She seems particularly adept at wordsmithing confidence in a dire report," the President requested.

"Uhh, if I may Mr. President," Colonel Terry Adams stepped forward, his uniform, as always, impeccably pressed, "I think we need to temper any reply until we have further details as to what actually happened down there. We don't even know if it was our boys. How can anyone determine whether the incident even was enacted from our side of the line? We don't want to offer validity to the incident until the facts are known."

"I understand, Terry. However, the public and the international community will hear about the incident and will react to what they hear. They need to hear the news from the Whitehouse. We do not need to lay blame, just deliver the substantiated facts and offer our sincere sympathy for losses that were sustained," the president declared.

"Just be cautious," the colonel urged.

"Of course, Terry. In the meantime, get me the facts of what did take place down there," Marshall demanded, turning to his Press Secretary, "Write it up, stick to the known variables and keep the slant as optimistically positive with our neighbors to the south. Let's just hope it was a drug cartel and not any of our own."

"Yessir."

"Oh, and Judith, I want to go on early," checking his watch, the president looked up, "I want to go on in fifteen minutes."

The initial vibe in the room was uncomfortable at best. Every member of the meeting had exchanged cordial greetings and then quickly retreated to their respective groups. The early morning news of the attack on Camello had swiftly spread, and despite it appearing to be an isolated incident, left the Mexican and American contingents unsure of how to proceed. Both of their respective governments had expressed genuine surprise with the attack, each condemning it. No one knew the impact that it might have on the accord or even if they should proceed as planned or quit and allow the dust to settle.

Senator Johnson's team had time to meet only briefly before entering the meeting, and that was primarily to cover ground on what little facts were known and what potential actions they should take at the NAEA conference. Their Canadian and Mexican counterparts arrived at the meeting room soon after they had debriefed what the White House spokeswoman had time to share with Johnson.

It was the senator who broke the thick air of uneasy silence, "Gentlemen. We do not yet have all of the facts. Both the Mexican and U. S. law enforcement services are engaged to sort things out. The early reports from our side do show some activity in an open rural area along the New Mexico – Camello border. Our first response teams have found remnants of U.S.-made Howitzer artillery equipment and a variety of spent shells and casings, most of which are consistent with those used by U.S. forces." The senator took a moment to allow that information to sink in. Information that had not been shared along the newswires. Information that Johnson had hoped would be an extension of an olive branch, indicating his desire for open and honest dialogue.

"Rogue military personnel?" Lamarillo asked, hoping to put the blame away from a U.S. commanded attack. Tensions were tight along the border, though the politicians had not indicated any further tightening of the border.

"It is too early to tell. I have been in contact with the White House, and there have certainly not been any actions sanctioned by the Executive Office or any of the military commanders," Senator Johnson assured the group which gathered intently around the massive boardroom table.

"What do we do now?" DuPont asked.

"I say we proceed business as usual. The best way to intercede in tensions is to forge a pact that is beneficial for *all* parties," the senator said, a smile breaching his face for the first time this morning, "Dissenters of this very accord were likely behind the atrocities that occurred last night. Do we let them win through these cowardly terror-based methods, or do we bring our three nations together as a powerful cooperative?"

The room erupted in eager applause, and the veil of unrest seemed to lift instantly. Sean quietly admired the senator and his decision to take on the level of discomfort by attacking it directly. He wasn't sure how much the folks back in Washington would have liked the senator's bold statements, as some of them were his assumptions. Still, he also felt he was right in encouraging them to forge on and allow the ongoing investigation to take care of feeding the media and politics.

Lance Corporal Enrique Guerrero was abruptly wakened by his sergeant. The man standing over his bed wore an anxious expression as held out the phone in his shaky hand, "Colonel Reyes, sir."

"What?" Guerrero asked, more to himself than anyone else, blinking, he tried to clear his head as he accepted the phone.

"Corporal, our sovereign nation has been attacked. Maybe it was a rogue terror cell, but it is time to enact our own plans!" the colonel's voice range through the receiver.

"Attacked, what…where?"

"In the town of Camello," Reyes snapped, "The details are irrelevant, just move up the time table and commence the assault immediately!"

"Yessir," Guerrero responded, his mind suddenly filling with a barrage of commands and steps that he would need to make while calculating how long it would take until they would be ready to strike. Suddenly a thought came to mind. They would have to attack in broad daylight. "Colonel, wouldn't there be additional scrutiny on the border from both sides?"

"Yes, Corporal, there will be. With luck, you will have a reaction from the states in which you can engage," Reyes concluded.

"Forgive me, sir, isn't that a little suicidal?"

"Only if you lose the fight, Corporal."

The phone went dead, and almost to his relief, Guerrero's years of military training kicked in, the assignments and tasks at hand filled in the gaps that allowed doubt and reasoning to begin arguing the merits of the mission. He had a job to do, and it was not his call to determine the course of action, it was his to ensure that what course of action was called upon was carried out and executed.

Tug reviewed the screen resting on his lap. He could see his men heading in the directions as assigned. They would rendezvous in twenty-four hours if more actions were sanctioned. Part of him hoped there would be. He missed the action of executing a full-on assault. Most of the missions that he had carried out as a mercenary were small in scale. Single target kills, simple interventions. His last mission had been a major assault. Only instead of having qualified ex-military personnel at his disposal, he was burdened with a band of fundamentalist radicals who were more adept at poaching baby deer than executing military operations.

He paused his thoughts as the screen showed activity up ahead. The sound of a powerful helicopter validated the information on his laptop. He was glad he chose to have a civilian vehicle stashed in an abandoned barn. Other than his laptop and sidearm, his vehicle would have to be stripped completely to determine if they were suspects in the assault. Noticing that the helicopter had begun to hover, he assumed they were coming upon a roadblock inspection. After glancing at the symbols on the map that covered his screen and seeing that his other teams appeared to be successfully making their escapes, he shut the computer down and stowed it under his seat.

Tug sat stoically as the truck he was riding in slowed to a stop. The early morning sky was ablaze with the rising sun and the flashing lights of law enforcement vehicles. One by one, the cars ahead of them trickled past the inspection. Each passenger compartment was opened for the attending officers to inspect, and a K-9 unit circled, sniffing for a sign of contraband.

Finally, their turn came as the officer waved his driver forward. The officer looked at the driver and then at Tug, "On your way to work, boys?"

"Yessir," the driver answered and drew a puzzled expression on his face, "What's going on? More cons gone missing?"

"Just a routine inspection. Trouble at the border, as usual," the officer replied and raised his eyebrows slightly, "May I check the back?"

"Sure, if you want to," the driver shrugged, "You want help?" He watched the officer walk to the rear of the truck and pry open the hatch. From the side mirror, he could see the trooper pull his head quickly back away from the open compartment and wave them through. Even the well-trained K-9 unit seemed to want nothing to do with the vehicle.

The disgruntled officer's face reappeared in the driver's side window, "You're free to go, enjoy your day fellas!"

The driver put the truck into gear and rolled through the inspection point. Chuckling as he watched the officers snicker to each other as they resumed their duties with the next vehicle. Shooting a glance towards Tug, he was rewarded with a rare smile from the mercenary. "Honey bucket truck, that is why you are the boss, boss."

The mood in the conference room seemed to return to normal. The members of the three different governments had resumed their talks in a cooperative and amicable spirit. Sean worked in a side group that was negotiating conservation space. The former Conservancy negotiator urged the members from both Canada and Mexico to follow his organization's lead – quit squabbling over policies and regulations and allow private groups to purchase lands that they felt were vital for preservation. Bureaucracy and expensive fighting amongst groups were reconciled in enabling parties to purchase tracts that they could establish as conservatories without the government needing to finance the land. It also kept the government out of the infighting from either party. Everyone won in the equation whether they were staunch conservationists or capitalists.

As DuPont was asking Sean about how these private lands allowed or refused public use, Sean's phone began buzzing him. Checking the screen, he recognized the call was coming in from Washington, D.C. Sean darted from the table and offered an apologetic look, "Sorry, gentlemen, I need to take this."

Sean walked towards the door, catching a look from Wilkins. Sean merely offered a shrug and stepped quickly into the hallway. Pressing the "Talk" button on the phone, he answered, "Sean Kendall."

"Oh, I am sorry sir, I dialed the wrong number..."

As the line went dead, he looked at his phone, seeing that Rachel York, his long- time friend and confidant, now the Northwest Regional Director of the Department of the Interior had also called. Dialing the number quickly, he decided to take the moment of recess to check in on her.

"Sean, it's good to hear from you. How are things going down there?" Rachel asked and relayed that she was in the Capital when she had heard the news. "The White House is freaking out about what happened. They have even talked about yanking you guys out of there."

"Do they think we're in danger?"

"I don't think they know just yet."

"Well, the only way to fuel terrorism is to show fear and break from moving forward," Sean reasoned.

"True, but I don't think anyone wants officials from any of the countries getting themselves killed either," York responded quickly, "I'm not sure how much made it down there, but let's just say you need to be careful. There are people on both sides of the line screaming for escalation."

"Over a terrorist attack? I know it doesn't look good coming from American soil, but people can't think this is anything other than a group of whackos, or heck, a cartel hit with nothing to do with the U.S.," Sean insisted.

"True, but, these were whackos with U.S. military equipment. And not old surplus, fresh off the line brand spanking new just issued gear," the Department of Interior Director shifted her tone abruptly, "Look, that's about as much as I am comfortable discussing over the airwaves, it'll on be on the midday news. What I really wanted to get across is, just don't stray too far from the farm, you be careful down there."

"Yeah, we learned that the hard way yesterday," Sean scoffed.

"What?"

Briefly, Sean relayed the events of the previous day. "I'm not so sure that was a random act. I think you guys may be targets," Rachel warned, "Look, I have to get to a meeting, watch yourself and watch the senator."

Sean hung up after promising. For a moment, he stared at his phone, taking in all of the information that Rachel had shared. Beyond the phone, his eyes picked up the whisk of a figure. Glancing up, he recognized Clarissa Lamarillo walking past. Smiling, Sean began to walk towards her to wish her a good morning. He stopped short as the Secretary of Commerce's wife slipped behind the door of the ladies' room.

Shrugging, Sean glanced at his watch and decided he had better return to the meeting. Just as he took his first few steps towards the conference area, he heard a shriek and a restrained call for help. Following his ears to the sound, his eyes locked on the women's restroom. Clarissa was in trouble!

Sprinting to the door, Sean laid his ear against it. Inside, he could hear her rustling as if there were a struggle taking place.

Banging on the door, Sean called out, "Clarissa!"

From behind the heavy wooden door, Sean could hear a second shriek for help. Pressing against the door, Sean quickly realized it was locked from the inside. Slamming his shoulder against the door, it refused to budge. Desperately, Sean scanned the hallways of the lobby. Throughout the conference, the halls had been packed. As the day's meetings were underway, Sean found himself alone with no one to help.

From inside the bathroom, Sean heard the sound of glass breaking and metal falling to the floor. Spying a large fire extinguisher mounted on the wall, he pried it from its moorings and used it to smash his way into the bathroom. With one hefty whack, he was able to break through the simple lock mechanism used to pin the otherwise solid door shut.

The clatter of Sean's efforts to get inside had attracted attention as heads poked out of their meeting rooms. Feeling he had no time to waste, Sean ignored them, focusing on rescuing Clarissa. Shoving the heavy door aside, Sean found a large window on the opposite side of the room shattered. Its frame tossed tattered on the floor. Whoever had attacked Clarissa, had taken her through the window. Running across the shards of glass, Sean poked his head out in time to see a delivery truck close its door, the Commerce Secretary's wife pinned down inside.

Sean leaped out of the window as voices began shouting behind him. Before he could sprint after the van, a pair of solid arms held him at bay. Twisting his way out of the hold, Sean was able to reach the curb in time to see the delivery van pull away into traffic. A crowd had formed behind him, two of them, *policia* with their handguns drawn.

"*Senor*, come with us, please," one of the policemen asked, his gun held out in front of him.

"But they're getting away. A green and white van with a florist logo on the side panels," Sean pleaded.

"Sir, we will handle that. Come with me please," the policeman continued, his body posture unwavering. Behind them, a crowd from the street as well as the conference hall had formed. Looking past the policemen, Sean saw the tall figure of Senator Johnson flanked by the staffs from both Mexico and Canada.

Relenting, Sean moved towards the policemen. As he neared, one of them produced a pair of handcuffs. Sean looked bewildered at the two officers, wondering why they were treating him as a suspect. A voice from the crowd stopped the officer with the cuffs.

"That won't be necessary," Secretary Lamarillo strode forward and turning to Sean, "What happened? Where's Clarissa?" The Commerce Secretary put an arm around Sean and ushered him through the crowd, the officers close in tow.

"I was out in the hall to check my phone. As I was hanging up, I saw Clarissa and started to say hello until I noticed she was heading for the ladies' room. As I turned to head back towards the meeting, I heard her call for help. Not seeing anyone nearby, I went to the door to investigate. I called out, and my call was met with another brief cry. Trying the door, I found it stuck and heard glass shatter. I grabbed a fire extinguisher and broke the handle, pushing my way through. When I got inside, she was gone, and the window was torn from its frame. I ran to it, looked outside, and she was whisked away in a floral delivery truck," Sean sputtered excitedly through the events.

"Oh my god!" Lamarillo exclaimed, turning to a uniformed man, "Captain, get the word out to begin trying to find that truck." The man nodded and stepped away to relay the message over his radio.

"I'm sorry I wasn't able to get to her in time," Sean said, looking into Lamarillo's concerned eyes.

"I am sure you did what you could," the Commerce Secretary sighed.

The security captain turned away from his radio. A concerned look had washed across his face, "Senor Secretary...I, uhh, I think you need to come with me to the security office."

Lamarillo looked at the man with curiosity, "Did they find something?"

The captain hesitated to answer and then stammered, "Something on the video, sir."

Lamarillo nodded and took the lead toward the security office of the new conference center. From his position, the police captain waved over two of his men and whispered to them. Within moments, they had moved in behind Sean and flanked him as the procession moved inside the building.

As they walked, Sean was closed in by Senator Johnson and Wilkins. "You are a magnet, my friend," the senator laughed.

"I guess. What was I supposed to do?"

"You did the right thing."

"This *is* Mexico," Wilkins hissed to his two comrades, his tone not adding confidence to the group.

The security office was cramped with the bodies that had followed the Commerce Secretary. Two guards that manned the room, listening to the radio and watching the dozens of monitors faced the large contingent. "Senor Secretary, if you please," one of the guards motioned Lamarillo close to one of the monitors, giving a nod of his head, the second guard pressed a button on the console in front of him.

The video showed Sean in the shadows of the hallway talking on the phone. In moments, Clarissa Lamarillo passed by. Giving a glance towards Sean, she shook her head and snapped her focus in front of her feet. The monitor then focused on Sean. He snapped the phone shut and moved quickly towards Clarissa, he paused looking disturbed and then abruptly moved towards the Secretary's wife. The video promptly panned to Clarissa, who glanced nervously over her shoulder and then disappeared into the ladies' room. Sean immediately came into view and began banging on the door. Turning away with a scowl, he tore a fire extinguisher off of the wall and slammed it down on the doorknob. With a kick, he disappeared from the video and into the restroom.

The audience in the security room fell silent. Sean felt the color drain from his cheeks as he watched the presentation. While all of the video was accurate, there were glaring omissions that made his actions to rescue Clarissa almost appear to be stalking her and then viciously breaking into the bathroom.

When the security guard stopped the playback, all eyes turned on Sean. Sean felt his entire body flush with heat, his mind churned, desperately trying to think of the correct reaction. It was clear the videos told a warped view of the story. He almost convinced himself not to worry until he saw the look in Lamarillo's eyes. The jovial, even-tempered Mexican dignitary burned with concern over his wife. In a blinded rage, he ordered Sean remanded into custody.

"Please, Secretary Lamarillo," Sean pleaded, "The video doesn't tell the accurate story!"

The two police officers standing at his flank moved in and placed their arms around each of his.

The guard at the console turned to Lamarillo, "It is as I watched it, sir."

Sean was horrified by the guard's statement. At first, he focused on the man's eyes, as if he could see the lies inside him. Then as he began to be drug away by the *policia*, his eyes moved to the ID clipped to the man's shirt pocket.

"This is some misunderstanding…," Senator Johnson began before Lamarillo cut him off with a wave of his hand.

"Silence, or I will have you all arrested for conspiracy!" the Commerce Secretary snarled, "Get him out of here."

The guards yanked at Sean's shoulders forcefully, directing him out of the office. Behind him, he heard the senator promise to clear things up. As they reached the hallway, the guard that had been at the console jogged out to his counterparts, "I'll take him in. I watched the *puta* attack one of our country's most giving people…on *my* watch!"

The guards exchanged looks and shrugged. They would just as soon review the tapes a few more times themselves to see if they could add anything to the investigation that might put them in good favor with the politician. Career advancement in their ranks was greatly predicated on who you found good favor with.

Gruffly, the guard who Sean had identified as Esteban Marquez, shoved his captive forward. Pulling a pair of handcuffs from their pouch on his utility belt, Marquez slowed his gait to slip one side around Sean's left wrist. Leaning in, he whispered, "If you don't corroborate our version of what took place inside the center, Senora Lamarillo *will* be killed."

In a moment of panic, Sean's mind battled over his suspicions and the complete insanity of fleeing. As the cold metal of the cuffs met his wrist, the suspicion side won out. Sean wrenched his hand away, as he did, he kicked his leg backward, catching Marquez in the groin. Instantly, as the guard doubled over, he lost his grip on Sean's right shoulder. Sean sprinted towards the large bank of lobby doors and into the crowd. Without turning his head, he sensed that a half-dozen handguns were already drawn and trained in his direction. Slicing through the crowd was the only thing that kept him from getting shot in the back.

Running wildly, Sean struck out in the same direction that the floral van had taken off in. Weaving his way past pedestrians, he often jumped into the road, nearly missing getting run over by pulmonia taxis as he avoided slower-moving groups on the sidewalks. He was barely two blocks from the conference center when he heard the first sirens coming down the street from both directions.

As his lungs began to burn, his mind began questioning his rash decision to run. There was something in both the guard's reaction as well as Lamarillo's that told him justice was not going to come down kindly on him. The video change had happened so cleanly and so quickly, the guard's in place…he almost stopped in the middle of the sidewalk, despite his eyes picking up the first glints of the red and blue flashing lights…the phone call that pulled him out of the meeting in the first place – he was specifically targeted.

Choking down the realization that he had been set up, he broke from the street front and sprinted down a nearby alley. The smells of fresh-baked bread and the sundries along the sidewalk churned with the foul stench of years of trash and slop that coated the warm and humid corridor. Suddenly, Sean found himself out on the beach. His slacks, dress shirt, and tie clashed with the thin bikinis and board shorts of those already out to soak in the morning sun.

Tearing his tie off, he crammed it in his pockets. Without slowing his gait, Sean rolled up his sleeves and unbuttoned his shirt to the top of his sternum. Ahead of him, rows of beach umbrellas rose from the vast glistening expanse of golden sand. He thought as the beach grew more crowded, he could at least slip away long enough to collect his thoughts and stage the next step.

His vision of escape dashed as the growl of an approaching engine tuned his attention to the grayish waters of the Sinaoloan coast. A large grey boat had come in from the channel, turning as it reached the shallow waters of the beach to race along the shoreline. Mounted towards the bow was a 40mm gun, its muzzle tracking Sean's every step.

Instinctively, Sean darted away from the shore and the boat. Moving towards the first alley, he again was forced to change course as a four-wheel drive with police lights rotating was using the lane to make its way toward the beach. Sean pushed further up the beach, trying to use every obstacle to break up a direct line of sight with the military boat.

Behind him, Sean could hear the gunning engine of the four-wheel-drive, making its way on the soft sand towards him. Picking up the pace, Sean tried to translate the shouts in Spanish called to him. Fragments of college-level Spanish afforded him the words "stop-shoot-police"- shoot in particular stung his brain. The bay was dotted with small fishing boats, both returning from the morning catch and heading out for an afternoon run of shrimp.

Sean used the heavily utilized waterway to force the gunboat to detour further from the shore.

The four-wheel-drive, too, fell out of real estate, having to backtrack to circumnavigate the bay. Sean found no relief as the drone of rotors roared overhead, a police helicopter had joined the chase. Sirens filled the streets of downtown Mazatlan from all directions. As Sean darted up the slope from the bay and back onto the busy sidewalks, he used every bit of his athletic ability to dart in and out of the vendor stands. He felt if he could get south of the city, from the bits he had seen by car earlier in the week, he felt he could find refuge, at least until dark, and then make an escape from the area altogether.

His peripheral vision told him that the gunboat was again coming in towards the shore.

Ahead of him on the coastal road, he saw the lights of a half-dozen police cars coming towards him. He knew there was a small army from the south. The sirens he had been hearing also alerted him that he was being squeezed from the east as well. He was quickly surrounded. As the helicopter roared overhead, Sean ducked under a vendor booth. Taking only a second to allow the vessel to fly by, he again poised to take off. Pausing, he looked at the merchandise of the booth that used for cover. Flippers, goggles, snorkels and scuba tanks for rent were neatly displayed in crates along the booth. The vendor was still setting up, making trips from his van parked along the street when the chaos began.

Sean spied a few items that he thought could be useful. Snatching a dive knife with leg sheath and a vest, he curled them under his arm and sprinted for the end of the merchant area. He didn't like his plan, but he thought that it might be his only way out – as slim a chance as it was. His pursuers closed in, egging him on to go forward with his foolhardy plan.

Streaking through the crowd, Sean burst up the steep row of stone steps to the platform at *Punta de Clavadistas*, a high dive platform that skilled entertainers used to delight the crowd and earn tip money as they launched themselves into a pool surrounded by a jagged, rocky crag.

Sean had watched the divers launch from the platform the previous day as they returned from the tequila factory. He recalled Silverio telling him how dangerous it was, with several deaths resulting each year from ill-advised dives. As Sean studied the assault of Pacific waves against the rocky shore, his pulse quickened, his escape plan was marred with the added risk of low tide. His leap had to coincide precisely with the rise of a swell, or he would collide with the jagged rocks under the current, a fatal proposition.

His senses felt overloaded with the sounds, and visual clues of his pursuers nearing his capture, even the drone of the helicopter rotors loomed so close, his chest shook with the vibration. Sean felt guilty as he chose a path that used bystanders as cover from the rushing police personnel's firearms.

A final glance out at the water, Sean hoped he timed his jump correctly. Only then did it occur to him that he wasn't sure the vest he snatched from the dive stand would work, and if he did make it successfully into the water without impaling himself on a rock, he wasn't sure where he would go. He didn't see the policemen merely shrugging and walking away. They would stand around the chasm for hours to ensure that he did in fact die, and only when a bloated body rose to the surface, would they be satisfied.

Give up or go for it. Sean chose the latter. His legs pumping, he glided up the rock steps. Clutching the vest, he launched himself into the air. He stared at the oncoming swell, arching his back as he jumped. Sean tried to buy himself precious seconds. Instinctively, he closed his eyes as his hands met the water, curling his body, he tried to limit the impact if he had guessed wrong. Pulling out of his dive, he pushed upwards towards the surface. He was horrified as he felt his abs being ripped to shreds by the coarse basaltic rock before releasing him to the water.

With a few kicks, he propelled himself into deeper water. Desperately, his fingers fumbled for the valve on the dive vest. Sean had limited knowledge of Aqualung vests. He couldn't remember if they lasted for five minutes or fifteen. Or if they had different models with different rescue loads. Or, which one he held in his hands. As he brought the valve to his mouth and he allowed his lungs to draw in their capacity of oxygen – at that precise second, that was the only thing that he cared about.

Even as he savored the breath of air, Sean pushed himself to fight the incoming current, diving lower, he found the outbound rip, propelling him out of the channel and past the swells. Sticking close to the froth, he had hoped the turbulent waters would provide him with a modicum of cover for escape.

His next problem was where to go. It would not take the police long to expand their search in the small probability that he could make it out of the chasm. Sean remembered from the brief tour he received as Silverio chauffeured them out of town, a near water level cavern tucked in along the shore, roughly half a mile south of Punta de Clavadistas – Caverna del Diablo – an old cave that linked the ocean to a lookout point through an underground tunnel. This historic soldier's escape route to the sea would be perhaps his best chance for escape, maybe his only chance.

Fighting the constant thrash of the shore break, Sean swam as efficiently as he could south. Constantly meeting obstacles, jagged underwater rocks, and discarded crab traps, he used the froth of the swells gurgling overhead to release lungs-full of air, hoping the bubbles would mix with the turbid water.

Colliding with a rock shelf that jutted into the open water, Sean fought the sting of salt in his eyes to view the obstacle. A long line of boulders stretched from the bank, looking to Sean like a man-made formation - likely a jetty from years past that had succumbed to erosion and settling in the silt and sand. He enjoyed a moment of hopeful relief; perhaps this was the cave he had learned about from Silverio. Sean's pulse quickened, as it did, he realized he was no longer receiving air from the mouthpiece, its volume had already spent, a victim of the arduous swim down the coastline.

Hand over hand, he pulled himself over the jetty, at the top, he felt exposure to the air, taking in a mighty gulp, he slid back into the water on the other side. Sean knew that the cavern was his only ticket for refuge, and if he was wrong about the location, he would quickly fall prey to the Mexican authorities. Using his refilled burst of air, he slipped through the water towards the shore. Halfway to the edge, his lungs began to burn. Each stroke made his chest scream as muscles greedily devoured the oxygen that was left in his system. Resisting the urge to pop his head out of the water and refresh his spent lungs, Sean pushed his hands forward and used subtle movement from his torso to propel him further.

Finally, his hands met with a row of steel bars - the sealed entrance to the Caverna del Diablo. Yanking frantically at the rough textured bars, Sean tried to free them from their hold. To his and his lungs' dismay, the entrance remained secure. His lungs depleted, he was forced to kick to the surface for a desperate gasp of air. Even as he rose for a breath, Sean could hear the drone of the police helicopters as it began to expand its search circle.

Quickly diving for the relative safety of the water, Sean, fumbled for the knife he had swiped from the dive stand. Bar by bar, he examined them for weakness. Decades of exposure to corrosive saltwater, he found a pair that seemed to be particularly soft. Choosing to work on one nearest the edge of the cavern, he began digging at the brittle metal. To his dismay, once the blade penetrated the outer layer of rust, the metal underneath remained solid.

Exasperated and desperate for air, Sean kicked away and, for only a moment, allowed his face to breach the surface. Out on the horizon, he could see the gray shape of the patrol boat, behind his head, he could hear the clap of the police helicopter. Quickly ducking below, his salt stung eyes scoured the massive metal grate that barred him from freedom. Once more, he attacked the steel piping that seemed to be the weakest, instead of digging into the bar itself, Sean focused on the solder ball that fastened the grate to the frame that surrounded the mouth of the cave.

As he dug the blade into the base of the bar, he found a little gap between the bar and the frame. Working feverishly, he twisted and hacked with the knife until he could see the connection had whittled. Using the blunt end of the knife, a hardened extension on the handle divers use to signal trouble by banging it on submerged objects. He hammered away at the weakened joint. Just as he thought his lungs would explode, he felt the bar give way from the frame.

With two feet on the frame, he grabbed the bar and yanked with every ounce of breathless power he could muster. The bar extended away from the mouth of the cave by barely four inches. In Sean's mind, he had hoped for a greater gap, but as his ears picked up the drone of the patrol boat, its sound waves rippling through the water toward him, like the insidious pounding of an on-coming army, he knew he had no choice.

Wedging his shoulder between the cave mouth and the rusted bar, Sean snaked his body between the two. Each inch he pulled forward, the rusty edge of the steel bars etched deep gashes in his back. Once he had his entire upper body over the edge, he was able to bend his way past the bar, his hip bone bearing the final settlement doled out by his escape path. Scrambling into the cavern, his mouth burst open as he choked in the stale air. His lungs wheezed as they refilled with oxygen. Sean remained on is hands and knees as his body recovered. Once his lungs were satisfied, his sore and bleeding back began to complain. He was relieved that he had recently received a tetanus when he was injured during the incident in Seattle. With the back of his hands, he tried to reach his wounds, trying to assess their severity. While his withdrawn hand was well covered with sticky, red substance, blood did not appear to be dripping down his back.

Collecting himself, he realized he did not know how much time this detour would allow him, nor what obstacles he might face on the other end. Rejecting the spent aqualung, he placed the dive knife in his waistband and felt his way along the cave. His eyes had no light to adjust to as he moved forward. Several times, he stumbled, the worst when his foot found the first of many steps carved into the hillside. Following the cadence of the stairway, helped him not have to rely on feeling his way along the walls, allowing him to make reasonable time until his eyes were once more, met with growing light.

The mouth of the cave was narrow, opening into a large chamber like a balloon. As Sean expected, he was met with another large steel grate, barring progress. Worse, beyond the grate, several merchants were setting up their wares along the

Cerro de Viggio lookout. A part of him wondered if he could wait out discovery and proceed after dark. The other part of him screamed that if he were to be caught there, he would be trapped. As the police helicopter that seemed to be omnipresent roared overhead, the merchants abandoned their duties to press their bellies against the rail of the lookout to observe the commotion down along the coast. Sean used this distraction to assess the proposition of the gate. To his relief, he found that the installation was concerned with entry, but not exit. The iron gate, in the middle of the large grate, was attached to hinges that had screws on the inside.

Rushing up to the iron door, he stuck the blade of the knife into the first screw head. Years of rust had locked it in place. Sean thought the blade of the knife would break before the head finally made its first turn. Excited, his wrist twisted at the decrepit bolt wildly until it was free from its place and clattering to the floor. As he went to work on the second screw head, he peered out at the merchants, focused on the manhunt conducted below. The second bolt freed as some of the merchants tired of the scene and began to return to their duties. Sean went to work feverishly on the third bolt of the bottom hinge. The screw was frozen in place. The veins in Sean's wrist bulged as he tried to free the bolt. More workers were returning to set up their booths. Sean felt trapped.

Along the street, Sean heard the screech of brakes. His heart raced, he figured it made sense for the authorities to post a sentry at the lookout, for its vantage if nothing else. To his relief, the vehicle came into view. A large tour bus had pulled to a stop along the curb. It's first stop in shuttling cruise ship guests into the Golden Zone. Desperately he gave a mighty kick to the gate, the lower hinge snapped free, to his amazement, the fervor of the crowd unleashed into the marketplace, provide adequate cover for the noise of his exit.

The top of the gate still intact, Sean slid through and out of the cavern. Straightening himself the best he could, he tried to appear as though he belonged instead of some reject from the sea. His pants remained damp, his shoes sloshed with each step, but he otherwise felt as though he would fit in enough. Carefully, he slid the gate back into place and melted into the human landscape of Mazatlan.

Sienna Gutierrez had awakened in a strange place. Alarmed, her eyes swept through the sparsely furnished room. A bed, a commode and a sink were the only items adorning the room. Light filtered through the single window on the outer wall, heavy iron bars casting a shadow against the wall. Sadness washed over the five-year-old girl, and she began to cry. She missed her father and her nanny. Her nanny…the thought of her caretaker lying on the floor of the entry of their brownstone home made her stomach feel ill.

Despite being hungry and thirsty, she dared not make a sound. More than she wanted food, she wanted to be left alone by the strange men that had stolen her from her home. Her body betrayed her desire to remain quiet, as her bladder screamed to be emptied. Reluctantly, Sienna rose from the bed and tiptoed to the toilet. She prayed silently that her captors would not hear her.

Instinctively, she flushed the toilet when she was done. Freezing in place, she chided herself for completing that automatic action. Within minutes, a key scraped into a lock, and the door to her tiny room opened.

"*Buenas dias*," a man entered the room, a bright smile spread across his face.

Sienna ignored him as he proceeded into the room, carrying a tray of toast, fruit, and juice. He did not look familiar to the little girl. He seemed different than the rest – more like a jolly uncle than the wicked bandits that had abducted her.

The man set the tray down on the bed, "It's okay little one. Cesar will not harm you."

Sienna continued to stare at the man as he turned back towards the door. She stood stoically in silence, her arms crossed in front of her body. The man closed the door, and she could hear the key moving the lock into place. Friendly or not, the man was still keeping her prisoner.

Chief of Police Raul Saboda stood on the sidewalk in front of the Punta de Clavadistas. Scratching his chin, he stared silently at the turbulent water lapping against the shore. The helicopter and patrol boat had picked up nothing. The now several dozen strong patrolmen combing the shoreline had reported no trace of the fugitive American. He might have died upon impact. The low tide certainly made that possibility more real. It is possible that the outgoing current had already drug his dead body out to sea, or the man had somehow become pinned on the bottom of the channel.

Swearing softly, he shook his head. All he knew is that reporting in with no trace of the suspect accused of kidnapping the wife of a statesman was not a good career move. Each crackle of the radio gave him hope and then ripped it away. All of his patrols reported in with regular intervals, all of them had nothing to report – no man, no clothing, no blood. He had called for a second helicopter to expand the search circle and summoned a dive team to inspect the bottom of the channel.

Saboda cursed again, how could a man vanish into the water and not surface in some manner? In minutes, the second helicopter roared overhead, buzzing the downtown Mazatlán airspace allowing the first chopper to concentrate solely on the shoreline. The divers arrived in two teams, one on a zodiac, hovering in the entrance of the chasm, the other coming in a crew cab pick-up. Men grabbed their tanks and made their way to the edge of the channel.

Sabado was confident that this search would yield the whereabouts of the American, and he was so sure of the results, he had already had a team ready with a body bag once the fugitive was retrieved. The police chief watched as the dive team set up spotters onshore, radioing instructions on sightlines to the team on the zodiac. Four men were already in the water, fighting the constant pull and push of warm Pacific water as they tried to remain clear of the jagged rocks that the waves wanted to propel them.

Nearly forty-five minutes of watching the dive teams work, Sabado was mortified when their search revealed nothing. Before he could release another string of curse words, the dive captain offered up a suggestion that it was likely that the body was flushed from the channel with the outgoing tide. He would have his team exchange tanks and sweep outward and along the mouth of the gorge for clues.

Once more, Sabado clung to hope. More and more, he wanted to see the body of the pig that thought he could commit such a heinous crime in his country, in *his* town. His hopes were dashed when nearly an hour later, the dive team reported that the gate to the Caverna del Diablo had been jimmied, and it was possible that a man could squeeze through.

The dive team captain ordered the zodiac to the cavern to inspect the scene. Within minutes, the radio crackled a report of blood visible inside the cave entrance. Sabado instantly commanded a team to Cerro de Viggio as he jumped into his vehicle to personally work the scene. As he arrived at the busy marketplace, his team was already at the gate of the historic cave. His head slumped as he watched his man move the gate back and forth, free from its hinges.

Lance Corporal Enrique Guerrero surveyed the horizon. He swallowed hard as he recognized the increased number of flybys that the U.S. fighter jets were making along the American side of the border. Without seeing them, he knew the AWACS drones were blanketing the atmosphere over his head. Still, he had a job to do. His best hope was that the U.S. would stutter in their response, and retaliation would be delayed. Ultimately, he knew it didn't matter. For years, Mexico was the ugly stepbrother to the south. It was high time that his beloved country became the pre-eminent American continental power they deserved to be.

Moving his sights to the target, he was pleased to see business was as usual. The employees of the Texas-based refinery were busy with their given tasks. No additional security seemed to be in place.

"It's ridiculous!" Adam bellowed, as Security Captain Garibaldo Riva explained why he, Laura, and Miranda had been sequestered. Each placed into separate conference rooms. Wilkins had joined them. He wanted to be sure that everyone was treated fairly and with respect. Different aides from both countries filtered into the conference rooms.

"Easy, Adam. I saw the video, while I am sure there is some explanation, it doesn't look good," Wilkins said.

"I don't give a damn about a video. Sean is not a terrorist. I don't know if you have a clue about last night in your wonderfully lawful and safe country, but we were all attacked, and if it weren't for Sean, Clarissa Lamarillo would have already been dead," Adam defended.

"Perhaps," Riva said, his hands clasped thoughtfully in front of him, "Perhaps Mr. Kendall needed Mrs. Lamarillo alive for a different means."

"This is a bunch of crap!"

"Is it? Is it 'crap' that Mr. Kendall is on probation in his own country for an attack on a tour boat?"

"You mean when he *rescued* the hundreds of people taken hostage on the boat?" Adam replied angrily.

"Yes, a vigilante. Maybe he feels that his activity today is for some greater good. Or maybe he is a lunatic that your country has been a little too lenient on," Riva retorted, before Adam could offer up his reply, Riva held his hand up, "Where were you an hour ago Mr. Raines?"

"I was on an excursion with about twenty other people until the helicopters came and snatched us up."

"Do you know where Mr. Kendall may have had Senora Lamarillo taken? A rendezvous point?" Riva continued.

"No, I don't. This is absurd! In fact, I'm out of here. If you want to talk to me any further, you can invite the U.S. consulate in with us."

"Adam, it is in all of our best interest, especially Sean's, if you cooperate. Like I said, I am sure there is some explanation. Captain Riva, why don't you show Adam the video, it may help him understand why Sean is under such scrutiny," Wilkins suggested, trying to keep heads cool. He was already trying to think of ways to remove Senator Johnson's name from Sean.

Maybe paint Sean as a hero suffering from post-traumatic stress disorder. As Adam watched the video clip, Wilkins excused himself to have his assistant in D.C. draw up a preliminary statement.

Miranda was stunned; she felt every hint of color seep away from her face. This could not be happening. She made the detective replay the video four times before she couldn't stand to watch it. It made no sense. But there on the screen, Sean appeared to confront Clarissa, when he was ignored, he ran to the bathroom door and broke in. Each time she watched, she hoped for something that didn't fit. The way Clarissa reacted, the camera captured her face perfectly. She did not want anything to do with Sean.

Sean's attack on the door seemed to be an attack made in desperation. She wished there had been audio to coincide with the images. Sighing, she took it all in as the detective, and Senator Johnson remained quiet, allowing her to come to terms with the situation.

"Sean must have felt Clarissa was in trouble. He must have heard something that made him break through the door," Miranda offered.

"I don't think so, ma'am. There was a security guard nearby at the time. He claims that he didn't hear anything until he burst in to see your friend crawling through the broken window, his accomplices having already received Senora Lamarillo on the other side," Detective Tavarez reported.

"He doesn't have accomplices. This is a misunderstanding!"

"I wish it were, Senora Shaw. Why not call for help? Why did the guard not hear her plight?"

"He must have had a reason. Sean is very reactive…"

"Ah, yes, the American cowboy…" Tavarez tossed the folder he was holding on to the conference table, so it landed with a loud smack, "It seems he is no stranger to trouble, in fact currently on probation and levied into your care, Senator Johnson?"

"Guilty of saving hundreds of lives. I am not sure how accurate your file is, but Sean was key in preventing hundreds of hostages aboard a dinner cruise from being blown up, he nearly died himself breaking up a terror ring in Seattle. Yes, Kendall may be impulsive, but he helps people, he doesn't hurt them!" Senator Johnson's tone was pointed, but even.

"But not a stranger to violence. Who knows what makes a man snap. The report paints him as a patriot. He probably is, but perhaps his patriotism wants to ensure that his country has leverage in these talks," the detective added.

"The talks? Is that what you think this is about? For one, the talks are going quite well. All of Sean's initiatives have been agreed upon. You're reaching a bit, I'm afraid, detective."

"You are aware of the attack that took place along the border this morning. Our intelligence has reported that it came from the U.S. with U.S. weapons. Mister Kendall is a patriot. I am sure those who attacked Camello fancied themselves patriots as well."

"Our intelligence indicates that there is no hard evidence as to who demonstrated that act of terror on your country. For all we know, it could have been your *own* countrymen," the senator cast a stern look toward the detective, "Let's stick to what we do know. The video *does* look suspicious, but again, there are tremendous leaps to conclusions going on.

"Then why would your man run?" the detective spat, slamming his fist on the table.

"Maybe he is unimpressed with Mexican justice and wanted to make sure he had an opportunity to clear himself," Miranda snapped.

"Fleeing from the authorities is not a signature of innocence in *any* country Ms. Shaw," Detective Tavarez replied, "I will ask you one more time, where would your friend go?"

"This is pointless. I'm out of here!" Miranda rose from her seat and pushed away from the table.

The two men watched her in silence as she made her exit. Senator Johnson turned towards the Mexican police detective, "I expect this manhunt to be conducted civilly, should you catch up with Sean, I want to be notified immediately."

"We will handle this matter in accordance with our laws. This horrible incident is a dark reflection on *both* of our countries, I am sure our governments will handle each other with respect," the detective looked into the senator's eyes, not revealing any insight into how he was taking the conversation.

Seizing the last word, the senator glared, "I'll be here to make damn sure that you will."

Seven

onitoring all law enforcement channels, Tug was surprised to hear the APB come across the Mexican national police channels for terror suspect 'Sean Kendall'. The Mexican authorities now wanted his nemesis who foiled the attack on the Seattle World Trade Organization conference. The hardened mercenary could not resist letting out a chuckle.

The pretty boy was on the run from the Federales. Tug tried to think how he could use that to an advantage. Kendall had slipped through his fingers twice, and here he was embroiled in the same country he was trying to evoke a war. Before his tactical brain could devise a plan, his concentration was broken by the cell phone ringing.

Looking down, he saw that it was his secure satellite phone. Snatching it from the console, he pushed the "receive" button. His senses tightened as the voice of Senator Small announced himself. "Senator, your phone is secure?" The seasoned special ops veteran purposely declared his caller's identity to drive home the fact that he had better be on a secure line.

"Of course. With me in the room is Jerry Rhinehart, no one else," the senator declared, "Is your team ready to reconvene?"

"Target two or three?"

"Does that make a difference?"

"Target two in daylight is incredibly high risk, approaching suicide. Target three is a little more doable without waiting for dark fall," Tug replied.

"Fair enough. Two holds a little more punch, but just keeping up the pressure is the goal, so three is acceptable."

"Consider it done. Are there any new particulars we should be aware of?"

"Well, the skies and the borders are hot, but that shouldn't surprise you. Nothing else, really. The Mexicans are grasping at straws, and D.C. is assuming either it was the Mexicans themselves or some vigilante wing of the Minutemen," Small replied.

"Then it is time to up the ante and show American military might at our southern border."

Sean chose a location where an American tourist would not be an unusual sight. That, and he was parched. The Pacifico Brewery was strategically located at the base of Cerro Creston Hill, a draw with the El Faro Lighthouse perched high above the city of Mazatlan. The brewery enjoyed easy access to the port for shipping, as well as the barrage of cruise ship guests that plundered along the docks. For Sean, this location served as excellent cover. He also was fairly certain that police would be expecting him to go into hiding, not sitting in a tavern pub drinking from a chilled pilsner and eating fish tacos.

As he placed his glass down, he reluctantly admitted that he had no idea what to do, where to go. His cellphone had died from his swim, and even if it were working, the feds from both the U.S. and Mexico would be all over him. As his waitress brought his second beer, she placed a complimentary shot of tequila next to the pilsner. Happily knocking the shot back, as the shelf pour burned down his throat, an idea came to him. As he mulled the idea, he realized that a return trip to the tequila factory was either his ticket to refuge or suicide.

Leaning back, Sean took a sip of his beer to wash down the tequila shot. He would travel at night, during the day, a spotter plane or helicopter would easily see him hiking along the barren landscape that separated him from solace. Even at night, he had bandits and the chance for police to catch up with him. Even if he made it to the distillery, he had no idea how Frederico and the others would receive him. Still, he surmised, it was his best shot.

Despite his sound reasoning and tequila-fueled encouragement, Sean nearly jumped every time the door to the pub swung open. He tried desperately to keep his cool and not appear nervous, so he buried himself in his plate of food. He sat strategically so that he maximized exits. He had even studied the staff and the direction that they came and went, noting all service doors.

Realizing that he couldn't stay in the pub all day, Sean grabbed some brochures of the area, trying to find suitable places that he could hole up until dark. Ultimately, he wanted to move towards the highway that would lead him to the tequila factory, yet stay off of the beaten path. As he finished his meal and tossed a handful of pesos on the table, Sean slipped a pair of sunglasses he bought at the counter over his eyes and proceeded into the harsh sun of the clear Mexican skies.

One brochure, in particular, seemed to hold promise for Sean, in the wooded hillsides leading out of town, a small cemetery dating back to the first European settlers memorialized salty sea captains. Here, removed from the bustle of town, the brochure stated that this site is visited by an evening "ghost pirate tour". The picture showed considerable overgrowth of the area; Sean saw this as a reasonable place to lay low until the sun began to cast sufficient shadows over the region.

The ambassador tapped nervously at his desk with his pen. The phone rang continuously; none of the calls were the one he wanted to receive. Hours had passed since the press conference. While the caller ID flashed with requests from the State Department, the President's Chief of Staff, and his counterpart in the U.S., the only call he was willing to pick up was the one that would reunite him with his daughter.

He was exhausted from the continuous worry and the ache that consumed his heart and his head. Gutierrez swore to himself and God that he would trade his entire career, or even accept death himself, to have his daughter back. His disciplined mind did at least reject going down the path of thoughts depicting what those heathens might be doing to her. He wondered who these men were. Reluctantly, he had to admit that they could be an outside entity or even rival factions of his own government. Corruption ran deep in his country's political framework, a fact that he had turned a blind eye to for so many years.

The picture on his desk made the pain in his chest drill even deeper, but he refused to take his eyes off and lessen his burden. Instead, he focused on his little girl's big brown eyes, disappointed in his naiveté. He wanted to create a better future in his homeland for his daughter. Now his anger at his own countrymen made him curse that he had spent his life trying to fix the ills of a nation that didn't want to be fixed. They exported their problems to the States, retaining the rest to toil and labor for a pittance in their factories, farms, and hotels. Now, if he got his daughter back, he would just as soon protect her from the people that he had served for so many years.

Suddenly, the flash on the call screen registered in his eyes. His heart skipped a beat, and he eagerly stabbed at the receiver. His voice was almost nil as he rasped a muted "hello".

"Senor Ambassador. You have done well so far. I am sorry for the backlash the administration must be levying on you," the voice on the phone hissed.

"How is Sienna?" Gutierrez blurted.

"She is fine. You have a very well-behaved daughter. You must be very proud of her."

"I am. Now when can I get her back?"

"Tut, tut. We still have work to do, though it seems our cause is being helped out by unforeseen similar interests. I assume you heard about the attack on Camello," the man asked.

"I did, was that you, too?" the ambassador asked.

"No, I do believe it was the Americans. And the trouble in Mazatlan?" the voice continued.

"Yes."

"Seems our neighbors to the north will make our job of ruining the trade conference even easier."

"Then give me back, Sienna!"

"I said easier, not complete," the man snapped, "What we need from you now is information. I assume your phone has been ringing off the hook. It took me several times to get through. Your superiors would like to have a chat with you, I presume."

"What kind of information?"

"Well, you *are* still the Ambassador to the United States. Our countries seem to be in conflict, and you have put forth a fair rationale for why you halted the trade agreement. I want you to do your job and supply us with all relevant information to troop movements, investigation reports, and real-time updates on the reactions from both governments," the demands rattled over the phone.

"You don't need to hold my daughter to receive this. Most of this information, I'd bet you are already privy to. I'll supply you with everything you need, bring back Sienna."

"Please, Senor Ambassador. You are a man of great integrity, but I think we both know that to make this relationship work, we need collateral. Think of Sienna as doing her part for her country. She is a hero, Senor Gutierrez. And whether you agree or not, you are working in the best interest of your country," the man paused and changed his tone to reflect that he meant business, "We will call you every half-hour. Every time you fail to answer, you bring discomfort to your child."

"But…what you are asking me to do, I'll be in meetings, I'll be at the podium, I'll…," the ambassador stammered.

"We live in a world of amazing technology. I trust you will figure it out. And oh, by the way, if we find you are holding out on us, well…that would not be in your daughter's best interest."

Colonel Reyes sat behind his desk. The smell of a Cuban cigar wafted in from the balcony where, Tiberon LaCosta chewed on the tip of his cigar. LaCosta beamed at his man who had just hung up the phone, "See, Reyes, the good ambassador is a very willing participant. He can provide insight into where the talks are and possibly even to the U.S. military's intentions along the border."

"If we know in advance, then we can position our troops to hit them before they are ready. Good, good," the colonel scratched his chin and then looked up, "Tell me LaCosta. What is in all of this for you? You have obviously gone to great expense, even contracted a mercenary force…surely you don't care about the environment. I hardly suspect you are so deeply devoted to your country…."

"There are those of us who profit tremendously from the current system. The false border, the conduit of desperate souls who will do anything to get into America…they are our pipeline. I could care less about the politics. I need a workforce desperate enough to risk everything to find that romanticized a better life to our north. I am merely maintaining the status quo," the mogul replied.

"Moving, LaCosta, very moving. Not sure I'll use your sentiment to motivate the troops, but whatever your reason, I believe our camps can work together."

"Our two camps are going to establish policy in the Americas moving forward."

Typically, the scene of afternoon sun shining through the fronds of giant palm trees against the backdrop of the gleaming blue Pacific would have delighted Miranda. Today, they served as a cruel reminder to the crisis that she and her friends were ensnared. The soft clasp on her shoulder diverted her attention to Laura Raines. Following Senator Johnson, congressional aide Wilkins and her husband Adam into the private balcony of the suite that served as their meeting room, Laura tried to offer comfort to her friend.

Miranda managed a weak smile in return. Turning her focus to the senator and his aide, she asked pointedly, "Have they found him?"

"No, we just received an update, it sounds as though he has led the police force of Mazatlan on quite the chase," the senator replied, the vision of Sean causing havoc amongst the local law enforcement almost bringing a grin to his lips.

"What about that van?"

"Still nothing. That really hurts Sean's story. People on the street don't seem too willing to come forward. They prefer to keep to themselves in matters like this, I guess," Senator Johnson said.

"What about you? Is there anything we can do for you?" Wilkins asked.

"Just keep me in the loop," Miranda shrugged. "I need to know Sean is safe."

"That guy is wiry. I have seen him wriggle out of more difficult situations," Adam said wryly.

"Oh, I know," Miranda pursed her lips, "I still can't figure out how he got into *this* one. I mean, he stepped out of that room for what, ten minutes?"

"He was set up. Anyone who does the slightest research would know he's an easy target – a boy scout who can't keep his nose out of trouble," Adam scoffed.

"And a government that is known to be a little reactive and police force overrun with corruption," Wilkins added.

"The question is, what do we do now?" Senator Johnson asked aloud, turning to Wilkins, "You have our man coming in, when?"

"Right, we have an FBI agent that has volunteered to come down here and lend support. He should be here in a few hours. We also have a U.S. Embassy envoy en route from Mexico City. The White House has been alerted to what is going on, but until they have a better understanding of what actually happened before they get involved on an official basis."

"What is that going to do?" Miranda asked.

"Well, if the Mexicans catch up with Sean, they will have to treat him a bit more kindly than if the spotlight wasn't on them. We can also start trying to negotiate for asylum or at least provide American legal defense," Wilkins replied, "What I wonder is, where in the world Sean could have gone. Any ideas where he might have taken off to?"

"Beats me," Adam said, "As far as I know, the only knowledge of Mazatlan is what he's seen in the past couple of days."

"This is the first time he's ever been here, I have no idea," Miranda agreed.

"My boy's gone in survival mode, he could be long gone in the middle of the wilderness or holed up in the basement of this very hotel," Adam supposed.

"I know it's difficult, but we may as well take care of ourselves. I have asked Silverio to book us in a private dining room. Let's go and try and relax. The authorities have Wilkins' cell phone, and they'll let us know if anything changes," the senator suggested. As if to avoid the possibility for Miranda to argue, the senator stood and held his hand out to help her from her chair. Reluctantly, Miranda succumbed and agreed to the dinner invitation.

Eight

Traveling through the brush in the twilight was slow going. The craggy hills, crumbling rock, and hot sand made Sean's trek away from town that much more arduous. With every passing helicopter and spotter plane, Sean dove into the cracks and crevices of the terrain with abandon. Each time, he grimaced, not knowing if he was going to share the space with a snake or scorpion.

The slowly retreating sun pushed its way to the west providing him with ample shadows in which to take refuge. These same shadows, which seemed to correlate with fewer fly-overs from the spotter craft, also hid the contours of the land, frequently tripping Sean up and sending him sprawling to the ground against jagged beds of red rock.

Ignoring the collection of bruises and trickling cuts, he pressed on. The heat of the day giving way to the slightly cooler onshore flow helped him maintain a quicker pace. Soon, he reached the timber and chicken wire fence that encircled the Hacienda Tioga Tequila compound.

While exhausted, parched and hungry, he wanted just to run up the drive to the heavy wooden entrance. Instead, he listened to a little voice in his head that demanded he use caution. He didn't know how he would be received. Frederico seemed amicable enough to Sean, but being accused of kidnapping the spouse of a country's high-ranking official tends to change people's opinions.

Sticking to the ravine that snaked alongside the drive, he made his way up towards the hacienda. His senses on high alert, Sean listened for any sign of someone coming down the driveway or someone having observed him crossing the lower edge of the ranch. Forcing himself to take it slow so that he did not make too much noise on the loose stones under his feet or the sagebrush that scraped along his legs, he found himself at the large circular drive of the tequila factory. The porch lights were ablaze, and several cars were in the driveway. Seeing so many vehicles made Sean even more wary of making any type of bold entry, not knowing who any of those cars might belong.

Crouching below the sill level of the windows, he crept to the far side of the building. Here, where the factory received and sent deliveries, there were not the large bank of windows that afforded the building its magnificent view. Sean knew that this would be his best chance to observe the scene and see if it made any sense to seek refuge with Frederico.

Slinking along the side of the building, he rounded the large delivery bay. A new scent met his nostrils. Sean paused briefly to determine what the smell was – enamel. Behind a cargo truck, was a grey panel-van that Sean's nose led him to. This van had recently received a fresh coat of paint. Studying it briefly, he thought it looked an awful lot like the florist's van that had whisked away with Mrs. Lamarillo.

His pulse quickening, Sean was on his highest alert. It was hard to keep his composure and not storm the building to demand answers. Instead, he continued to sneak along the side of the building in silence. Closing in on the corner of the hacienda, he heard voices out on the back veranda. Several people were engaged in what sounded like a heated conversation. Craning to see around the corner, he saw Frederico with two other men. Each held half-empty glasses of tequila. A server came out on to the veranda and brought a fresh drink to a woman who had her back to Sean as she leaned over the iron railing, staring out at the rugged terrain of the ranch.

The woman turned to accept the glass, and Sean's heart nearly leaped out of his throat – Clarissa Lamarillo was leaning casually against the rail, sipping her drink. Spinning back behind the concealment of the far corner of the building, Sean desperately tried to make sense of what he just witnessed. Clarissa seemed to be wholly unharmed and unfazed by her recent abduction.

Sean reasoned that there had to be an explanation. Maybe gunmen were holding her there, so she decided that she may as well not fight it. Maybe here captors don't see her as a threat and agreed to allow her to be comfortable. Sean struggled to piece together a plausible rationale for this situation. Instead, his ears made the whole thing that much harder to stomach.

Above the murmur of conversation, Sean could hear Clarissa laughing with one of the men who approached her. Whatever the situation, Clarissa did not appear to be in any apparent danger or stress. Sean knew he had to get closer to catch the conversation. Looking around, he tried to locate a way to move around the backyard unnoticed, but the only way under the veranda would leave him fully exposed.

Behind him, he studied the large pallets used to transport the cases of raw goods to the factory for making batches of tequila. Tipping one on its end and then stacking a second on top of it, he used the slats as ladder rungs and was able to reach up to the roofline of the portico covering the loading bay. Grasping the edge, he was able to pull himself up to the top. From here, he could reach the roofline of the hacienda itself and duplicate his effort.

Slinking carefully along the red clay roof on his belly, he made his way until he was just over the veranda. He could hear the conversation getting heated again. Clarissa's voice rose above everyone else's.

"No, I won't have it. This little stunt was supposed to help the cause *and* my husband. This sounds like you will hang him out to dry!"

"Clarissa, you know the risks. Unfortunately, your husband is not worth the harm it will do the project. He is a loose cannon. We gave you time to control him, and you failed. Now, we must take control. He will either do as we say and reverse his pro-U.S. stance, or he will be removed from office. One way or another, Clarissa...," one of the men said. Sean's brain worked overtime to translate from Spanish to English – a task he had not done to this level since his sophomore year in college.

"He *will* turn. You'll see. Give him more time. I will go back and work with him. After my supposed kidnapping by the American, he will be much more open," Clarissa pleaded.

"He might. But Clarissa, we have been given our orders, we cannot take that risk," the man responded defiantly.

"No, I won't have it!" Clarissa repeated, her voice escalated. The sound of her heels against the stone floor of the veranda suggested she headed towards the door to the factory.

"Hey, leave her alone!" Sean recognized Frederico's voice, "It's not supposed to be like this!"

Sounds of a scuffle followed by a single gunshot and a piercing scream Sean assumed belonged to Clarissa filled the air. Trying to peer over the edge, Sean scooted forward, but he felt if he crawled any further, he would fall over. Seconds later, he could hear the sound of tires squealing in the driveway and a large engine growling as it sped towards the highway.

Moving as quickly as he could, Sean retreated the same way he had come – to the roof of the portico, to the loading bay, to the side of the house. Glancing around the corner, he found the veranda vacated. Grasping a rung of the iron rail, he hauled himself up to the stone-clad porch, crouching behind a massive planter housing a palmetto. Peering around the stone pot, he could see a pair of legs sticking out of one of the large French doors separating the tasting room from the porch.

Not hearing any noises from within, Sean slowly moved towards the body. A river of blood was oozing its way into the doorjamb. Tracing it to its origin, Sean found the gasping body of Frederico. His eyes met with Sean's in desperation.

"Don't move, I'll help you!" Sean said hurriedly, trying to console the man.

"No," Frederico pleaded, "You must help Senora Lamarillo. They have taken her."

"Where? Do you know where they were taking her?"

"There is a compound, a drug lair east of Canoas. They will take her there. They feel invulnerable there," Frederico wheezed.

"Alright, but first, we must get you some help…"

"Sean," the Frederico's body was growing cold, his hand grasping Sean's, "Tell Silverio I am sorry…I was wrong…"

Sean's stomach churned as the man at his feet released his grasp, his head slumping to the floor. Reaching out to his carotid, Sean could find no pulse. Dejected, he rubbed his jaw, trying to determine his next step when a figure came out of the shadows, a large gun in his hands.

Panicking, Sean searched desperately for cover, but the man was right on top of him before he could move. For a moment, the figure stopped, still cloaked in the darkness of the room. Then he took a step closer. The gun was leveled at the floor, not at Sean.

The house server approached him tentatively, and in rough English, he said, "Here, Senor. You get her back. I take care of things here." Abruptly, the rifle was shoved in Sean's arms.

Stammering, Sean responded, "I will."

This exercise for Tug held little risk. In the cloak of darkness, he checked his illuminated watch and calmly began unbuckling the case that he knelt beside. Pulling the long tube out of its foam packing, he clicked open the site, armed the trigger and pointed it towards the sky. He watched a cloud work to swallow the moon. He preferred it remained covered, the people who would like to come after him would benefit from it more than he would.

On the horizon, the blinking aircraft navigational lights came towards him. They seemed to be moving so slowly, while in actuality, they were traveling at nearly 500 miles per hour. His pulse nearly still, Tug gently applied the slightest pressure against the trigger. One final breath before he held the weapon steady - an ingrained habit after decades of marksman training. The mercenary could hear the slightest dull roar overhead and squeezed the trigger. A brilliant streak raced skyward until it met with the starboard engine of the defenseless target. Delta Flight 683 burst into a giant fireball and disintegrated into the night sky.

Placing the tube back into the case, he fastened the buckles and slung the kit over his shoulder. Abandoning the stolen car that he had used to cross the Mexican border and sit outside the Nogales airport, he began the hike in the opposite direction towards a second vehicle that was awaiting him.

As ordered, he found a dilapidated Volkswagen Rabbit, parked along the side of the road. The front passenger tire deflated, discouraging anyone from taking it and providing a reasonable explanation of why it sat vacant on the side of the road.

Popping open the hatch, he pried the plastic wheel well cover away from the body, exposing the rear strut. Velcroed to the strut housing, Tug found a can of compressed air and a key taped to the cylinder. Peeling away the Velcro, he tossed the SAM case in the hatch and quickly made his way to the flat tire.

In minutes, Tug was streaking south on Highway 15 towards Mazatlan. In contrast to the numb, matter-of-fact manner in which he dispatched the missile that just killed 243 passengers on the airliner, he was boiling over with excitement that he could catch up with his unlikely nemesis, Sean Kendall. It is not that he never had a failed mission or one that left a loose end hanging, but never had a civilian caused him so much trouble. No, to Tug, Sean Kendall was a personal target that he *wanted* to take care of – an emotional desire that violated every code that made Tug the successful mercenary that he had become.

Sienna Gutierrez was awakened by a commotion outside in the courtyard. Scrambling out of her bed, he dashed to the barred window of her room. Several of the men were shouting at one another. The mean man that seemed to lead the group of thugs appeared to be the most upset. He bellowed a hysterical rant of cuss words while flailing his arms wildly in such an animated fashion. Sienna couldn't help but giggle.

Looking on, the young girl wondered what could make this surly man act in such away. A gleaming black car had pulled up and the driver, along with two other men exited quickly and were busy explaining that whatever brought them there was not their fault. The head man kept peering past the driver and into the vehicle. Each time, he shook his head disgustedly. Finally, he threw his hands up in the air and growled that they should bring the passenger in and find her an appropriate room.

Turning back towards the hacienda, the angry man saw the tiny face of Sienna Gutierrez peering out between the bars. "You have company Sienna!" the man scoffed and disappeared into the building.

Sienna wrinkled her brows, wondering who it could be. In her heart, she hoped it would be her father, although that would mean that these bad men would have him too. As she watched, the men by the car yanked a woman from the back seat. She was an attractive woman who looked much like the ladies that her dad knew. She had an elegance about her that was in stark contrast to the setting that they were immersed in. The woman seemed to be very unhappy to be at the compound and, like Sienna, appeared to be there not of her own accord.

"So, what do you suppose is going to happen?" Laura asked Senator Johnson, the serious, dark conversation in stark contrast to the serene setting of the moon streaked ocean framed by the silhouette of gently swaying palm trees.

"I honestly don't know. The attack on Camello, the incident with Sean and Clarissa, the sudden change in the Mexican contingent's stance on the accord, it doesn't look good. I haven't

seen tensions this high with the U.S. and her neighbors in my
entire career," Johnson shrugged. He paused as Wilkins pulled his
cellphone from its pouch and excused himself from the table. "My
biggest concern is for Sean's safety at the moment. The current
mood among the *policia* doesn't suggest that they will deal with
him kindly."

"They had better…," Adam growled, "I wished he would
contact us."

"Yes, but I bet the Mexican authorities do too," Johnson
sighed, his lips forming a tight seal revealing his concern.

"You think they're listening in?" Adam asked and received
the senator's response in a sullen nod.

Wilkins approached the table, his affect grim. Miranda's
heart sank, fearing the news was negative about Sean. "Sir," the
aide called as he neared the group, "There has been another
tragedy. An American-based airliner has just crashed outside of
Nogales. I don't like where things are going, and the Department
of Homeland Security recommends we move to the embassy
compound immediately."

"This just keeps getting worse. Did they say why the plane
crashed?"

"No, sir, just that it was a complete loss with no survivors.
Emergency response crews are on the scene, and investigators are
en route."

"Make the arrangements for the embassy and have a driver
pick up everyone's things from the hotel. Then have the driver pick
up The Raines' and Miranda. I would like you and I to meet with
Lamarillo and DuPont," the senator replied. He wanted to try and
keep a medium for communication open, as well as be able to
monitor the pursuit of Sean directly.

Wilkins began to protest the senator's decision, but reading his boss' expression, knew his stance would not change. Instead, he nodded and strode to the corner of the room to place the necessary calls.

"I'm sorry, guys," Johnson announced to the table, "I hope you are all okay with moving to the embassy, at least until we sort things out and can assemble some sort of risk assessment."

"What about Sean?" Miranda asked.

"There is a situation room at the embassy. I will make sure that they allow you access to monitor the official channels. That will be one of the best ways to keep in tune with Sean's plight. In the meantime, they will be able to ensure your safety and make arrangements to evacuate you if the situation calls for it," the senator replied, scooting his chair from the table, "Please excuse me. I am going to try my best and keep the channels with our Canadian and Mexican friends open the best that I can. Try and enjoy dinner, and I will see you at the embassy later on."

Getting Wilkin's attention with his hand motioning, he was ready to go. The pair left the private dining room.

The three remaining diners sat in silence as they attempted to reconcile the events of the day. Adam was the first to speak, "It looks more and more to me as though Sean was a convenient goat for Clarissa's disappearance. I think it was her that the bandits were after last night."

"I think so too. Anyone who knows Sean would have known he was easy to bait. There are obviously people somewhere that want friction between the two countries. I just can't believe they somehow got Sean into the middle of it," Miranda agreed.

"He'll be alright, Miranda. Sean is very resourceful. If he can survive the wilderness of the North Cascades, he can manage the desert of Mexico," Laura exclaimed.

"He's probably kicked back, sharing a bottle of tequila with a lizard right now. Swapping stories, roasting flies on the fire while staring at the stars…," Adam chided. Both Laura and Miranda laughed in spite of themselves at the picture.

Monitoring the airwaves, Tug received yet another break. Senator Johnson's delegation requested a driver and police escort to bring them to the U.S. Embassy in Mazatlan. Glancing at his watch, he calculated how long it would take the group to be picked up and approximately where they would be when he could intercept them. Flashing a rare grin, he relished the prospect to invoke even more international havoc while exacting his revenge.

Pointing his car towards the outskirts of Mazatlan, he decided Sean Kendall could wait. He hoped that the delegation might provide some clues as to where his nemesis might be holed up, providing this chance as a hat trick of fortune. Thumbing his way through the touchpad of his handheld device, he found the map of the Golden Zone. Tracing the route for the delegation to transit from the restaurant to the embassy, he found a point that was out of the fray and would be a point of vulnerability.

Gunning his rickety car through the desolate stretch of western Mexico real estate, he hastened to set up an appropriate ambush site. He hoped his guess would be correct, and the spot would be relatively free of local traffic.

Nine

The Land Rover Sean took from the hacienda rambled down the poorly maintained highway. He followed the vague directions he was provided as best as he could. Further and further away from the Pacific coast, he drove, entering the rugged interior of the Mexican mainland. He left behind the final traces of civilization as he pursued his quest to bring Clarissa Lamarillo back and clear his name.

As he drove, he enjoyed the bottle of water and paper bag filled with tamales. After his long hike from Mazatlan to the tequila factory, he was starving and in bad need of replenishing the fluids in his tired body. Just sitting in the leather seat of the SUV was a comforting rest. He felt like he had completed a triathlon, and while he longed to curl up for sleep, the food and water helped to reinvigorate him.

His mind began to walk through his next steps. First, he had to find the drug cartel's compound. He was guessing that there would not be signs along the highway to point the way. Sean also knew that asking a bunch of questions in the nearby town was also not an option. He was concerned enough, just showing his Caucasian face. Still, armed with a general idea of where to head, he was determined to find the Commerce Secretary's wife.

The second step he pondered was what to do when he *did* find the compound. Armed with a single 7mm rifle, he was pretty sure that he would be well out-gunned. His mind ground through various scenarios, each more ridiculous than the one preceding it. None relevant without having a clue of what the lay of the land would be like. He envisioned having to get to the core of a massive hornet's nest. Getting stung there would be deadly.

Having not seen a single light or sign of humanity since the hacienda, he found the drive east of Mazatlan kind of eerie. Surrounded by darkness, he sped across the flat desert only occasionally dotted with canyons to break up the dim and monotonous terrain. In the distance, he could see hills looming, barely visible in the pitch-black sky. As the hillside neared, Sean found himself descending another canyon.

After hours of nothing but lonely cactus breaking up the beam from his headlights, Sean was almost startled to see the burning lights of a settlement backed up to the hillside. He slowed the Land Rover as he decided how to enter. It was the middle of the night, and his headlights might have already warned of his approach. He hesitated in turning them off, as he did, the road in front of him disappeared.

Waiting, the engine idling, Sean had hoped his night vision would afford him enough to sight to make his way quietly down the road and into the canyon. Slowly and not nearly as well as he had hoped, his eyes did adjust enough to vaguely make out the rough side of the road from the aged blacktop. Cautiously, almost as though he were feeling his way along, Sean crept towards the little canyon town.

He watched diligently for any signs of another vehicle, but no headlights met his view. Growing more comfortable, he accelerated slightly, eager to see what he could learn. Aiming directly for the town, Sean did not catch the slight jog in the road in time and for a split second, he felt his heart leap into his throat as the tires of the Land Rover left the pavement and rambled over the rocky ground towards a ravine. Sean yanked the wheel and pressed hard on the accelerator, but gravity had already taken hold and sent the SUV careening sideways into a massive stand of boulders at the bottom of the dry creek bed. The horrible sound of metal crunching simultaneously met with the loose rifle taking flight and knocking Sean in the head.

Groaning, he rubbed the site of impact as a knot already begun to form. He tried turning over the ignition to see if he could maneuver his way back onto the road, but the engine wouldn't start. Grabbing his gun, he slid out of the cab and inspected the vehicle. The collision had been violent enough to slam the metal grill into the radiator, rendering the truck useless. Sighing, Sean gingerly crawled out of the ravine and onto the highway.

He halfway expected someone in the little town to hear him and come to investigate. But as loud as the sickening collision ways to his ears, he was still a couple of miles outside of the town, far enough that only he and the creatures of the night had bore witness. Rifle slung over his shoulder. He hiked towards the little settlement.

Nestled against the hill, Sean deemed that this must have been an old mining town. As the buildings came into view, he found most of them decrepit, with siding missing whole boards and porches with roofs that seemed to be sagging towards rotting floors. Trying to peer through dusty windows, Sean found most of them dark and lifeless. The few that had their lights on were devoid of life. One was a general store, another a tavern, and the third a little taqueria. The lights, Sean assumed, were to help monitor pilferers, though he couldn't imagine they received that much traffic, this far out from other points of civilization.

Keeping to the shadows, Sean investigated each building. The town was made of three streets, each running further away from the old highway and closer to the hillside. The three little storefronts were primarily what made up the first street. Each appeared to be vacant and locked up for the evening. Not wanting to pass by the lights in the front, he kept to the darkened rear of the buildings. The dusty alley behind the tavern littered with cases of bottles stacked outside, the scent of stale beer swirling in the evening breeze. Approaching the rear window, his foot caught a glass bottle and sent in end-over-end into several others, resulting in a teeth-chattering crash. Sean pushed his back to the darkened wall and waited for a reaction.

A chorus of dog barks began to fill the night air. Starting with a dog tied to a post within easy earshot and view of the tavern and spreading to the row of ramshackle homes lining the next avenue where two more dutiful canines joined in, summoned by the first. Slinking behind a dumpster, Sean saw a porch light click on a house on the second street. A small man pressed his face against a crooked screen door, and with a sudden loud creak, the door flung open. To his amusement, the man began cursing loudly in Spanish and flung what seemed like a shoe in the direction of the dog.

Slowly the barking abated, and Sean continued on his search, placing greater care where he planted his feet. The tavern was completely dark, and despite the dogs, not a single noise emanated from the town in or outside of the building. Finding the door as weak and worn as most of the surrounding buildings, Sean grabbed the handle and forcibly yanked on it several times until the primitive latch gave way, ripping from the aged wood that held it shut. Cautiously, Sean peered inside. Placing deliberate steps forward, he winced with each creak of the floorboards. The hum of two refrigerators gave him some solace that it might mask his noises.

Feeling his way along, Sean found himself in the back office, which was no more than a cramped hallway between the back door and the service side of the bar. Roaming his hands along the desk, he found an old flashlight. It was heavy steel with its beam on a right angle from the body itself – the type used in years past by minors who would attach it to their helmets or on a belt so they could operate hand-free.

Further along, he found a rag. Placing the rag over the head of the flashlight, Sean flipped the switch. The muted light would be soft, and he hoped not visible through the dirty windows to anyone awakened by the barking dogs. With the light, he carefully angled it towards the floor and began sweeping the contents of the office. His Spanish rusty, he could make out some of the documents that seemed to overflow the old wooden desk. Most appeared to be invoices, the word *cerveza*, Sean readily recognized.

"Speaking of which, I doubt any will mind." Reaching into one of the refrigerators, Sean liberated a chilled beer from the rack. Hooking the jagged cap on the side of the desk, he pressed his palm firmly down on the bottle, sending the cap flying. Taking a sip, his mind followed the cool liquid down his throat. Though he had been given a jug of water at the hacienda, the cold beer was a pleasant treat. Removing a few pesos from his pocket, he tossed them on the desk.

A corkboard over the desk was ringed with pictures, many of them taken in the bar. Leaning in, Sean studied them, finding them just to be a random collection of smiling faces around buckets of beer and small glasses of tequila hoisted in the air. About to turn away, one thing caught Sean's attention. There was a stark contrast among the patrons. Many, especially the bartender and the waitress, appeared to be very poor. Their clothes were simple and shabby, their hair rough and slightly unkempt. Others, however, were quite different. Their clothes were newer and more stylish, a couple of them wore linen jackets, their overall appearance much more polished. Looking closer, Sean noticed a leather strap just hidden by one of the jackets. The man was wearing a shoulder holster.

Trying to imagine the presence of this dichotomy seemed to fit with the tip he was provided by the assailant at the hacienda. There was another element of this seemingly dead town. An element of wealth and individuals who felt it necessary to be armed. Sean was sure he found the town where the drug cartel was, now he had to find where. It made sense to him that the layout of each street being more removed from the highway, with the final street and row of buildings with its back to the hillside, would make an excellent setting for a cartel hideout. Swigging a throat full of beer, he turned to make his way out back out of the tavern.

Back into the cool night air, Sean was careful not to make any undesired noise this time. Sticking to the shadows, the weary fugitive made his way to the last street in the little town. Sneaking past the row of humble homes, some with only curtains for windows, others with no coverings at all. As he reached the last road, Sean met with a tall chain-link fence that stretched as far in each direction as he could see. Cautiously using the rag covered flashlight he took from the tavern, he studied the obstacle. In contrast to the rest of the town, the fence seemed to be new and in excellent repair.

"If I was going to hide a drug-making facility, I might put a fence around an old mining operation in the middle of nowhere," Sean mumbled to himself.

He thought about climbing the tall fence, determining how he would scale the razor wire at the top when a light bobbed in his direction from the other side. Caught out in the open, Sean whipped his head from side to side, desperately trying to find a place to take refuge. Fifty yards away, he spied an old trough, like those used to hold water for horses and cattle. Trying to sprint as fast as he could and still maintain silent footfalls, he slid to a stop behind the large wooden container.

Peering around an edge, he saw the bobbing light come closer. As the figure appeared near the gate, Sean could identify a man holding the leash of a German Shepherd. The guard shook the gate to ensure that it was secure. Suddenly, the German shepherd began to growl and bark, its nose pointed directly at Sean. Wincing, Sean readied his gun. The flashlight beam swept through the night, making an arc towards the spot where Sean took cover. The light flashed overhead and continued on its circular path. As his hideaway returned to darkness, Sean again peered out from the edge of the crate.

Scolding the dog in Spanish for what Sean assumed was reacting to nocturnal critters, the guard continued on his circuit, away from Sean. Deciding this was his best opportunity, Sean raced in the opposite direction of the guard, following along the fence, searching for a logical point of entry. Finally, he found what he was looking for. A two-foot section of razor wire was flattened against the top of the chain-link fence. On the other side, the trunk of an old tree surrounded by sawdust told Sean how this break in the armor of the compound came to be. It appeared as the tree, or at least a limb from it had recently fallen, crushing the razor wire top of the fence and hadn't been repaired yet.

Accepting the gift willingly, Sean wasted no time scrambling up the fence. Reaching the area of sharp blades, he gingerly selected fingerholds that would allow him to vault over the top without coming into contact with the razor wire itself. Swinging over the top, Sean jabbed his toe into an opening in the chainlink, allowing both hands to glide over the top until they were clear and they could arrest his fall, safely on the other side. Freeing his toe, Sean hung from his fingers and dropped softly to the dirt below.

Feeling exposed, Sean darted for the first thing his eyes made contact within the compound. A row of trucks and machines sat waiting for the morning where they would be called into duty. Feeling temporarily safe in this cover, Sean checked himself for injury. Aside from a tear in his shirt and a superficial scratch, he had escaped harm, clearing the razorwire clad fence.

From his new vantage, he studied the compound. At the base of the hill, in front of the three-story high building that connected the conveyer from the mine to the loading zone for hauling the ore out, sat a series of small buildings. Each was well lit, several with new SUVs parked out front. In the center of the smaller buildings was a large adobe, seeming out of place amongst the backdrop of the mine. In front, parked next to a babbling fountain, was a large Mercedes sedan. Sean felt even more assured that he was on the right track. Now he just had to find out where Clarissa Lamarillo was being held.

Ten

S ienna Gutierrez stared in silence at the fuming
woman placed with her in the small room. From the
moment she arrived, the woman failed to
acknowledge Sienna, but instead paced back and forth in front of
the door, periodically calling for one of the men to let her out and
that she had to speak with LaCosta. Her rants were met with deaf
ears as no one even respond to her demands. Finally, she gave up
and looked across the room to find a place to sit. Looking at
Serena, she offered a weak smile.

Seeing her face in full view, Sienna paused. She recognized
the woman from one of the photos in her father's office. "Are you
a friend of my Dad's?"

Clarissa almost appeared uncomfortable with the question.
A frown swooped down her face, and she stammered as she begun
her reply, then straightened up and announced, "Yes...yes, I am.
Your father and I go way back. Sienna, isn't it?" The look on the

girl's face told Clarissa how desperate and overjoyed she was to make contact with someone who knew her father.

"Yes, ma'am. I remember you from one of the pictures in my Daddy's office."

"I am Clarissa Lamarillo. You may call me Clarissa," extending her hand she, grasped Sienna's diminutive grip warmly, "Are they treating you okay?"

The girl looked up at the woman in front of her. Her voice trembled as she spoke, Sienna had been so strong and defiant in front of the bad men, now, all of the pain of her journey exploded in a stream of tears, her reply in broken gasps, "They are awful, I just want to go home. I want my daddy."

Reaching out and almost to Clarissa's surprise, Sienna collapsed into her, hugging her waist and nuzzling tightly. The impact of this little girl's emotion and pain seethed deep into Clarissa's soul. A plan hatched to use some spoiled ambassador's daughter to force his hand seemed so easy to discuss and to be a part of, until she was face to face with the human reality of who the plan affected. "I know, dear. We'll get you back to your daddy," looking out at the barred window, "I don't know how, but we will."

Sean crept from shadow to shadow until he was upon the row of cabanas, flanking the adobe. He was grateful for the constant murmur of the fountain, masking the crunch of coarse sand underneath his feet. Combing carefully over each building, trying to catch any sign of where a hostage might be held. He slunk back into the wheel well of a large pickup as he saw a guard exit the main hacienda and approach the small cabana just to the left from Sean's vantage.

Quietly drawing a set of keys from his pocket, the man inserted one into the lock and seemed to take great caution not to make any noise as he entered. Sean took the guard's actions as enough of to reasonably assume they had someone locked inside. Fearing that this could be his only shot at entering the cabana, he risked leaving the cover of the pickup. Racing across the open space, sticking to the shadows as best that he could, Sean bolted to the front door of the cabana. He noted that the guard must have feared closing the door would have created too much noise and left it ajar.

Deciding speed was a more significant advantage than stealth, Sean slid his fingers in the opening and swung the door just enough to allow his own slender body to slip through and into the cabana. Only the soft glow of a penlight down the hall illuminated the small building. Sean took several cautious steps forward as his eyes adjusted to the darkness. Flattening his body against the wall, Sean could see a hand gingerly try a doorknob, finding it secure, the man seemed satisfied and began to retrace his steps – heading straight for Sean.

Launching himself, Sean took two great strides, lowering his shoulder and plunging every ounce of force he could muster into the midsection of the unsuspecting guard. Maintaining follow-through of his tackle, Sean drove his victim to the floor. The resulting noise was loud, but brief. Sean didn't have time to assess whether or not it had been enough to alert the main house. He delivered a brutal slash of his elbow to the side of the guard's head, leaving him slumped and motionless under Sean's weight. The keys the guard carried clanked to the floor just as Sean scooped them up in his fingers.

Snatching the penlight as it rolled along the baseboard, Sean pointed the feeble glow at the doorknob the guard had just checked. By his fourth attempt, he found a key that slid all of the way in. Taking a deep breath, unsure of what or who he might find, he yanked the door open. Moving the penlight back and forth through the room, Sean was surprised to see two figures asleep in a pair of beds. One started to stir, and at the site of the light, lifted her head and opened her mouth in fright. Diving across the room, Sean cupped his hand to the girl's mouth and shushed her in a breathy voice.

In the dim light, Sean noticed the startled captor was a little girl, her eyes wide in fear. Taken aback, he almost let go of her mouth, but was able to stifle a building scream.

"Kendall?" a voice called from behind. Sean instantly recognized that it was Clarissa's.

"Senora Lamarillo, who's mouth am I holding shut?"

"Her name is Sienna," Clarissa replied and scurrying out of bed, and across the room, the stateswoman cooed to the frightened girl, "It's okay, Sienna, don't scream."

"They're holding a little girl captive?" Sean asked incredulously.

"They are. Listen, if they find you here, they will kill you without hesitation," Clarissa hissed.

"I know. That is why we have to go now," Sean replied flatly, with hesitation, he took his hand off of the little girl's mouth. Leaning on one knee, he whispered, "Sienna, I am going to take you out of here. You have to be very quiet. If I tell you to run, I need you to do just that. If I tell you to hide, find the best place you can find quickly, especially a place that you'll fit and no one else can. Can you do that for me?"

Sean could see the girl's silhouette nodding in the frame of the window. "Okay, let's go. Follow me out into the hallway." Poking his head out of the doorway, Sean motioned for Clarissa and Sienna to follow. Sienna gasped at seeing the unconscious man lying in the hallway.

"Stay here for a second," Sean hissed as he grabbed the guard by the ankles and drug him into the room Clarissa was held. The guard stirred as Sean turned to leave the room, with a quick kick of his leg, Sean caught the guard on the chin snapping his head backward, returning him to slumber. Reappearing in front of the anxious escapees, he urged them to follow. Moving toward the front door, Sean thought the better of it. Instead, he locked it and headed for a window on the opposite wall.

Sliding the jam open, Sean helped Clarissa out of the window and held Sienna up for Clarissa to catch. In reasonable darkness, they were able to skirt behind the cabana and lurk through the shadow between it and the next. Looking at the keys in his hand, Sean realized that none of them belonged to a vehicle. Stuffing them in his pocket, he motioned for Clarissa to remain in the cover of the shadow. Sprinting, Sean crossed into the open, and to the four-by-four he had used for cover during his search. Reaching his hand up, he opened the door and slipped into the cab. With the penlight, he was about to pull down the ignition wires when his head nudged the visor dislodging a set of keys into his lap.

"I guess in a locked compound. They're not too afraid of car thieves…" Sean muttered to himself. Finding the interior light switch, he clicked it off and leaving the door open, ran back to Clarissa and Sienna. "Come on," he called, "It's time to go!"

With Sienna under his arm, he led them to the truck and piled inside. Shoving the key in the ignition, a flick of his wrist bought the big machine snarling to life. In seconds, lights flicked on in the adjacent cabana, and a silhouette appeared in the doorway of the hacienda. Shoving the truck into gear, Sean stomped on the accelerator as he wheeled the pickup away from the buildings.

Behind the spray of dirt and gravel the big truck's tires sent airborne, Sean could hear the reports of handguns and semi-automatic weapons. "Get down!" Sean yelled to his passengers as he sent the truck flying in the direction of the cyclone fence. Flipping the headlights on, he saw the guard with the German Shepherd steady to take a close-aim shot at the truck. Drawing his weapon, Sean sent a poorly aimed shot at the guard.

Rolling away for cover, the guard looked up to see Sean change course and aim straight for the fence where the guard lay. Abandoning his weapon and his hold on the leash, the guard leaped out of the truck's path and safety with his well-trained K-9 at his side.

With a crash, the truck slammed into the chain-link fence, the tall, heavy-duty bumper of the truck knocking it down as the over-sized tires easily rumbled over. Sean hoped the force of the fence coming down would limit contact with the razor wire and, more importantly, not allow it to wrap around the axle. As he gunned the truck towards the highway, fears calmed as the four-wheel-drive chugged to speed. In the distance, Sean could see headlights. The cartel members had wasted no time getting into the chase.

With a sizable lead, Sean felt confident that he could outdistance between them and his pursuers. Racing down the street that connected the outside world with the mine, Sean kept close watch on his rearview mirror. Slamming the truck into fifth gear as they reached the intersection with the highway, Sean was too late to see the large van scream from the alley behind the stores and slam into the truck broadside.

The tall four-by-four tipped on its side and rolled over in a horrendous cacophony of twisting metal and shattered glass. Careening to a halt in the middle of the intersection, the truck spewed steam as a milky blend of fluids oozed to the ground. Tiny Sienna slid to the floorboard under the wide vinyl-covered bench seat. While bruised and battered, she avoided the head trauma that rendered her compatriots unconscious. As she crawled up from the tangle of limbs she was pinned under, Sienna suddenly wished she too, was not alert to see the armed men rushing the truck.

Pushing away from the upright end of the cab and closer to Sean's limp body, Sienna tried to avoid the outstretched arm that probed through the shattered window of the pick-up truck. A hand was just able to reach the foot and ankle of the girl with enough grip to drag her closer to the crumpled door that had been wrenched open.

"Take the girl back to the compound, tell Segurio that we have been compromised," the only man without an assault weapon in his hand spoke in Spanish, "Ask him what he wants to do with these two, they aren't looking too good."

Another man spoke rapidly into a walkie-talkie, in moments, a crackly voice responded, "Take them to the bend in the hills, toss them over the edge into the ravine. Haul the wreckage on a flatbed and leave them behind. They'll think the American kidnapped her and lost control, killing them both. A perfect scenario. The Secretary's wife was getting out of hand."

"You heard him, get a machine and a flatbed, make it quick!"

Wilkins looked over his shoulder as he placed the call. Tapping his foot impatiently, he waited for the line to be picked up. After hearing a simple "Halsey," he spoke quickly, "Listen, I don't have a lot of time, but I need this done quickly. Find out everything you can on Sean Kendall. Where he has worked, gone to school, who he's voted for, girlfriends he has had, any unusual ties."

"Sean Kendall…I've heard of him, he's the guy who saved Johnson…," Halsey replied.

"Yeah, well, for that reason, the Senator has kept him like a pet, only I think he's a dangerous one. See what you dig upon him and the whole mess in Seattle. I am sure there is something more than meets the eye," Wilkins shared.

"A political sinkhole. You want me to bury him?"

"Maybe. Let's just see what you find, hopefully there's something to convince the Senator that he needs distance. If not, then we'll go to plan B."

Senator Timothy Small returned to his office, ready to celebrate a significant victory. He had tied the hands of the Democratic majority leader bundling a bill to extend the Endangered Species Act with an allowance to allow additional offshore oil exploration – a deal that will add millions the portfolio of his most prominent backer, oil tycoon Harold Billings, the very day it is announced to the public.

As he filled his snifter glass with his special Johnny Walker Blue, his phone rang. Over the speaker, his receptionist's voice called, "Sir, a Mr. Halsey for you."

Agreeing to take the call as he wet his lips with scotch, "Halsey, what do you have for me?"

"I just got off of the phone with Senator Johnson's aide, Wilkins," Halsey replied into the phone, "It seems he his hell-bent on digging up dirt on that Kendall guy."

Small let out a loud laugh, "Not too much of a surprise, that guy is like a cloud of mosquitoes caught in your duck blind. I have heard he was getting into trouble down south, too close to our friend, I presume."

"That seems to be the size of it. Wilkins wants a little archeological dig on the guy's past and is hoping will act like repellant between him and the Senator."

"Let me know what you find. I wanted that twerp out of the picture, but this could be even better. Let me know what you find before you let Wilkins in. This sounds promising," Small requested.

"You got it."

Small smiled widely. This had been a good day indeed.

Silverio pulled in front of the hotel in the gleaming black Humvee. Adam, Miranda, and Laura were ready and jumped inside almost before he was able to come to a complete stop. Beaming at his American friends, he grinned, "Amigos, I thought you could use a friend."

"You've no idea, Silverio. We couldn't go to the Embassy. They would trap us there like prisoners. We have to find Sean. I figured the first place I would go if I were him was the Hacienda," Adam said, clapping Silverio on the shoulder.

"We can't thank you enough. I think most of the folks in this area have had their fill of us Americanos," Miranda sighed.

"I guess. Not their fault. They don't know you, they believe what they hear on the news. Especially here in Mazatlan, the Lamarillos are heroes," Silverio admitted.

"I don't blame them. It's just tough to swallow how quick to judgment the police have been," Miranda replied.

"Didn't look good when his chase down the boardwalk was all over the news, not to mention the thousands of witnesses," Adam cautioned and then grinned, "Still, pretty impressed with our boy being able to get away. Maybe he's not the soft pretty boy, after all."

"Senor Kendall? On the street, they are calling him the *fantasma*."

"What's that mean?" Laura asked.

"The ghost," Silverio grinned.

Gunning the engine, Silverio pointed the heavy SUV up the hill towards the highway that travels away from the coast. He was as anxious to get to the Hacienda as his passengers were. He had been calling Frederico all morning without a response. If Freddie wasn't there, someone else was always available to pick up the phone. He didn't want to place an additional burden on his American friends, but he was very concerned.

The call came into Tug just as he passed the sign for the "Golden Zone" intersection. His targets had eluded their escort to the Embassy and were seen heading for the inland range. The mercenary smiled. This group of civilians was as bold and open to risk as some of the mercs he had worked with. This time, their willingness to disobey the authorities was going to cost them – to his favor.

Instead of continuing to Mazatlan, Tug pulled over to the side of the road, a cloud of dust rising into the air as the dented and rusty vehicle slowed to a stop. Making his way to the trunk, popped open the lid and selected a couple of choice items before calmly walking to the passenger side, leaning on the hood. Adjusting the sights, he felt confident that his fortune was going to hold. Taking a long drink of water, he set the bottle down and returned his eye to the sight.

Glancing at his watch, Tug grumbled in the rapidly increasing heat. According to his sources, the target should have come through by now. Just as he took the time to wipe the sweat off of his brow, the reflecting sun off of a gleaming chrome grill bounced into his line of sight. From years of honing his skills, his body instantly snapped into posture, and his finger readied on the trigger. His well-trained mind ignored the impulse to fire too soon and allowed the heavy vehicle to continue until it was less than thirty yards away – so deep into Tug's kill zone that he could pinpoint exactly where he wanted to strike. Snapping off a shot, Tug sent a flurry bullets into the radiator of the massive V-8.

Steam instantly spouted from the hood of the SUV. Tug watched as the glow of brake lights briefly broke through the cloud. Without the slightest movement that would have alluded to the mercenary appearing rushed, he casually strode to the driver's seat. He wheeled the weathered economy car in the direction of the ailing Hummer. Following the steam cloud for roughly a quarter of a mile, Tug found the SUV on the side of the road. The driver had just stepped out when Tug brought his car to a stop right beside the other vehicle.

Silverio looked up, happy to see another motorist stop to lend support before he saw the gun pointed in his direction. The man behind the weapon motioned for him to move to the rear of the Humvee.

The passenger door opened, and the red hair of Adam Raines poked over the hood of the car. "Tug Gaskill, what the hell…"

"Ranger, stand down and proceed to the rear of the vehicle, or your friend here is splattered all over the Mexican blacktop,"

Tug spat before Adam could finish his statement. The gunman followed Silverio to the rear, his semi-automatic trained on the concierge's skull the entire way.

As Adam walked by his still open door, he motioned with his hand for Miranda and Laura to remain silent in the back of the SUV. Laura reading the look that had crossed her husband's face, sank into the leather of the bucket seat, dropping her head below the heavily tinted windows that surrounded the vehicle. Miranda wore a look of both surprise as well as anger, but she too relented to remain silent and as much out of view as possible.

"Funny meeting you here, still plotting against your country?" Adam sneered despite the muzzle of the pistol swinging in his direction.

"There's nothing funny about it. Not sure if you guys are lucky or incredibly unlucky. You seem to have embroiled yourselves into another mess - this time a war. And your nosy friend, labeled the cause of the whole damned thing. The good news is, he might wind up in the history books, the bad news is, you'll all be dead," Tug growled at Adam. The Fish and Wildlife agent had the ability to get under just about anyone's skin, no matter what the circumstances, he usually had some joke or sarcastic comment to spit out of his mouth.

"Not very sporting of you, just shooting a couple of unarmed men," Adam retorted, and then despite the gun trained on his midsection added, "Hey, I heard that Chavez guy was a friend of yours. Man, watching his head squish under the car tire…messy, messy, messy."

The icy core of the mercenary was seared in his emotionless gray eyes, "Chavez lacked discipline, I don't. And if I were after sport, I'd shoot pigeon."

"If you truly want sport, you'd tackle my boy, Sean. Too bad you can't handle him," Adam shot back.

"Hmmm," Tug scratched his fingers against his chin, "Kendall. The one thing keeping me from blowing a hole through your head right now. Then again, I don't need all of you. First things first. Call the ladies out."

For the first time since he squared off against the mercenary, Adam's permanent grin fell from his face. "No. Fire away then," Adam held out his arms and expanding his broad chest to create an open target.

"In due time," Tug said calmly and then yelled toward the cab of the Humvee, "Mrs. Raines, please join your husband. And have your friend Ms. Shaw exit on your side as well. No games, I truly don't need all of you."

Without delay, the rear passenger door opened, and the two ladies appeared behind the SUV. "On your knees!" Tug commanded and then looked towards Laura, "Not you. Here, put these around their wrists."

The mercenary reached in his pocket with his free hand and pulled out several plastic zip cords. With his outstretched hand, he held them for the frightened woman. Reluctantly, she accepted the cords and began one by one, placing them around the joined wrists of her husband and friends.

Seeing that Laura was not drawing them taut, Tug snapped, "Tighter!" A flick of his gun-toting wrist gained her compliance.

As soon as Adam's wrists were properly bound, Tug kicked his boot hard into the helpless man's chest, knocking him to the ground. Swinging his weapon at Laura's head, he snarled, "Tell me where Kendall is, or I blow her head off!"

"I don't know!" Adam screamed, the ordinarily jovial man's voice was full of fear and desperation.

"Hmm, I believe you. You can still help, though. Where is Johnson being moved to? The embassy?"

"After he meets with his Mexican and Canadian counterparts, he is. Probably late this afternoon," Adam admitted.

"He is still at the convention center?" Tug asked and was met with an earnest nod, "Alright, consider yourselves bait. I think I can draw Kendall out. Too bad you won't all fit in the car."

The mercenary swung his gun in the direction of each of his hostages. Pausing with each of his victims, he finally settled on Silverio, decidedly the least connected to Sean, "Duck…duck…goose…."

As he began to squeeze the trigger, a caravan of vehicles screamed towards the scene. The sound of roaring engines and pulsing sirens caused Tug to pull away. "Into the car. All of you, now!"

The bound victims were slow to rise, trying to manage balance with their arms behind their back. "Damn!" Grabbing Miranda by the shoulder of her blouse, began dragging her to her feet. The wail of the police cruisers drew nearer, as Tug tried to coerce her towards his vehicle. Adam hopped to his feet and lunged forward, knocking Tug and Miranda to the ground. Before they could completely untangle, the Mexican *policia* closed in. Leaving his hostages behind, Tug fired a series of shots at the advancing police officers and was able to climb into his car and gun in it away from the scene. From a small duffel on his passenger seat, he grabbed several avocado-shaped items and tossed them out of the drivers' side window. Behind him, the already pot-hole strewn blacktop exploded into rubble. The police cars in pursuit careened wildly to avoid the new obstructions. One was able to avoid the mess as well as the ditches dug on either side of the highway to accommodate flash-floods. Tug merely continued tossing his arsenal of grenades until the final vehicle, too, was unable to follow.

In his review mirror, the mercenary's eyes glanced at the carnage in his wake. Relieved that he was able to make his escape, he was still disappointed that he lost his leverage in hostages. While the plans for Senator Johnson's relocation to the American Embassy would assuredly change, he could at least try to think ahead of them to anticipate when they might move. He could also use his sources to better hone in on the agenda. Still, the annoying Fish and Game officer in his grasp would have been an excellent bonus to his trip south.

Sean arose with every fiber of his body, screaming in pain. His senses argued over which body part held claim to the most severe agony – the two that surfaced to lobby for top honors were his throbbing head and his bone-dry mouth. The taste of cured blood stained his tongue, which felt as parched as on an old piece of sandpaper. As bad as his mouth felt and tasted, he decided his head won the dual. It pounded so hard, it was difficult to think, which was contrary to the notion that it was trying to convey – through the hammer-like blows to his temples, his synapses bellowed for him to get up.

Forcing his sore eyes to open, he pushed up from the awkward position of his face being squished against the windshield of the truck. Once more, he faced the assault of his neuropathic pain pathways as inch by inch, each muscle group he called on groaned vehemently. Beside him lay a cold and clammy Clarissa Lamarillo. Studying her in his dizzy haze, she lie motionless, streaks of blood caked to her forehead, cheeks, and clothes.

Ignoring the calls of pain, he stabbed his fingers quickly to her carotid artery, relieved to feel a feeble, but present pulse.

Pulling himself straight, he moved his hands along her slumped body, feeling for any obvious trauma or bone breaks. When he was finished, Sean tabulated two broken bones and dozens of lacerations and contusions. As long as there was no internal bleeding, he concluded, if he could get her help quickly, none of the injuries should be life-threatening.

Looking beyond the cab of the truck, he began to take stock of the situation. What he saw was quite grim. The truck was sandwiched between the sides of a ravine. Each door was pinned against walls of rock and sand. Positioning his body against the back of the bench seat, he kicked against the windshield. On his fourth attempt, the tempered glass broke free its seal and tumbled to the dusty ground below.

Crawling through the newly created opening, he spun to gingerly free Clarissa from her tomb. Finding no ideal location to lay her down, Sean set her softly on the dirt at the bottom of the ravine. Reaching back into the cab of the truck, he ripped away the vinyl fabric from the seat and used it to serve as bedding for the unconscious woman. Scanning the area for unsavory creatures, he felt confident to let her rest as he climbed out of the gully to scope out their surroundings.

What he found caused great alarm. For miles in each direction, the view held an endless panorama of desert sand and the occasional agave. Given Clarissa's condition, she could not survive alone in this terrascape, never mind himself. Slipping over the side of the ravine, he noted his shadow, giving him both the relative time of day as well as their general bearing.

Sliding back to the bottom of the gully, Sean glanced at the still body of Clarissa Lamarillo and then dove back into the truck to see what he could pilfer. Recovering a small toolset, he began tearing away parts of the truck he felt could prove to be useful.

Starting with the foam padding that was made bare from his removal of the vinyl seat cover, he tossed wads of it out on the dirt next to Clarissa. Finding nothing of further use, he turned his attention to the exterior of the vehicle.

The truck turned upside down, Sean had easy access to the fuel line. Using a wrench form the toolkit, Sean pried a split in the line and soaked one of the foam wads of padding. He didn't know how long they were going to be out in the desert, and as the sun fell, they were going to need warmth. As he wiped away the deluge of sweat from his brow, he thought it ironic he was already thinking about needing a fire. By his estimation, the temperature had already climbed into the neighborhood of one hundred degrees.

The relentless sun spurred Sean to focus on their primary need – water. He hoped the cartel members who cared for the truck were cheap in their service. Removing the windshield fluid reservoir, Sean filled as much liquid from the radiator as he could. Swirling it around in the yellow-aged plastic container, he was satisfied that it was satisfactorily clear. Putting the outlet to his lips, he winced as he tried the stagnant juice. Despite tasting like a mouthful of pennies, he was satisfied that no other impurities or potential toxins were at least prevalent to taste.

Absconding with what he could from the destroyed pickup, Sean turned his attention to the fallen Clarissa. All of her lacerations appeared to have coagulated and did not pose a risk of excessive bleeding, much to Sean's relief - first aid supplies were scarce. Collecting what he had, he slung Clarissa over his shoulder and began walking east, following the tire tracks in the dirt. He hoped that he would find civilization before nightfall. Instinct told him that the cartel knew the area better and left them in a spot that even if they had not died from the crash, it would leave them dead just the same.

Eleven

The cabinet meeting adjourned, as most of the key members filtered out, President Marshall caught his Secretary of Defense by the arm, "Mike, will you join Tom and me in my office?" The request more of a statement, the Secretary nodded his head and followed the president and his Chief of Staff.

Inside the closed door of the Oval Office, the air was thick, and the mood somber. Mike Thompson and Tom Chambers sat across from the president. "Mike, since the first debate over immigration reform, there has been a level of contemptuousness, from whichever side of the fence. Do you believe President Lopez when he says that his side of the border had nothing to do with the attacks?"

"I don't know, sir," Thompson's words came direct and pointed, "I have my doubts. Our intelligence sources haven't been able to prove or disapprove the Mexican government's claims. More disturbing, we haven't come close to determining who's been firing from our side."

"How can that be?" Chambers blurted, "It was U.S. military issue weapons used in that attack on Camello."

"Yes, we have already determined that and *where* they were taken from, but from there, they could have been delivered to anyone. Rogue military, terrorists...the Mexican's themselves," Thompson replied.

"We can worry about the why's and how's later, we spent enough time on that at the cabinet meeting. The question is, what do we do in the meantime. Our cities along the border are shut down. The people are afraid to go about their normal lives, and I can't blame them. I am crossed up between two competing thoughts, and that is why I have brought you guys in here apart from the rest of the cabinet," the President shared.

Casting a stern glance toward Thompson, "I need you to mobilize our troops. I want the navy to begin slowly deploying out of San Diego and El Paso. I want troops at the ready from Louisiana to California. I want the Air Force to have the Raptors on standby with full payloads. Try and keep the movements subtle and the scale hidden from the media."

"That should be no problem, sir. I think under the circumstances, anyone would expect our presence to increase. It is the lines behind that first wave that we will have to keep from view."

"Sir, is this really the best answer? From a global perspective, others might see this as aggressive and escalating the conflict. What if there was rogue military involvement. You, the entire nation, will be vilified," Chambers cautioned.

"I know this. That is why you will set up a face to face meeting with Lopez. We can even do it in Mexico. We will continue to air our regret over the issue and propagate the message that we are extending the olive branch," Marshall replied, "We will run both plays in congruence. We *will* try and end this quickly and peacefully.

If we find their government did have anything to do with these attacks or willingly failed to prevent them, we'll be ready to serve justice swiftly."

Senator Johnson paced in front of the black Suburban, "No. We need to get you back to the embassy. We'll send an agent with the Mexican police to the Tequila Factory. If they find anything, they'll call us immediately."

"Sir, Sean could be there. Where else in Mexico would he have gone?" Adam pleaded.

"Yes, and if anyone else knows that, then that place is even more dangerous for you three to be. Listen, we cannot have any more incidents down here. We are on the brink of war," Johnson reasoned.

"Rick, if it were you out there, what do you think Sean would do?" Miranda asked.

"If I were Sean, I'd probably already be there, but…,"

"We are closer to the hacienda than we are the embassy. Moreover, Tug Gaskill doesn't know about the Tequila Factory, but he does know that you are being moved to the embassy, and I am pretty sure you are his target. I suggest the hacienda is our safest choice until the compound is fortified, and that could take hours," Adam argued.

The senator looked around at the scene uncomfortably. He didn't like his choices. The fact that a skilled mercenary could have already established an ambush between their location and the embassy did not ease his comfort. Reluctantly, he nodded, "I'll see if the police officers will provide escort. *But*, I will also arrange for a helicopter, and when it arrives, we are all leaving."

In minutes, they were piled in the Suburban, following a pair of police cruisers and being trailed by another pair. Adam could see the anxiety in Miranda's eyes. Reaching over, he squeezed her hand, "He's okay you, know. Sean's probably kicking back, drinking an ice-cold Corona."

As comforting a thought as the words were, Miranda couldn't help but to fear they were hollow. Had he made it back to the hacienda, he would have notified them somehow, even if he was concerned about the call being picked up. What made her even more uneasy was the fact that they had withheld from Senator Johnson – Silverio had been unable to reach anyone at the factory all day.

Miranda's thoughts were replaced by intense anxiety and excitement as they approached the long drive up to the incredible tequila-making facility. The scene seemed to unravel painfully slow for Miranda. Inch by inch, the beautiful building came into view. First, the red clay tiles of the roof, then the magnificent archway supported by massive adobe pillars and then the fountain in front of the building.

The procession of cars wrapped around the fountain and doors began swinging open. Before anyone had been able to take a step towards the stairs leading to the entry, a meek figure appeared in the doorway. Miranda recognized him in passing during their tour of the factory. It was the expression the man wore on his face that made the hair on her neck stand up. He had the countenance of someone who was about to deliver bad news.

Silverio paused in his tracks for a moment and then raced up the steps. In rapid Spanish, the concierge rattled off a series of questions, "Pablo, is everything okay? Where is Freddie? Why does no one pick up my calls?"

Pablo's mouth opened, shut, and then finally, the little man replied, "Senor Frederico is passed."

Silverio stared at the houseman, stunned by the news, "How…what happened?"

Waving everyone into the Hacienda, "Come, I tell you everything."

Sitting everyone in the parlor, Pablo first led Silverio alone to where he had laid Frederico's body. Almost requiring him to see proof of his cousin's death, he demanded a moment before he could hear the houseman out. The police called in for the coroner as they waited.

Finally, a hollow, flat-affected Silverio joined the group, followed by Pablo. The houseman related the events in Spanish, and Silverio repeated them back to the group in English, stumbling over the details of his cousin's death. Then Pablo told the group of Sean's appearance and how Frederico sent him off to rescue Clarissa Lamarillo from the cartel. Miranda and Adam shot each other mixed looks. It was positive to hear that Sean had made it that far, but they also realized he might have jumped into a more horrifying pit of snakes.

The travel through the heat of the day wore on Sean. Carrying the load of the limited supplies, he was able to liberate from the dilapidated truck, as well as Clarissa Lamarillo's limp body would have been enough to drag him down. The addition of the dozens of cuts, bumps, and bruises along with the massive concussion, made his trek absolutely brutal. As much as his weary muscles begged for water, Sean wanted to save it for Clarissa.

Concentrating on his path as opposed to his body's demands, he trudged one foot after another in machine-like doggedness. Sean kept an eye on the track of the sun, hoping to find either civilization or at least a viable campsite before the day gave way to night. As the horizon closed in, Sean noticed a wall of rock inch closer and closer. Spanning his field of vision, the desert terrain he traversed turned into a mountain of rock and rubble. Shifting his load, he carefully picked his footpath to climb the hill that confronted him. He considered putting either the Commerce Secretary's wife, or the supplies down, but he seriously doubted whether he could make it back up the hill twice. Shaking his head, he fought off the concern that he might not be able to make it once.

Sidestepping boulders and imposing thorny plants that seemed to stab at him from all directions, he managed to reach the top. His entire body wailed in pain. His head spun from dehydration and response to his injuries. Ready to set his entire load down, he saw something that caught his eye. Something that didn't fit with the terrain that he had trudged across the untold miles he had endured. Something natural, yet manmade. His dry throat seized as his eyes recognized what it was he was seeing.

With a sudden burst of energy, Sean moved quickly towards this structure. He feared a mirage. No longer did he wince with each footfall, no longer did his shoulders complain under their load – he was wholly focused on his goal. With each step, he believed he was closer to sanctuary. Gently laying Clarissa down on the sand, Sean cast away his other items with abandon. Placing his hands on the stone structure, he looked deep into its mouth. The cavern seemed to sink for miles. Cool air met his face as he stared deep into the well.

Nearing exhaustion, he searched for a pail and rope or other device he could use to extract the badly needed contents of the well. Snatching up the emptied windshield fluid reservoir, he produced the screwdriver he had shoved in his pocket and began relentlessly driving it into the seam of the plastic container. With his forearms about to explode, the vessel finally burped as a corner opened. Squeezing his fingers into the narrow opening, Sean strained to pull the container apart. Ripping into two halves, the reservoir flung apart in different directions.

Looking back down the well, Sean tried to estimate its depth. Grabbing a nearby stone, he let it drop down the black fissure. Straining his ear, he waited for the splash, trying to estimate the ratio of time to distance. His heart sank, when instead of the expected splash, he heard a dull thud. Staggering back, exhausted and disheartened, Sean fell mercy to fatigue and collapsed at the base of the worthless stone structure.

Knowing that his vehicle was marked, Tug had to dump it. He also knew that he had miles of empty highway in front of him. If the Mexican *policia* had access to a helicopter, he would be made in minutes. Pulling to the side of the road, Tug tossed his duffel over his shoulder and popped the hood on the decrepit car. Not knowing who might happen along first, Tug armed himself for a battle.

Knocking back two bottles of water as he waited in the searing heat, Tug was relieved to hear an engine roaring down the road. At this point, he didn't even care if it belonged to the *federales*. He was going to liberate it for his own. Through the distorting haze rising from the blacktop, Tug could recognize that the vehicle was not the police. Stooping over his engine, he rolled the dice that in this barren land, any motorist would at least stop to lend assistance.

His hopes were realized as he heard the car's engine wind down and stop just short of his vehicle. "*Necesitas ayuda?*" called across the pavement. Smiling, Tug reached to his side and brought his left hand around. Locating the driver, the mercenary squeezed of a pair of shots into the samaritan's throat. Slumping to the wheel, the hapless motorist fell silent. The sedan rolled slowly forward before Tug could reach inside and slip the brake into park.

Grumbling, the mercenary stretched through the window and yanked up on the handle of the brake. Swinging open the door, he pulled the driver free and drug him several yards from the side of the road. Scanning the empty highway, Tug slid behind the wheel and jammed the car in gear. He had a bead on Senator Johnson and wanted to complete this portion of his task.

Pushing the stolen car to its limits, Tug sped down the coastal highway, returning towards Mazatlan. His phone buzzed by his side. Hoping his contact had a more accurate location for the senator, Tug eagerly snatched the cellphone from its holster.

"Gaskill, we need you to regroup with team Gamma. The White House is spinning this thing as just a couple of extremist activities. We need to up the American military fingerprint on actions against Mexico," the voice crackled through the secure phone.

"I will as soon as I take out Johnson. I'll have him in thirty."

"Negative, you need to arrive at Laredo to rendezvous with your team by 1500. They will bring the hardware, but we need you on point."

Calculating the time it would take him under ideal circumstances. He knew that he had no choice. As it was, he was unlikely to meet the infil time. Grumbling, he pulled the parking brake as he spun the wheel, executing a clean 180-degree turn and head north towards his new objective.

Colonel Reyes trained his field glasses on the San Diego border crossing terminal. Law enforcement on both sides of the heavily used transit point had blocked off access. On either side, thousands of passenger cars and cargo trucks were stacked up in immobile rows. The overwhelming presence of military and police personnel, as well as civilians, made this the perfect target. The very activities of the past several days had created this captive pool of potential casualties. With his equipment fed through Central America, the culmination of years of failed and foolish policies to arm and fund the various fragmented groups by both the Russians as well as Americans had allowed them to get close enough to avoid alarm, yet close enough to inflict massive losses.

Dropping his glasses, he paused for just a moment. A part of him almost felt sorry for the mass of people that were about to lose their lives. The fleeting thought passed, and he gave the signal. In moments a massive barrage of shells lobbed through the air. Soltam K6 and Russian M43 mortars suddenly came alive. Each unit capable of launching their payloads thousands of yards in the air, taking out everything within hundreds of feet with each shell. With a dozen launched into the air, the devastation was going to rival that of any other terror attack ever lobbied on North American soil.

After each gun had exhausted six revolutions of shells, Colonel Reyes demanded the immediate withdrawal and disbursement of the squads. He knew by then, the American military would be on the ready and had probably already tracked their heat signatures or established their location on satellite. Fewer than two minutes later, his assumption was born out. The delay likely to the hasty yet necessary discussion that had to take place within the Pentagon as to should they strike their southern neighbor.

Several A-10 Warthog Tank-killers swooped along the skyline and proceeded to take out Reyes' arsenal, driving each mortar into the ground as a crater of molten and fragmented steel. The Mexican colonel's fast attack four-wheel-drive vehicle sped rapidly away from the scene. He estimated roughly 30% loss of personnel and equipment on the raid. He quickly realized that the swift American response could reach 70% loss amongst his ranks. Disappointed in the casualties of his good men, it was a boon for the purpose. This was the first official American retaliation. Everything that had let up to this was branded as mere terrorism. This attack was the start of the U.S.-Mexican war.

"This unprecedented attack on our nation is the destruction of centuries of an allied partnership. This act can only be seen as gross aggression by the American elite," Ambassador Gutierrez spat into the microphone, his words met with a roar from the press pool, "Both of our countries have met with unfortunate attacks. Until now, each has met with the appropriate discourse and cooperation of our two governments.

A few minutes ago, a Mexican infantry unit stationed miles away from the U.S. border was fired upon by United States military bombers. Not long before, a horrific terrorist attack had occurred on the Border Station south of San Diego, California. Without due process, the U.S. military acted unilaterally against the Mexican government in response to a terrorist attack. I have always loved our brother to the north, but now, I must urge my government to take arms. No questions please."

Walking away from the podium, Ambassador Gutierrez felt like a traitor to both countries. He was hoping that he would just be fired for talking out turn with the officials within Mexico City, but he knew he was in a losing proposition. If the terrorists could not use him, then they did not need Sienna. That was not a scenario that he wanted to come to fruition.

Walking past the mob of staffers and reporters, a thought crossed his face – a thought that drained the color from his face. There was no way out with Sienna. If he was successful in the kidnappers' bidding, Sienna was dead. If he failed, Sienna was dead. Gutierrez had to get help. But who, and how? If the group who held his daughter found out that he was soliciting help from the authorities, they would undoubtedly kill her on the spot.

His cell phone began buzzing. A quick flick of his wrist showed that the caller was his boss. Sliding the phone back in its holster, he continued his exit of the United Nations press hall. Deciding to avoid a return to his office at the embassy, Gutierrez instead made the tough call to go home. He had not been back to the townhouse since he had found out that Sienna had been kidnapped. Somehow, he felt as though he had avoided some of the stabbing pain of reality by not having to be in those lonely rooms. He was right.

Each step taken to the front door held increased anxiety for the ambassador. As he slid the key in the lock and twisted the handle, a flood of images slammed into his head. Gutierrez backed the door shut, leaning against it, he slid down to the floor, awash in tears. His daughter was everything, and yet, he had been sucked up into the progression of his career. Slamming his fists into the floor, he blamed his absence and his push for his position for Sienna's abduction. Right now, his life was as clear as it had ever been. Nothing was more important than his daughter.

Twelve

T he mongrel dog tore away from his boy. Inexplicably, the canine darted recklessly towards the flat. The sandal-clad youth labored to keep pace, losing sight of the excited pooch as it disappeared behind the family's dormant well. Rushing to see what had tickled his dog's olfactory senses, the boy was shocked to see two pairs of arms and legs sticking out of the narrow shadow. A look of horror crossed the boys face, "*Muerte!*" Taking several steps backward, he stared wide-eyed at the tangle of bodies under the strange vinyl cover.

The boy let out a shriek as one of the hands moved. The cover slid to the side, and a man rose from the ground. "Papa!" the boys screamed at the top of his lungs.

"It's okay. It's okay…uhm," Sean thought for a moment, fighting for the Spanish words through the dense fog in his head. Holding his hands up in front of him, he wearily whispered, "*Agua. Aqua.*"

Nervous, the boy paused to hear Sean out, "*Tengo ayuda por la mujere, por favor. Comprende?*"

Silently, the boy nodded and disappeared in the direction that he had come from. Sean leaned his back against the well and checked Clarissa's vitals. As many times as he had performed that procedure over the course of the last twenty-four hours, he still winced as he waited for the results. Once more, he was relieved to detect an ever-faint pulse.

Waiting for the boy to return pained Sean. It felt like the boy was gone for hours. Even as the thought that the boy or his family might call the authorities, he knew that he and Clarissa were in a life or death scenario and just couldn't care any longer. As the sun rose higher over the ridge, Sean felt himself begin to slip back into unconsciousness. His head spun, and the world narrowed to an uneven tunnel of haze. Suddenly, before him, a man appeared, his lips moved, but Sean could only hear muffled sounds. He felt something pressed against his lips and a damp towel wrapped around his neck. Slowly, the world came back into tune, and his senses once more accepted the stimuli around him. A flask of water was once more brought to his lips, and the weathered face of a smiling man materialized into view.

The simple offering of water was like a miracle tonic to Sean. His aching body and his foggy mind once more gave way to the impetus to revive and find the helpless Sienna. His attention returned to Clarissa, where the little man silently resumed his efforts with her. After a few failed attempts to stimulate her with the flask of water, he signaled for his boy. The boy who found Sean that morning walked by, grinning at Sean while tugging on the lead of a burrow. Behind the gray, dirty beast, trailed a cart with an incredibly squeaky wheel.

Sean watched as the man, barely five feet tall, hoisted Clarissa into the cart with ease. Once the Commerce Secretary's wife was properly stowed, the man ambled towards Sean. With a wave of his hand, Sean rose with surprisingly wobbly knees. His intention was to walk alongside but instead relented to ride along with Clarissa to wherever the man and his body intended to take them.

The burrow-drawn cart bounced along the terrain. The beating sun did not faze Sean now that help had arrived. The entire trip to the modest concrete block house was performed in silence. The boy kicked stones, pat the donkey, and peered curiously into the cart, yet not a sound was heard other than the rhythmic, grating squeak of the cartwheel.

When the carriage stopped, Sean scooted out of the back, his legs more able to manage the strain of standing. Despite his condition, he insisted on helping to carry Clarissa into the house. Sean was amazed at the temperature difference that the structure provided. The small house was at least ten degrees cooler than the outside air temperature.

Clarissa was laid on a bed in the back of the house, where a woman was waiting with a bowl of water and a cool compress. The woman quickly went to work assessing the Commerce Secretary's injuries and began applying to compresses to Clarissa's forehead, neck, and wrists. Propping Clarissa's head up, the woman gently poured water into her mouth.

Sean's arm was grasped by the man, pulling him into the main room, which comprised a small wood-fired stove, table, and chairs. Set down in one of the chairs, Sean was provided a plate of tortillas and pinto beans. The boy appeared with a pitcher of water, and the two encouraged Sean to consume everything in front of him. The oddest thing to the weary American, was the complete lack of communication given the incredible hospitality he had received.

Finally, having completely returned to feeling human again, he attempted his best to thank his hosts. *"Hablo Espanol un poco.*

Gracias por tu hospitalto. Es la mujere muy enferma?" Sean strained to find the right words to thank the family. More crucial to his dialogue was to explain that the family had to get Clarissa to proper help. He also attempted to tell them that he had to go. Reluctantly, he admitted he needed directions as well as supplies. To Sean's surprise, the man shook his head "no" and then pulled away with a thoughtful look on his face.

"Mi esposa, she take care of *mujeres.* We get her to hospital. I take you now to village," the man said defiantly as his wife handed him a sack full of tortillas and a bottle of water.

"Muchas gracias, senorita," Sean said, smiling at the happy woman. He was surprised when he was met with a disapproving look. His Mexican hostess looked him up and down and began ranting in Spanish to her husband. A reluctant look crossed the man as he scurried off in response.

Soon, the man returned with a clean, folded shirt. Shrugging his shoulders, *"No pantalones, muy pequeno."*

Accepting the shirt, he nodded that any pants in this house would likely be too small. Unbuttoning his filthy and tattered dress-shirt, he donned the grey t-shirt he had been handed. It fit snugly across his broad back, but at least it didn't carry the scent of near-death and forty-eight hours in the desert.

Meeting mixed approval from the wife, Sean walked to the back of the small house for one final check on Clarissa and then headed for the door. On his way, he once more thanked the wife and paused to pop the bill of the young boy's hat, resulting in a wide grin on the face of the true hero who saved his and Clarissa's life.

The American Embassy satellite compound in Mazatlan was a fury of activity. Miranda figured all of the sites around the country probably were. Sensitive files were either sealed in crates and carted off to a loading dock or shredded and placed in an incinerator. Embassy workers, officials, and their families threw bags together of their belongings. They waited in staging areas for their turn to be shuttled to one of a dozen Chinook helicopters secured in a nearby vacant field.

Miranda avoided the frenzy and focused on the continuous news broadcast and, as much as she could, peer over shoulders to read the various reports that streamed in through a bank of fax machines and printers. The tension between the two countries had exploded. It seemed like the leadership in either country was responding in reactionary statements and actions as opposed to any signs of willingness to collaborate.

The writing was on the wall for her, Adam and Laura – they were all being remanded back to the states. There had been no further news on Sean, and the last thing she wanted to do was leave the country. As things were now, if the Mexican authorities caught him, he would probably be held for war crimes, that was if they allowed him to live. The thought sent a chill down Miranda's spine.

Knowing Sean, he would either try and find her or Clarissa Lamarillo. She feared with the former. He would risk his life returning to Mazatlan for nothing. With the latter, he was probably in way over his head, and…she refused to finish that line of thinking.

Looking up, she saw Adam and Laura walking towards her. She didn't like the expression on Adam's face. "What is it?"

"We have to get on the next shuttle, or we will be arrested," Adam informed her.

"But what if Sean comes here looking for us and we're not here? What if he gets caught? What if he needs us down here?" Miranda pleaded.

"I know. I have the same concerns. It was one thing with running around out there on his own but now that we are at the brink of full-scale war…," Adam began.

Miranda's eyes brightened, "We need to get a message to him."

"How can we do that? We don't even know where he is?" Laura asked.

"The news. I've been watching it. The broadcasts from each country have been gathering viewpoints from citizens from both sides. We have to get on the news!" Miranda cried triumphantly.

"We do have a friend who is a U.S. Senator," Laura suggested.

"No," a voice chimed in from behind them. A flat-lipped Wilkins stood, his arms crossed, "I'm sorry, he can't. The Senator is under guard and is boarding a special helicopter as we speak. He sent me up here to apologize for not being able to tell you himself and that, unfortunately, you three have to go with the staff since he is flying to a military base. I'm heading to his helicopter right now."

"But Sean, he's…," Miranda started.

"He's on his own. I'm sorry, Miranda," the senatorial aide pursed his lips and scurried down the steps where several men in military uniforms were waiting for him.

Miranda's spirit was unwavering. "The turtles!" she exclaimed.

Adam's face screwed into an expression of confusion, "What about them?"

"Since all of this stuff has started, the whole event to release the turtles has been completely forgotten about. The sanctuary couldn't be more than five miles from here. I am sure I can convince the people I met there to continue with the release. We can get media coverage of Mexican and Americans working together on a common cause, despite the crisis!" Miranda said, her voice with a ring of excitement.

"We can tell them that it is our final act before we head back to the states. Maybe Sean will see it, maybe not, but it is our only shot," Laura added.

"Yes! And…," Miranda pulled at her lip, "We'll make a run for it. Attract as much attention as we can. It's not like they're going to let us go willingly."

"You're getting as screwy as Sean!" Adam grinned, "I like it. Let's do it!"

Looking around the cluttered rows of desks, he found what he was looking for – a set of unclaimed car keys. He figured in the haste to evacuate, at least one set would be left behind. Snatching them, he walked to the window and began pressing the unlock button. Three rows out in the parking lot, the lights to a white sedan began to flash.

Without a word, the trio slipped through the crowd waiting in their cue and raced to the parking lot. Behind them, soldiers and officials shouted for them to return. As Adam opened the driver's door, he saw one of the officials speaking with a soldier and pointing. Moments later, the soldier trailed after them as a second joined the chase in an open-top Jeep.

Flipping the key in the slot, Adam cranked the engine and sped forward. Confused, the guards at the gate were prepared to stop people from getting in, not out. Whirling to see the racing vehicle drive through the stone pillars of the gate, they hesitated, not knowing whether they should take aggressive action or not. It was enough to allow Adam to gun the engine, spinning the car sideways as they hit the street. Immediately behind them, were the two soldiers in the Jeep. As they reached the entrance. They stopped. Their post limited to the compound.

Along the sidewalks lining the embassy, protesters and camera crews were greeted to the scene. One reporter and his cameraman jumped into their compact SUV and sped off in pursuit. Seeing the television crew following, Adam slowed his driving just enough to allow the SUV to keep them in sight.

In the backseat, Miranda was calling the sanctuary to receive their buy-in. She had made quick friends on her first visit and was confident that they would also like the idea. In minutes, she had their overwhelming confirmation for the plan.

Pleased with the camera crew's ability to keep pace, Adam took the sedan through its paces. In no time, he had the vehicle screaming into the sanctuary parking lot. Jumping out of their seats, the three Americans were greeted by their Mexican counterparts. Behind them, the television station SUV pulled to a stop. Conservationists from each country welcomed the reporter who wasted no time kicking off the interview.

Walking through the small building, each wall lined with aquariums, the center of the floor dotted with half-a-dozen small pools, Miranda and the conservation team took turns declaring the partnership between the two countries on the rescue of the endangered Loggerhead turtles. As the team began loading pails of water with tiny little sea turtles, Miranda explained that despite the incidents across each border, they felt it was necessary to complete their shared journey before they were evacuated that afternoon.

The language barrier made the car ride a particularly quiet one. As the Mexican farmer neared the old mining town of Sombrete, Sean had him slow the truck and pull to the side of the road. The man shot Sean a quizzical look. "*Peligro*, danger," Sean replied.

Nodding his head, the farmer stopped the engine and retreated to the rear of the truck. Leaning over the gate, he produced a well-used spade. Smiling, he handed the tool to Sean. Without another word, the man hopped in his truck and turned back on the highway. With a wave from Sean, he was gone.

Once more on the outskirts of the mining town, Sean began the hike back towards the cartel compound. He knew this time, his approach would have to be drastically different. He lacked the cover of darkness as well as the element of surprise. While they would assume that he was dead, his earlier infiltration would have put them on high alert. Lengthening his trek, Sean made a wide berth, skirting the small town. The tall mountain in the backdrop helped to cast early shadows for Sean to follow on his approach.

With the village in sight, Sean paused to recon the level of activity, as well as where he could choose as his access point. His patience paid off as he caught movement all along the fence line. Security heightened on the compound with sentries stationed every fifty feet. Sean's challenge to breach the mining compound was now a near-impossible task.

As he watched, he could hear the low drone of an engine chugging down the highway towards him. A large dump truck was laboring up the hill. Scrambling from his perch, he sprinted towards the truck as it crested the low rise, heading towards the town at the base of the mountain. Just as the truck passed, Sean left the shadows and broke for the road. Running as fast as he could, he leaped and grabbed the edge of the tailgate. Pulling up with his arms, he vaulted over and into the bed.

Bracing against the bumpy ride, Sean tried to judge where he was. To his relief, the truck slowed as it reached the single road entering the town. Fearing an inspection at the gate, he leaped out of the side and darted behind the dumpsters stationed at the rear of the tavern he visited during his last venture. The screen door opened up, and a young man in a filthy apron carried a bundle of trash towards Sean's hiding spot. Readying the shovel supplied to him by the farmer, Sean accidentally nicked a bottle with his foot. Tossing the garbage in the container, the boy began to walk behind the dumpster. Tensing his muscles around the handle of the shovel, Sean prepared to attack.

"Julio!" a voice called as soon as the young man neared the corner, "*Andale!*"

Sean could hear the busboy grumble and jog towards back towards the tavern. Scanning the area, Sean felt comfortable to move to the next row of buildings, the homes that lined the entry of the mine. Pulling some of the tortillas that the farmer's wife had given him, Sean tossed them at the two dogs that raised the ruckus on his last visit. Satisfied that he had made new furry friends, Sean sprinted to the corner of the first house. Crouching behind a pile of old tires, Sean peered out towards the compound. The activity was tremendous, both with workers bustling about as well as the additional security.

Sighing, Sean was struggling to develop a plan that any decent odds of success. As he scoured the fence line for any sign of weakness, a figure caught his eye entering the house next door. The man wore a guard uniform. Sean developed a risky plan to get inside the compound. Darting across the yard, he pressed his back against the side of the house. Peering into a window, he watched as the guard turned on the TV.

The hair on his neck stood up when he recognized a face on the television. Miranda was talking as a telestrator converted her discussion to Spanish – she abandoned the evacuation to complete the mission of the sea turtle release. As soon as she and her friends were finished, they were returning to the United States. At first, Sean didn't know what to make of it but then realized that they probably had no choice. All of the U.S. embassies were evacuated for fear of violence. The guard opened a beer and plopped down on a tattered couch.

Ducking under the window, Sean crept to the door. Slowly opening the simple framed screen, Sean slipped in silently. Wrapping his body around the corner, he flattened himself against the wall adjacent to the living room. As he moved across the hall, a floorboard creaked. Freezing in place, Sean gripped the handle of the shovel hard. Sean's heart raced as the sound of a pistol being cocked rang through the house. Sean held his breath, his eyes widening as he watched the muzzle of a gun slowly protrude from the corner.

Using the length advantage of his spade, the former baseball player let loose with a home run swing, finding its mark on a solid form in the hallway. Sliding out into the hall, Sean took another mighty hack knocking the weapon free. As he made contact, the figure fell back onto the floor. Fearing an imminent call for help, Sean drove the spade towards the man's throat, stop just as he pressed against his larynx.

With a finger up to his lips, Sean hissed, "Shhhh!" The man on the other end of the spade nodded his head. "*Donde es la nina?*" Sean asked where the girl was. He feared that they would not have kept her in the same place.

"*Ido. Ido.*"

"*Donde es?*"

The man stammered, his eyes searching around the room. Sean pressed the blade of the shovel harder against the man's throat.

"*Estados Unidos*," the man replied.

"The United States?" Sean exclaimed, not believing what he was hearing.

"*Si*. Phoenix…*El Pato*."

"*Que es El Pato*?" Sean asked, realizing that he had managed the most he could from his limited understanding of Spanish.

The man looked up at Sean, and finally said, "Quack."

"Quack?" Sean looked on incredulously, "A duck!"

Initially, excited to have interpreted what the man was trying to say, he then frowned, not understanding what a duck had to do with the girl's disappearance.

The man nodded while Sean stood, holding the blade to his throat. He tried to think of his next steps. He had no ID. Even if he had, he was a fugitive from the law. He had no money. He looked at the frightened guard. He almost felt sorry for what he was about to do.

"Auto?" Sean asked

The man nodded slowly, an unhappy look across his face. Sean held out his hand and allowed the man to fish them out of his pocket reluctantly. A single key hung from a Camaro key fob. "Sorry about this…," Sean said, grabbing the key. He started to swing the shovel hard against the man's skull, stopping short, he couldn't complete the strike. "Shhh!" Sean hissed with his finger to his lips.

Sean swiped the assault rifle from the floor and quickly peered out of the window. Parked beside the house was a yellow Camaro with its T-roof open. "That'll do," Sean muttered. Quickly searching around the house, Sean found a small envelope of money. Enough to buy him some gas and food, he presumed.

"Ayuda!" screamed from the hallway. Sean swung the gun in the direction of the guard who took off out of the house and toward the main gate to the compound. More shouting rang through the air, and the sound of the big chain-link gate opening was followed by the roar of an engine.

Taking a deep breath, Sean swung the door open and broke for the yellow car in a mad sprint, as the first volley of bullets sprayed from the sentry towers. Willing his legs to go faster, Sean jumped on the hatch of the Camaro, leaping through the T-roof and slamming hard into the driver's seat. Jamming the key in the ignition, he roared the V-8 to life and wasted no time pushing it into gear. Sending a wild spray of gravel behind him, Sean gunned the engine, speeding it towards the road that linked him with the highway.

Rapid gunfire erupted behind, several rounds finding their way into the sheet metal of the Camaro. The guards by the gate swung their attention to Sean and readied to take shots of their own. Pushing the pedal hard, Sean shot the car onto the road through the town. Throttling the muscle car to its peak, Sean streaked through the neighborhood. From either side of the side streets, vehicles emerged to block him, as they had the first night he escaped from the compound.

Prepared and with a much faster vehicle, Sean was able to slip between, leaving the cartel's security trucks to catch each other head-on, blocking the road from further pursuit. Sean grinned as the engine growled, sliding the car onto the blacktop of the highway quickly into the distance.

The Chinook was flanked by a pair of Apache attack helicopters, each hovering menacingly in their escort. The aircraft contained all of the highest-ranking officials from the Mazatlan satellite of the American Embassy. Senator Johnson was in such deep thought over the events. He nearly jumped when the soldier's voice came over his headset, "Sir, a call for you."

Johnson nodded and waited for the call. "Senator Johnson, we have three fugitives here at the Embassy. They escaped and now want back in to accept their evacuation. They said you would authorize it."

Instantly knowing what three individuals the embassy guard was referring to, Senator Johnson sighed, "Let me guess, two attractive ladies and a goofy, big red-headed guy?"

"Uh, yessir. What should I do with them?"

"Put them on a chopper and take them...bring them to Lackland, and I will see that they are properly dealt with."

"Yes, sir."

As Johnson ended the call, Wilkins' voice came over the speaker, "What the hell was that?"

"Apparently Adam, Laura, and Miranda took a little excursion prior to evac. I'm having them brought to the base," the senator replied.

"What? Sir, this is a time of crisis, not a time to be babysitting a bunch of civilians. Civilians linked to a fugitive who is largely to blame for the border tensions," Wilkins argued.

"I trust them, and besides, I'd rather keep them close and hopefully out of trouble," the senator smiled into his headset.

Wilkins disconnected the com and slid out his Blackberry. With his thumb, he tapped out a hasty message. He couldn't have these idiots screwing things up - friends of Johnson's or not.

Thirteen

The low roar of the Senate reporter's pool drew to a hush as Senator Small stepped to the podium. He stood tall and silent as he tapped his index cards in front of him and sized up the crowd that waited for his arrival. On his lapel, a small American flag glistened in the lights trained on the speaker's stand. Placing his hands on the podium as though it were a large steering wheel, he addressed the audience.

"We have suffered some despicable acts. Acts of cowardice aimed at the good people of the United States of America. We are a nation that has taken in the sick, the weak, and the poor of our neighbor to the south. We have nurtured their economy and supported their development of industry. We have protected their sovereignty and endured their relentless push of drugs and unwanted ilk of their society in return. Today, we were repaid for our generosity by the Mexican government attacking our civilians."

Taking a pregnant pause, he looked at the reporters, pens poised on their pads, thumbs on their digital recorders, cameras aimed at the podium, "Honestly, I'm not surprised. I am not surprised that a third world nation would take a jealous aim on the hard-working people of the United States of America. What I am surprised about is the pathetic response by our own leadership. President Marshall has not displayed the fortitude and courage to quell these terrorist attacks. Since he's been in office, he has catered to the Mexicans. He did not protect our border when he could have. He did not stop the deluge of unwanted, indigent, *illegal* aliens. He supported tying our hands and locking us into the North American Ecological Alliance – an innocently titled act of NAFTA that would force unfair trade tactics and environmental standards that only hurt us and help them..."

"Now, today's not the day to point fingers and lay blame. That's not what I am trying to do here. All I am saying is, we are not here by accident. If there are those that cannot make the hard decisions, then we in the senate and our counterparts in Congress need to be prepared to ourselves. We have a fight in front of us, whether we like it or not. And let's be honest, of all the enemies in the world, this ain't the toughest who would like to take a shot at us. How we react to them can send a message to the rest that we are the United States of America, and we will not tolerate *any* act of aggression against our people," the senator closed with his arms held high. His face twisted into a defiant expression.

Instantly dozens of hands and a chorus of calls for the senator's attention rang through the room. Nodding towards one hand in front held high, Senator Small accepted a question. "Senator, given the state of conflict between the two countries, how would *you* have reacted?"

"Good question, Candace. It is one that I have to answer in two ways. For one, I never would have allowed them to rise up to a degree where they could possibly think they could strike in such a manner. All of this pandering with the WTO, lop-sided trade agreements, our porous border...your elected government allowed this to occur. Those that our citizens trusted to make good decisions set the stage for these events. My second response is that as soon as any of these murderous attacks began, Mexico City would have been visited with a military reply," Small answered.

"What if the attacks did not come from the Mexican government?"

"The attacks came out of their country, they are responsible," the senator replied flatly, looking towards another reporter, "Jonas?"

"Thank you, senator, my question is, where are the strong leaders such as yourself? You seem to be the only one outspoken in alignment with the American public?"

"Well, Jonas, I don't know about that. There are a lot of good people in our government. Whether they are in the right roles or not, I just don't know," Small laughed, "I thank you all very much. I have to go, God Bless America!" The senator turned from the podium. His hands again held high before collecting his notes and leaving the reporter pool abuzz behind him.

Tug Gaskill met his team. Surveying the group as well as how they were equipped, he was impressed. Somehow, the powers that be had assembled a crack squad with serious firepower. A dozen sidewinder missiles and dragonfire mortar rigs were stacked and ready to go. Finding the operative who was identified as his point of contact, he asked, "What is our target?"

"The town of Nuevo Laredo, you pick'em and hit'em. A specific air flight has been selected for us to take down with the sidewinders. Supposed to be heading north out of the Mexican west coast destined for an airfield in Texas," the operative relayed.

"And the occupants?"

"Unknown, sir. They will provide FAA designation for our tracking system. Simple point and shoot, I don't ask questions, sir."

"Fair enough, what's our ETA?" Tug asked.

"Less than twenty, glad you came when you did. We would have had to start without you," the operative declared.

"All right. It sounds like the flyover is a clean and jerk, let me see what our options are in Nuevo Laredo town."

Miranda couldn't help but stare out of the window and search every inch of the Mexican Sonoran desert that the helicopter crossed for the figure of Sean Kendall trekking north towards the States. She knew it was a ridiculous cause, but couldn't resist succumbing to the task. Every shadow, every human-like figure that the helicopter whizzed past at nearly two-hundred miles per hour, gave her some feeble reach at hope.

Her heart tightened as their path flew over a military stand of the Mexican army. Rows of tanks and personnel carriers pointed towards the north. She wondered how the most civil part of the world had become so unstable to be at the brink of war. Just a few days ago, she had been welcomed by the kindest contingent of people she had ever met. Now their two nations were at odds. It didn't make sense. Reasonable leaders ought to be able to come to amicable conclusions. As the helicopter left the Mexican installation behind, she heard the pilot speak over the intercom, "We are entering U.S. airspace."

To Miranda's surprise, she saw a flash near the ground ahead of the helicopter. Before her mind could process another thought, an explosion rocked the aircraft. Her stomach lurched as the vehicle suddenly lunged towards the ground, twisting to the left and then the right before seemingly falling straight down. Her heart sank further as the pilot screamed, "May Day, May Day…!" over the headsets.

Her back pushed deep into the seat at the helicopter rocketed downward. Tears swam towards her eyes as her brain sympathetically sent her into unconsciousness.

The flight tag supplied to Tug from through the Defense Department database, the string that his sources routed to the smartphone of James Wilkins, appeared on the screen. "Target acquired!" he roared. Within seconds, a flash burst to his left as a rocket was sent skyward. Moments later, an explosion lit up the sky just to the south of their position as the object it struck plummeted towards the ground.

"Team two, fire at will and do not cease until I say!" Tug shouted into his com. In an instant, the sky was peppered with mortar shells arching through the air. The loud concussive shots played like a symphony to his ears. It had been years since he was able to launch an attack with state of the art equipment instead of the Soviet and U.S. relics that littered Central America.

Swinging his view back to the airborne target, he located the cloud of smoke billowing from its shell, but was surprised at the seemingly gentle rate at which it fell considering.

"Winged it, sir, should we take another shot?"

Waving the operative off, Tug had already dispatched a small contingent to intercept, "Negative. This could be even better."

Tug watched through his field glasses as the Humvee lurched forward and bounced across the meadow towards the crash site. They could deposit any casualties across the border and hold survivors as hostage until they are sacrificed – all at the apparent hands of the Mexicans. He hoped that a dignitary or ranking military officer was on board - the more significant the figure, the greater the impact.

Through the hefty binoculars, Tug could see a brief firefight break out before one soldier was killed, and the remaining passengers of the Chinook raised their hands in the air in surrender. Over his earpiece, his crew lead told him that there were two casualties, the pilot and co-pilot. One other soldier fired upon them and was fatally shot. The crash yielded half a dozen hostages, most of them civilians. What the mercenary saw next near caused him to choke. The angry visage of Adam Raines was one of the hostages. They sat on their knees, lacing their fingers together. "The wildlife officer, this can't be luck. He must have pissed off one of my bosses again or God himself," a rare smile crossed Tug's lips.

"Sir?" one of the soldiers next to him asked.

"Nothing. As soon as they are in custody, let's move out. The stingers and mortars will have shown up on either radar or satellite. We need to move fast to our next checkpoint."

Ambassador Gutierrez paced back in forth in front of the Tavern on the Green Restaurant, perched just inside the entrance of New York's Central Park. Ever since he made the call, he wondered if he had done the right thing. He expected at any moment for his phone to ring and to be scolded by a voice on the other end of the line. Riddled with exhaustion and haunted by thoughts of how his daughter might be treated, the Mexican Ambassador was at the doorstep of a nervous breakdown.

Each set of footsteps drew his gaze. Every pedestrian was stared down in mixed excitement and fear. Finally, one of the passersby slowed as he neared, a roll of the eyes showed his disdain for the obviously nervous man's demeanor.

"Mr. Ambassador, let's take a walk," the man said, his face barely visible through the updrawn lapels and low slung hat. Heading for the darker bowels of the park, the man led the ambassador away from prying eyes and ears.

"You have experience at things like this?" Gutierrez asked as he walked.

"I'm not here to be interviewed. I am here to learn about your situation and determine how I may help you. If you got my number, then you asked a trusted source."

"Yes, I'm sorry, I just…," Gutierrez began but was quickly cut off.

"I know your concern. You needn't worry. I don't exist. I don't use ordinary channels. I am a ghost. I understand a ghost is just what you need," the mysterious man replied, "Tell me what you know."

The nervous ambassador shared everything that he knew from the phone calls with the kidnappers. He felt a mixture of relief and despair. He didn't know if he signed Sienna's death certificate or gave her a chance at life.

The man listened. He gave no sign of whether the information was positive or negative. He offered no words of hope, just that he understood. Once the ambassador's extent of knowledge was exhausted, the man said he'd be in touch and disappeared into the bowels of the park without another word or glance.

The rust-spotted, yellow Camaro slowed to a stop beside the gas pump. Sean pushed the door open as a loud creak announced his presence. A man clad in coveralls sauntered out of the gas station office and wiped his hands on a rag he pulled from his pocket. When he got close enough to Sean to gather a good view, he stopped Sean. "Sorry, *gringo*, out of gas!"

Disappointed, Sean slumped is shoulders and considered his next steps. His growling stomach determined that the eatery adjacent to the fuel stop would be a fine oasis. "It's okay. I'll grab something to eat."

"I don't think that's a good idea, *gringo*," the attendant said.

Frowning, Sean ignored the man and willed his weary body toward the café. Pushing the door open, a series of heads turned his direction. Each stopped and stared as Sean entered the roadside eatery. Pulling a chair at the bar, Sean faced a man who had stopped mid-stream, putting glasses away.

"*Cerveza, por favor,*" Sean called, eagerly anticipating a cold beer.

The man behind the bar glared at Sean and shook his head, "No, *gringo*. No *americanos*."

Seeing where this exchange was going, he sighed. Hungry and out of gas, he was not in the mood to leave empty. Sliding a gun out of his pocket that he had swiped from the sentry had he stolen the car from, he slammed it on the counter, "*No problema, por favor!*"

The man behind the bar's eyes widened, "*Si, senor, no problema!*" Pulling a Negra Modelo from the cooler, he slid it to Sean and took his order for *pollo en mole*. Despite the discomfort of a dozen patrons never once taking an eye of him, Sean eagerly dug into the meal that was ultimately presented in front of him.

Another cerveza later, Sean fired up the black racing stripe clad Camaro, watching the fuel gauge bounce back to full. As he ate his meal, he watched several cars fill up at the pump, realizing that he had been lied to about the station being empty. Pushing the transmission into gear, he pressed on the accelerator, sending up a slight cloud of dust as the engine roared down the highway northward towards the border.

Fourteen

Bound at the wrist with plastic zip ties and his mouth crammed with a soiled rag, Adam Raines ignored the discomfort, which was immense. He, Miranda, and Laura had been shoved in the cargo box of a transport truck. The heat of the day had been baking them in excess of 100 degrees, dehydration and the gag preventing him from even wetting his lips would otherwise have plagued him. Even the concussion that caused every pulse of blood in his head to pound relentlessly or the cracked rib that was hammered with every bounce of the suspension as the truck rambled down the rutted road failed to get his attention.

All the wildlife officer could think of was his wife. Laura had not regained consciousness following the crash. He was forced to watch helplessly as he was held down by two of the mercenaries. Even in her state, she was bound and gagged before she was tossed in the back of the truck like a load of lumber. His mind was eased only by one of the gunmen checking her pulse and acknowledging that she was alive.

Miranda had appeared to be okay though in a serious state of shock before she was unceremoniously pushed to the floor of the truck. Adam could feel the vibration of approximately four pairs of footsteps enter the container before the doors were rolled shut, undoubtedly, there was a gun trained on him even as the thought crossed his mind. Had he been able to somehow get free from the zip ties, he would be instantly subdued if not shot.

Adam just wished that he could check on Laura. Had she become conscious yet? How bad was she hurt? Being this close to her and unable to help was the worst torture that he could imagine. While he doubted he would have the chance, in the slim hope they did survive and ultimately get free, he promised that he would get to whoever was behind this.

"Colonel Reyes, Senor La Costa, is on the phone for you," the soldier held up the receiver towards his superior. Taking his attention away from the preparations for the next proposed strike, he reluctantly accepted the phone.

"Colonel, I need to request a favor from you."

"Senor LaCosta, while I appreciate the support you are providing, I continue to take my orders from…"

Cutting off the military leader, LaCosta broke in, "I completely understand, these are extraordinary circumstances. My intelligence reports have identified a rogue American, who has recently attacked my facilities, is heading north, in your direction."

"You have your own people, I understand, that should be more than capable of containing one man."

"While true, there is a benefit to you and your entire outfit. This man can be tied to terrorist and espionage efforts in our country. To be frank, win or lose, your actions are going to put you in front of a firing squad. Acting against and insurgent such as this, could go far to clear you from criminal scrutiny and instead to being a national hero acting in *response* to actions like this rogue," the drug lord suggested.

"Who is this man? CIA?"

"We don't know Colonel. He is very unorthodox in his methods. His description appears to match that of the suspected kidnapper in Mazatlan," La Costa added.

"Hmmm. This is sounding more interesting. Tell me what you know," the Colonel asked.

"Reports have him most recently stopping at a fuel stop on Highway Two heading towards Sonoyta."

Despite not knowing where his captors where taking him, just the relief of large door to the rear of the truck opening up to allow fresh air spill in, was enough to Adam the slightest bit of encouragement. Pushed and jostled until he was thrown to the floor, he winced as his head bounced off of the concrete, unable to arrest the fall with his hands bound behind his back. He hoped, somehow, the mercenaries took greater care of Laura and Miranda.

Adam felt a foot hook his sore ribs with a steel toed boot and roll him over onto his back. Suddenly, his blindfold was stripped off. Wincing, Adam's struggled to adjust to the light. His ears hyper-present to the sounds around him, he listened as a pair of boots stopped at his feet. Looking up, Adam took in the image, a look of amazement crossing his face. What he saw was a death sentence.

"Wildlife officer, Raines. It is a pleasure to see you again," Tug Gaskill grinned at his captive.

"That makes one of us," Adam rasped, his throat dry and body weary.

"Oh yes, you were the funny one, weren't you," Tug sighed, "I'm sorry if I take some of the fun away this time. I can't imagine even you will find humor in what you have brought your wife into."

Adam's eyes narrowed as he strained against his bindings, "I'll rip your heart out!"

A heavy boot was brought down against Adam's head, slamming him to the concrete floor. Tug waved off his operative, "Relax. Mr. Raines cannot harm anyone. At least not this time."

"Where is Laura?"

"I have a medic tending to her. She is no good to me dead…for now," Tug conceded, kneeling close to Adam's head, "You should have minded your own business the first time around."

Adam stared at the mercenary, emotionless.

As he neared the border town of Piedras Negras, Sean noticed a increase in law enforcement and military presence. As he turned off of the highway, he noticed a black car behind him do the same. Coming to a stop, he watched as the car in the mirror had also slowed to a halt. What struck Sean was that the vehicle seemed to stop short, so that it didn't get too close.

Shifting into gear, Sean made the turn onto the main road that led to town. Pulling out, he found himself behind a slow moving truck loaded down with dozens of crates. Occasionally white feathers would fly threw the wire over Sean's head. A quick look ahead in the on-coming lane gave Sean an idea. As he glanced at the mirror and saw the black car emerge again behind him, he waited until the oncoming bus was close enough that passing was a bad idea, dropping a gear, he slammed his foot on the accelerator, launching the old Camaro into the oncoming lane, careening wildly amidst the bellowing horn of the bus, he swerved barely back into the proper lane. Keeping his foot on the gas, he sped down the road towards town. Behind him, he saw the black car narrowly swerve back behind the chicken truck until the bus passed before attempting to leapfrog back into position behind Sean. By then, the yellow Camaro was barely in sight.

Even more sure that he was being followed, Sean kept his speed up as much as he could. Nearing the edge of town, he decided to chance some side streets until he felt comfortable in ditching the car. At this point, he figured that he was going to be forced to move on foot anyway. There was not a chance he could navigate a border check. As he swung down the first side street, he felt he had a good chance that driver of the black car was far enough away not to have seen him.

Looking back in the mirror, he thought he saw the suspect vehicle race past on the main road. Turning left, he tried to move parallel to the main street, watching carefully for that black car or any other signs that he was being followed. Grumbling to himself, he should have figured the incident at the diner would have alert someone to his presence – the cartel, the feds, just about the entire northern hemisphere wanted Sean's head right about now.

Motoring through an outskirt neighborhood, he continued toward the center of town. As the buildings began to change from residential to industrial, he felt like he was going in the right direction. Seeing a police vehicle up ahead, Sean swung the car down a quiet alley. If he wasn't so stressed about running for his life, he might have enjoyed the drive, the powerful V-8 engine rumbling off the concrete walls through the open T-top of the muscle car was a piece of American musical heaven.

Snapped back into reality, his heart dropped as the grill of a black sedan swung into the same alley that he had turned down. Slowing to a stop. He watched as the sedan made a beeline towards him, taking up the entire alley. Shifting the car into reverse, he quickly began backing down the alley. Looking over his shoulder, he saw an identical black car pull into the alley, trapping him between the two. Snapping his head back to the first car, he saw it had actually picked up speed. Behind him, he heard the roar of an engine. A quick look in the mirror told him that the second vehicle too, was picking up speed. He was trapped and they were going to crush him.

Stopping the car, he searched desperately for a way out. There was nowhere to go and no time. As he stopped, the car in front of him slowed to correct his angle. Looking over his shoulder, he saw the second vehicle was right on top him moving at high speed. Summoning every ounce of power in his muscles, sprang from his seat, planting a foot on the steering wheel and the other on the headrest, he leapt out of through the open T-roof as the car to the rear struck, just seconds before the first car. The faster moving car behind Sean's carried more momentum. As Sean tread in midair, the second car pushed his Camaro from underneath him in a horrible collision before being halted by the car to the front joining the demolition. Miraculously, Sean landed on the ground inches from the rear bumper of the sedan that had trailed him. Slamming hard on the pavement in a sea of shattered glass, he rolled to a stop, bloody, but alive.

Viewing the aftermath, the Camaro was nearly disintegrated between the two large sedans. Both the rear hatch and the engine bay of the muscle car were gone. To his surprise, one of the sedan doors began to open and the barrel of an automatic weapon poked towards Sean's direction. Leaping to his feet, Sean sprinted down the alley. Just as he reached the street, a spray of bullets peppered the brick walls. Turning towards town, Sean saw the police car approaching with its sirens wailing, no doubt in response to the commotion of the wreck. Reaching the alley, the police sedan was ripped with bullets from the automatic weapon. Taking advantage of his pursuers having to deal with the *policia*, Sean continued his escape. He heard two shots fire from the policeman before his gun fell silent. Sean assumed that the men chasing him didn't waste anytime dispensing with the officer.

Deciding he didn't want the same fate, he kept his head down utilized the speed he possessed as a former athlete and put as much distance between him and his pursuers as he could. Seeing a black sedan approach, Sean ducked into the entryway of a small store. The car sped towards the alley he had escaped from, Sean assumed reinforcements had been called in. He didn't have much time to disappear.

Checking his pockets, Sean realized that he lost his gun in the escape from the car. He was weaponless and penniless. Still, he reasoned, immigrants found their way across the border everyday, he could too. Sean chose this town because of an expose he remembered from a news show about the border crossings and heavy coyote trade that the culminated from the town. The reporter in the expose located a small shanty settlement at the northeast edge of the town. That was the staging area for the crossings. Sean was sure that the week's terror and military actions along the border had deterred some from crossing, but those whose livelihood were based on it, would find a way.

Effectively avoiding detection, Sean found the area the reporter had mentioned. Without money, there was no way one of the coyotes were going to help him. Watching a group sitting in the shade of a crude lean to, most had small bags with them and jugs and bottles of every shape and size of water. This was a group ready to make a crossing. Sean decided to shadow them and watch where they went. If he got caught, the coyote might kill him. Still, he reasoned, it was as good of a plan as he had.

As he watched, a van pulled up and two men jumped out. Sean was afraid this meant his plan had fallen through. If they crossed in the van, he wouldn't be able to catch up. To his relief, the men that jumped out wore backpacks and quickly began shouting instructions to the group sitting on the ground. One of them began moving from person to person, stopping at a young boy Sean figured to be no older than twelve. As the coyote held out his hand for payment, the boy shook his head. In a torrent of Spanish insults, the boy was expelled from the group.

In moments, the boy was stuffed through the still open van door and whisked away from the scene – firsthand exposure to Sean what happens to anyone wanting a free trip across the border. Sean shuddered to think what fate the boy was likely to face en route and upon his ejection from the van. Sean quickly decided quietly shadowing the group was indeed the best way to get across the border. As an added thought, Sean also decided that with the extra scrutiny, of the border tensions, he might as well let this group test the waters ahead of him.

Pleased he didn't have long to wait, Sean watched as the coyotes collected the money, handed some off to a courier, grabbed their own supply of water and began herding the group on foot away from town. Slipping from his hiding spot, Sean carefully jogged across the street and set behind a nearby building. As soon as the entire group had moved forward, Sean continued his pinball movement from obstacle to obstacle, avoiding being seen.

After just a few miles of walking, Sean realized that avoiding detection was going to be a difficult task as the outskirts of town quickly gave way to open desert. The sun still high in the air, offered little cover for Sean to move in. He regularly observed, one of the coyotes circling back and looking in the direction they had come. If conditions didn't change, Sean knew that he would for sure be caught. Lying flat on the hot desert sand, Sean found that he could allow the entire group to get out of sight and still be able to follow the wisp of the dust cloud that cycloned up into the air.

Feeling dehydrated and exhausted under the late day sun, Sean continued to press on. Maintaining his pace behind the troop of immigrants, Sean was surprised when he spied a figure lying in the sand. Initially fearing it was a coyote lying in wait, he paused before moving forward. Hearing a weak moan, he cautiously stepped towards the figure.

Instead of one of the smugglers, he found an immigrant, motionless against the desert floor. A young woman, sobbing against her arms, clutching a half-drunk water jug held in one hand, a tattered picture of a young man in his other. Kneeling to see if she was hurt, he was startled when she shrieked and pushed frantically away from him.

Holding his hands in front of him, he tried to reassure that he was not a threat. The woman looked up at him, tears streaking down her face. Noticing her soiled and tattered clothes, he realized that she had been raped and left behind to be a victim of the harsh desert. Sighing, he rubbed his jaw both in disgust as well as trying to think of what action to take. He couldn't just leave her there. Going back was not a good option, nor did he like the concept of toting her across the border – for increasing the risk and burden as well as his convictions of illegal aliens entering the United States. Still, he knew he had to do something to help this girl.

Slowly, Sean reached his hand out to the frightened girl. Gently, he tugged away the water jug. Loosening the cap, he offered it to her lips. Reluctantly, she took a sip, as the liquid hit her lips, she swallowed. Nervously, she returned the gesture, offering a drink to Sean. Hesitating, not wanting to take away her precious commodity, especially after what she had just been through, he relented as she insisted. His mouth was so parched; he allowed the liquid, refreshing yet warm, to coat his mouth before he swallowed. Quickly he screwed the cap on the bottle and handed it back as he gently lifted her to her feet. Watching the sun begin to make its way towards the horizon to the west, he looked for the now faintest trail of dust in the sky, barely visible.

"We need to go…uh, *vamanos*?" Sean urged.

Nodding her head, the girl seemed to understand and allowed Sean to lead her in the direction that he last saw the now-vanished dust trail of the coyote-led migration.

"Who the hell is doing this?" President Marshall bellowed at his National Security Advisor Bruce Adams. The president slammed the file down on the table. The report detailed the latest shelling of Nuevo Laredo. The policia headquarters, town bank, and a market were destroyed in the attack. "Are the Mexicans bombing themselves? Is there *really* a rogue U.S. military group doing it? Terrorists?"

"Sir, every one of our troops is accounted for. Though we now have a sizable force spread along the southern border, none of our boys have fired a shot across the border," Adams said.

"That's not what the Mexican government nor the media think. Word of *our* military initiating the attacks is what every news and social media outlet is suggesting," Press Secretary Judith Myers shared.

"Great, as if we don't have enough pressure in many of those areas," the president shook his head, "Where is our intelligence. This isn't taking place in some bunker in Afghanistan. This is right in our backyard. I want results immediately!"

"Sir, we have traced some missile deployments in parts of southwest Laredo. We've flown in a team. They did find some traces of artillery fire in the area. We also have an evac helicopter from the embassy in Mazatlan down in the area. Our techs are on the scene, and their early indication is the missile that shot it down was American," Adams replied.

"But we give the Mexicans plenty of our defense surplus. Anyone on this continent could have fired those weapons!" President Marshall pleaded.

"Two issues with that, sir. First, the angle of the missile and its origin on radar were from the U.S. side. Second, it was new technology. We haven't distributed them outside of our military," Secretary of Defense Adams said.

"So, we *do* have a rogue squad. That would explain why we can't find them. They re-assimilate into position," President Marshall asserted.

"Perhaps, sir. We can't rule that out. I can give the air force flybys and the satellite recon notice to track our troop movements," Adams suggested.

"That is a start," President Marshall agreed, and then a look of despair crossed his face, "What about the helicopter, who was on board?"

"Some civilians who were taking part in the alliance talks in Mazatlan and the soldiers from the flight detail," a screwed look crossed Adam's face.

"What is it, Bruce?"

"The marines were shot *after* touchdown. The civilians were nowhere to be seen. We are trying to get a satellite image of the area. Still, I don't think we are going to be lucky with that. Our attentions were on other areas along the border," National Security Advisor replied.

"U.S. soldiers killing our own marines...," President Marshall mulled, "I'm even more convinced this is the work of terrorists. Our weapons fell into the wrong hands and are being used against us."

"It wouldn't be the first time, sir," Adams agreed.

"It might be the first time that it has caused a full-fledged war," Marshall cautioned.

Fifteen

As the sun began to set, Sean had a harder time following the migration from the distance that they had gained. To ensure that he was able to exploit the chink in the U.S. Border Patrol's capabilities that the coyotes knew, he decided to risk picking up the pace and closing in on the trail. The girl he was helping seemed exhausted but willing to push as hard as Sean urged her. Soon, their increased pace allowed them to hear occasional voices emanating from the group. Sean felt that they were safe from detection, though he had to remain vigilant in being wary of the occasional patrols to the group's flank.

Overhead, Sean heard the occasional roar of a helicopter flyover, often accompanied by the sweep from a powerful searchlight. He deemed this a sure sign that they were near or just across the border. His biggest concern was the military with thermal scanning FLIR cameras, which could instantly give away their position.

Directing the girl forward, he was suddenly alarmed by another sound, rustling from a nearby mesquite tree spun him to the side of the path. Sean tugged on the girl's shoulder, dropping each of them to a knee. Stepping from the cover of the desert tree, one of the coyotes stood menacing a long knife. He heard the girl gasp as she slid behind him.

"*Puta!*" the smuggler spat at the girl and turned his attention to Sean, "*Como estas, gringo?*"

"The end of the road, for you, *amigo*," Sean replied, dipping his hand into the sand and flinging a cloud of dust in the coyote's eyes. Using the distraction, he scrambled quickly to his feet and immediately launched into smuggler's midsection, driving the full force of the impact with his shoulders. Sticking with the assailant, Sean followed through with the blow until he drove the smuggler into the ground. Letting out a gasp, the coyote instinctively let go of the knife. Snatching it, Sean slipped it into his waistband and grabbed the smuggler by the throat.

"You like to rape little girls as you traipse into *my* country?" Sean snarled. As the coyote began to struggle underneath him, he lifted his knee and drove it into the man's groin, "You're not going anywhere!" Rolling off of the smuggler, Sean slid off his belt.

Using the opportunity to try and crawl away, the coyote was quickly met with the sole of Sean's shoe, sending him sprawling into a nearby yucca plant. Void of compassion, Sean sneered, "Serves you right."

Plucking the man off of the thorny plant, he spun him on the ground so that his face was against the desert floor. Kneeling back down on him, he coupled the smuggler's wrists and pulled the belt into a loop and strung it tight.

"Good luck, *puta*," Sean growled and motioned for the girl to follow him. Seeing the girl pause, staring at the bound man, Sean shrugged, "Maybe the desert will get him, maybe the border patrol will find him, maybe he'll make it back to Mexico." Unsure if she understood him, he watched as she walked over to the man and delivered a severe kick to the stomach. "I think she understood," he mumbled to himself as he marched them northward.

Adam struggled at the cords that bound him. The result was the same as the other hundreds of times over the past few hours – bloodied wrists as the ties dug into his skin but failed to give way. He had no idea how long he had been tied up. Stuffed in a dark room that was sealed from the outside, he explored his prison by scooting along the floor, feeling what he could along the way. He hadn't seen Laura or Miranda since Tug's team first recovered them. Assessing the situation, Adam counted about a dozen men, each heavily armed and wearing marine uniforms. Being a former marine himself, they seemed authentic to Adam. Each weapon was consistent with current arms used by the United States Marines and infantry. The mercenary had certainly seemed to have paired with a group far more sophisticated than the one Sean and Adam tangled with the first time.

Outside, the heavy door that entombed him was unlocked and opened with a loud creak. Light streamed in, causing Adam's eyes to struggle to make out the figure in the doorway, the man's voice gave himself away. "Your wife won't shut up. I figured you could talk some sense into her, and perhaps you both might be more willing to cooperate."

"I'd be a hell of a lot more afraid of her than me, Tug," Adam laughed, glad to hear that she was okay and giving them a hard time. Two men on either side of him helped him to his feet. Guiding him out of the holding room and into the hallway, they pushed him by Tug.

Looking at the blood caked around the wildlife officer's wrists, Tug taunted, "How did your escape work out? That looks real uncomfortable."

"Let me out of them for a minute, and I'll show you uncomfortable," Adam sneered back.

"I don't think so. I underestimated you before. You have proven quite capable, and I have no intention of affording you any opportunity to cause problems again," the mercenary conceded.

"What do you need from us?" Adam asked. Knowing how men like Tug Gaskill worked, he was surprised that he and the ladies weren't shot right alongside the marines at the crash site.

"Friendly persuasion," Tug commented, as they turned into a well-lit room, Adam found Laura lying on a bed. Sitting up, she began to rise to greet her husband. "Just stay where you are, Mrs. Raines. This is not a conjugal, just merely reassurance that you are both alive and well and now maybe you can shut up."

Steaming, Adam knew reacting aggressively would only yield a negative effect, he tried to keep his rage in check, winking at his wife he jabbed, "You should hear her at home, she's *always* nagging me about something. I'm surprised she hasn't bugged you to fix this place up a little, it's a disaster. Where the hell are we anyway?"

"Home sweet home, for now," Tug replied, "Now, you have seen each other, this has all been pleasant. Know if you do not do as my men and I say, the other will feel the consequences. Take him back."

A look of panic washed across Laura's face as the men on either side of Adam wheeled him around to take him back to his separate room. Looking back over his shoulder, he called, "I love you, sweetheart!"

"Adam...," she called. Rising from the bed she was sitting on, she was rewarded with the door to her room slamming shut and bolted closed.

"Tibby, it's Alex. The Ambassador just hired me to find his little girl. Do you know anything about this?"

"Alex, what would I want with a little girl?" Tiburon LaCosta asked incredulously into the phone.

"Hmmh, I think the ambassador's about-face on the love fest between Mexico and her northern counterparts now seems to suddenly make sense. Nice plan, but a little girl...."

"It had to be done. We needed leverage. All of our more reasonable attempts to influence him were turned down. He turned down a substantial donation, political appointments...a very impractical man," LaCosta said.

"So, what you have me do, Tibby?"

"I believe our time with Senor Gutierrez may be done. Why don't you visit my team? They have relocated to the United States. Send a message with this unfortunate girl and make it very clear that it was an American intervention," LaCosta commanded.

"It's gonna cost you, Tibby."

"For what? Sentimental value because it is a child? That's ridiculous. There's no resistance. You have her location – all you need to do is show up, do what you do, and place the appropriate evidence. Come on. It doesn't get any easier," LaCosta posed.

"Fine, the usual fee, you're lucky you supply consistent business my way."

As the phone went dead, LaCosta mumbled, "You're lucky you don't find your head floating in the Rio Grande."

Senator Johnson fretted over the disturbing news regarding his friends. He stood in a crowded room of other dignitaries and officials that had been evacuated from various sites around Mexico. They were allowed to take over one of the base's situation rooms. Monitors covered one whole wall with scrawling news reports, satellite maps that tracked military movements along the border, and a feed from the White House that currently displayed the Presidential Seal against a blue background. The last report that he had received was of the dead marines and missing civilians.

He couldn't believe that scarcely a few days ago, he was on a mission to bring unparalleled cooperation between the U.S. and their southern neighbor, and now they were at the brink of all-out war. Somewhere in the middle of it, his friends that he drug to Mexico, were caught in the crossfire.

"Mr. Senator, the FBI has completed their satellite review of the helicopter crash site," Wilkins interrupted Senator Johnson's thoughts, "They have images of Adam, Laura and Miranda being captured."

The senator spun to face his aide.

"Mrs. Raines appeared unconscious, the others seem to be in relatively unharmed condition," Wilkins consoled his boss.

"Who grabbed them?"

"That is unclear, sir. The images were inconclusive. Some of the equipment seemed like our military, but the unit's overall configuration was not consistent with any of our regimens. It should be displayed on monitor B," Wilkins pointed toward the bank of screens.

One of the screens displaying a newsfeed suddenly changed to a slightly pixilated satellite feed. In surreal silence, the events in the vacant field just north of the Mexican border unfolded for the Senator to see. The vague images of his friends flashed on the screen. Had he not known it was Adam, Laura, and Miranda, he might not have identified them, but he knew. The pit of his stomach washed in acid as he watched the unfortunate events. His despair and melancholy suddenly gave way to resolve. He wasn't going to be a bystander to the events. The friendships that he had built in Mexico, the common goals they each shared, were real, and they weren't one-sided. It was time to reconnect and begin putting sense to the insanity that had taken hold along the border.

Sean pushed the girl to continue trudging over the sandy ground northward. In the distance, he could hear the spillover murmur of the migration party. Not wanting to risk interaction with another coyote or be near when they realize one of their own was missing, he veered his path west of the group. As a growing mass of clouds obscured the moon, visibility across the rough terrain became more challenging. Occasionally, Sean's shin would meet up with a cactus or yucca, and instinctively, he would lash his arm out to stop his companion. One such incident, he paused long enough to hear faint voices drift in from the north. These were different than those of the migration party – these voices were American.

Spinning to his tag-along, he held his finger to his lips and hissed, "Shhh." Motioning for the girl to squat behind a mesquite tree, he slunk off towards the voices. Creeping closer, he could make out vague shapes, four men huddled on a hill.

Silhouettes of each figure with long arms framing their group posed in front of him. "Minutemen," Sean whispered to himself. He had read articles and seen news stories on the loosely organized band of patriots that took upon themselves to close the border. Not wanting to elicit an adverse reaction from the bunch, Sean spoke out to warn them that he was approaching.

"Minutemen? I am an American. I tracked a group of coyotes migrating a large cohort of immigrants nearly twenty strong!" Sean called out.

He was met with the beams from several flashlights. Sean was nervous. His disheveled appearance would not convince the group that he was indeed American. "One of the coyotes raped a young woman traveling with the group. I caught up with and him and left him disabled, about two miles back. The rest of the group is just over that rise."

"Nice work, but who the hell are you, one of us?" one of the men behind the flashlight beam asked.

"I'm definitely a patriot," Sean replied, "Look, the girl back there needs medical attention. She's pretty shook. See, she gets help and care, will you? I'm a little worse for wear and not much help at this point."

"You got it. We'll take care of it. You need some help yourself?"

"No, just get the cavalry to round up the bad guys," Sean was hoping the men would spring into action and forget about him, and they did. In a flurry of radio calls to the border patrol, and their own colleagues further down along the border, the men burst into action. Sean had the luxury to melt into the night and disappear into southern Arizona without further attention.

Another dark room. Sienna opened her eyes, trying to accept any light to allow her to see. She sat up on her musty bed and moved her eyes around the room. A small blue line seemed to glow behind a thick tapestry. Moving across the room, the girl pulled aside the curtain. Shards of moonlight cut through the darkness of her room and illuminated the world outside. A row of dilapidated wooden buildings lined the rough dirt road outside of her window. There were no street lights, cars, or any sign that people had been here in a long, long time. The scene reminded her of a ghost town she and her dad had visited on a trip to New Mexico. Thoughts of her dad caused the girl to slump. She remembered pretending to serve him Sarsaparilla at the saloon after a day of riding horses and touring the town. They always had so much fun together. Staring out at the abandoned village, she couldn't help but think of how much she missed her father.

As the tears had just begun to stream down her face, the door to her room opened. She spun in fear. As scared as she had been in the beginning, since the failed rescue attempt, the men who held her captive had begun acting even more strangely. They seemed nervous and excited. Something told her this change in behavior was not a good thing. The man paused in the doorway, staring at the startled little girl. Walking past her, he checked the window to ensure that it was stuck tight and then paused on his way back out. Looking at Sienna, who tilted her head up at him with tear-filled eyes, said, "*Lo siento*, I'm sorry, *la nina*," he handed her a bottle of water and a candy bar and quickly walked out of the room and locked the door behind him.

Alex glanced at his passenger as the rented sedan passed under the street lamp. The unconscious body of Butch Harvill, a vocal anti-immigration activist, lay slumped in the back seat. Less than twenty minutes after being released from jail for harassing a group of Mexican ranch workers, Alex' men nabbed him. His preoccupation with staving the flow across the border was conveniently coupled with his hidden passion for narcotics. His men lured him in with a fix after his jail stay and ensured that he would sleep soundly for their boss' purpose.

Alex knew the drugs he administered to Harvill would last through the night, allowing him plenty of time to reach the site and complete his task. Take out the target and conveniently place the near-over dosed, publicly proclaimed opponent of Mexican immigration policy Harvill to take the fall.

Normally, Alex would have succumbed to the "buzz" of the job, but this time, he was conflicted. For one, he liked the ambassador. From what he knew of him, he was a good man. Second, killing a child…he had taken countless lives. None had made him the slightest bit squeamish until this one. The consummate professional, he knew he had to be extra cautious. Thinking too much could make him lose his edge. In his line of work, losing your edge can be fatal.

For the third time in as many days, Sean was in a position where he had to commandeer another vehicle. This time, his donor nearly handed him the keys. Walking past a nightclub that had apparently issued last call, a drove of revelers streamed out into the adjacent parking lot. Sean watched as several escorted their dates, some they came with, some they may have just met, to their cars.

Sean chuckled as more than one seemed to struggle to get their keys from their pocket to the lock. He watched as one young man, in particular, seemed to struggle more than others. Yelling across the lot, he exclaimed his need to urinate to a friend and his date and stumbled awkwardly into the alley, just beyond his Jeep. The friend seemed to be more interested in his date and simply waved off his intoxicated buddy as he jumped into his own car.

The man in the alley crashed into the side of the building as he fought with his zipper. After relieving himself, he staggered towards the topless Jeep, keys in hand. After a zig and a zag and another zig, the party-goer somehow made it to the driver's seat. Fumbling with the keys, he dropped them to the floorboard. After seeming to search for them for a few moments, he lay still in the bucket seat.

One by one, the parking lot emptied. During a lull of traffic, Sean stole across the parking lot to the Jeep. Taking a quick look around, he started to yank the man from his seat. Sean was startled when the driver spun his head and looked at him. With a teetering head, the man looked at Sean with vacant eyes, "Dude, I think I'm going to yack!"

Swallowing a laugh, Sean offered assistance, "C'mon man. You don't want to do that in your ride." Holding out his hand, the man leaned into Sean and allowed him to pull him free from the Jeep. Nearly carrying the drunken partier to the curb, Sean propped him against a concrete wall.

"Thanks, dude, righteous."

"No worries, man, no worries. You going to be alright?" Sean asked, looking down, he realized that the kid passed out against the wall, a pile of vomit streaming down his side.

Without another moment wasted, Sean jogged to the Jeep. Sliding behind the wheel, he patted at the floorboard, his finger nicking a set of keys. Holding them in front of him, he found the one for the ignition and started the four-wheel-drive up. Jamming the stick shift into reverse, he pulled out of the parking space and wheeled the vehicle onto the road and towards the highway.

Despite being near exhaustion, the adrenaline of the heist woke him up. After miles of hiking, he was just glad to be sitting down and off of his feet. Even in the Arizona desert, the wind whipping in the doorless, topless Jeep was chilling. Cranking the knobs for the heating system, Sean enjoyed his first convenience in quite some time.

With the roar of the road, he didn't hear anything, but a glow from the passenger seat alerted Sean to a cellphone. He assumed that the call was from the friend that became worried about the owner of the vehicle. Allowing the call to drop, Sean took advantage of the device and quickly punched in some numbers. Looking at the clock on the cellphone's screen, he wondered if the call would be answered at all as it read three o'clock in the morning. It was not. Hitting redial, he tried again. Three more tries, Sean relented to the fact that his friend, for whatever reason, was not going to answer. Staring crossly at the glowing phone, he decided to try another loyal friend.

"Rachel York," a sleepy voice called through the phone.

"Rachel, it's...me," Sean yelled back, the howl of the highway rapidly moving passed the Jeep made hearing very difficult.

"What? Sean...where are you?"

"I'm in Arizona."

"You have every federal agency in Mexico and the U.S. looking for you. What the hell is going on?" Rachel demanded, her brain jolted wide-awake by her friend's voice.

"I don't have a lot of time. There is a little girl who has been kidnapped. I'm trying to find her," Sean replied, "I need your help."

"You know you can count on me," the Northwest Regional Director agreed, "Who's phone are you on?"

"You don't want to know. Sorry to bother you so late, I called Adam..." Sean started but was abruptly cut short by Rachel.

"You don't know? The embassy was evaced. Their helicopter was shot down. The marines were sent in, but by the time they got there, the place was cleared out. They are assumed hostages."

"Any idea by who?"

"Not yet, the boys at the Pentagon are reviewing satellite data," Rachel said.

Sean's mind reeled with this information. His instinct was to react, but he lacked the intel to do so.

"Maybe if I can help this girl," Sean sighed, needing to focus on one crisis at a time, "I was told by a thug at a Mexican drug cartel I infiltrated..."

"You infiltrated a Mexican drug cartel?"

"Listen, if you repeat everything I say, this is gonna take a lot longer," Sean scolded.

"Sorry, I shouldn't be surprised anymore by what comes from you," Rachel conceded, "So what do you have?"

"The cartel guard told me that a Mexican Ambassador's daughter is being held at a place near Phoenix that means roughly "duck" in Mexican. Can you find a way to look that up?" Sean called into the phone.

"Yeah, sure, but how did…"

"Don't worry about it right now. I'm sure your phone is monitored. Just call me back at this number. Did it show up on your screen?"

"Yeah…yeah, I have it," Rachel replied.

"Good, call me when you have an answer!"

Sean flicked off the phone and returned his full attention on the road. He was quite sure that when he reached Phoenix and if he found the site, that he was going to be up against a crew of well-armed cartel guards. And all he had was a severely exhausted body. As usual, he was in way over his head.

Sixteen

The highway was nearly empty from the border town of Lukeville to the outskirts of Phoenix. Rachel York had called Sean back nearly immediately and gave him detailed instructions on how to find the Drake hotel. Rachel had described the Drake, the closest translation to "duck" that he could find on Google, as part of an old mining town – a part of Arizona just outside of Phoenix that hadn't seen humanity for nearly fifty years. Just outside the reach of the Scottsdale suburbs, several contractors had made bids for the area to either develop or turn into a tourist destination, but had been turned down as the land was part of a grant afforded native Americans.

Sean used the primitive map on the cellphone that the owner of the Jeep left in the passenger seat to guide him to the area. Averaging a speed of eighty miles an hour, Sean made good time in the crude four-wheel drive. As proud of himself as he was as to how things had turned out so far this evening, he knew it was all for not if he did not reach the Drake on time. He was confident that Clarissa's safe return would resolve his issues with the Mexican Government, but the Ambassador's daughter was still in the clutches of the cartel, he had to save the girl. Images of her frightened brown eyes were burnt into his memory. He couldn't imagine what the child must be going through.

He fought fatigue as he scanned the horizon. To him, each desert road looked the same. "Turn left at the nine-hundredth cactus…," Sean mumbled to himself.

Finally, he reached a major intersection, the split in the southern highway that would swing him west to city center or east to the suburbs and beyond. Slamming the Jeep in gear, Sean sped towards the location that Rachel had identified. Soon, Sean saw the break in the road he was looking for – a seldom-used dirt road that headed into a box canyon.

The unarmed man feared a direct confrontation. Surprise was the only thing he had on his side. Switching off the headlights, he used what moonlight shone down to pick his way through the bumpy terrain. As the roofline of a building crept into view as Sean navigated a curve, he pulled the four-wheel-drive off of the road. Switching off the engine, he sat and listened.

Relieved, the only noises that met his ears, were those of the insects that took advantage of the cooler night air to become active. Slipping out from the driver's seat, he rummaged through the contents of the Jeep. Under a jacket in the tiny compartment behind the rear seat, Sean found an aluminum softball bat. Snatching it free, he slung it over his shoulder and began his march toward the building.

Slinking behind a boulder, Sean watched the house. Occasionally a flicker of light would bounce through the first story and shine through the windows. "Either this place has ghosts, or I'm in the right spot," Sean muttered. Advancing, he arched his way around the building, noting what movements he saw. At two

different times, he saw lights downstairs and once upstairs. None of
the lights aimed outside, telling Sean that he had not been spotted or
heard.

The rear of the dilapidated building seemed void of activity.
A shattered window under the shadow of an old mesquite tree made
an excellent opportunity to enter undetected. Sliding around the side
of the boulder, he began his approach. Nearly leaving his
concealment, Sean saw the slightest movement near the window he
targeted as his point of entry. Pulling back, he peered out from the
edge of the boulder. Staring through the broken window, Sean's eyes
strained to determine if he saw anything in the dark abyss of the
hotel. Holding still, a faint shape again appeared in the side of the
window bay. A sentry posted in that back room. Sean's point of
entry would have to be somewhere else.

Rolling to the other side of the boulder, Sean spied a veranda
on the side of the building. Below it, a steel drum, once used to hold
rainwater from the defunct gutter, stood as Sean's new point of
entry. Following a gully that ran along the back of the property, he
moved down to the corner of the house. Poking his head out of the
gully, Sean found that he could follow the shadow line of the
mesquite tree.

Still clutching the aluminum softball bat, Sean raced along
the treeline, out of the moon's spotlight. Without breaking stride, he
leaped with one foot on the steel drum and pushed up into the air.
Gripping the bottom of the veranda, he swung his body up until he
was able to add a leg to the hold on the wood decking. Sliding the
bat onto the deck, he was able to use both hands and pull himself up
and over the rail. Landing as softly as he could, he crouched against
the side of the old hotel out of the view of the windows and the
doorway.

Sean's ears worked overtime to detect the sense of anybody in the adjacent room. Cautiously, he gripped the bat and spun into the open doorway. Scanning wildly around the room, he was relieved to find it empty. Taking cautious steps, he moved through the dark hotel room. Maneuvering to the doorway, he was able to follow the sound of voices, deeper into the building. Among the voices, he could hear the diminutive voice of a little girl. The little voice amongst the chatter spiked Sean's will. His affect changed from one of concern to one of defiant resolve.

While not entirely ignoring stealth, his anger pushed him on with a renewed vigor. His eyes narrowed as blood pushed through his veins. Wielding the bat over his shoulder, he slid the door to the room open, ignoring the loud creak, readying himself for a battle.

Expecting the conversation in the room down the hall to cease and a half-dozen men wielding firearms to come barreling toward him, he was pleasantly surprised to see that he was able to move completely across the hallway without such a confrontation. As he rolled his back to the open doorway of the room, he struck quickly as the first head appeared to investigate the creaking door. Grabbing the man by the collar, Sean pulled him into the hallway. Before the kidnapper could draw the gun from his side holster, the softball bat cracked him on the wrist, sending the man reeling back with his Springfield .45 falling to the floor. Holding the bat menacingly in the air, Sean watched the man back himself against the rail and unwittingly flip over backward to the first floor below.

The calamity summoned the entire force of the kidnappers to converge on the area of the open stairwell. Sean snatched the Springfield off of the floor and spun back to the wall. Swinging an upward arc, Sean caught the next assailant in the hands sending his gun flying and then backed him into the room with the muzzle of the .45. Slinging the bat to the side, Sean kicked the door shut with his foot and scanned the room. One man sat on a bed across from Sienna, who sat up expectantly. Sean smiled briefly at Sienna and demanded to the man on the bed to toss his firearm over. Sliding to the side of the room, Sean motioned for the man he had disarmed to move against the closed door and hold it shut.

Nodding toward the door, "Andale!" Sean urged the man on the bed to join his partner. "Sienna, how're you doing, sweetheart?"

"I'm okay. I knew you'd come for me!" Sienna called happily from the bed.

"Alright, how about you stand behind me while I figure a way out of here," Sean said, his semi-automatic trained in the direction of the two kidnappers. His mind calculated the enemy count against him. He knew there were at least two downstairs, maybe a couple more. There was the man that fell over the railing – doubtful a considerable risk at this point, and the two that he faced and had disarmed. Bending down, he retrieved the handgun that had been slid across the floor. Stuffing the gun in his waistband, he moved to the window with Sienna shadowing behind.

Before he could look out, the door to the room rattled violently, accompanied by shouting from the other side. As the two detainees looked at each other to decide whether to let their partners through, Sean fired a series of shots over their shoulders. Moments later, angry, painful screams emanated from the hallway. "At least one more down," Sean mumbled amidst his detainees shrinking to the floor, their faces washing pale.

Stealing a glance over his shoulder, he decided that dropping out of the window was his best chance of escape with Sienna. Searching the room for something to use to rappel down to the ground, his search was cut short as a renewed effort to get in through the door began. "If anyone gets through that door, you two are the first ones getting shot!" Sean warned the men blocking the door. His warning was met with them planting the soles of their shoes against the floor.

Snatching the sheets from one of the beds, he twisted a crude knot through a bedpost and hoisted Sienna in his right arm like a football. Firing a final shot in the direction of the doorway, just over the heads of the two disarmed kidnappers, he shoved the pistol in his waistband and grabbed a handful of the sheets. Without hesitating, he kicked his legs through the open window and hugged Sienna tight to his ribs as he slid the length of the crude rope and dropped the remaining ten feet to the ground.

In an instant, the house exploded with excited shouting, and heavy footsteps could be heard on the old stairway. Still holding Sienna under one arm, Sean raced as fast as he could down the road, making a bee-line for the stolen Jeep. Scarcely a hundred yards away, he heard the first shot fired and the too-familiar zip of bullets flying overhead. He was confident that his head start would get him and the girl far enough away that a pistol would no longer be accurate, he just hoped that they didn't have any long guns in their arsenal.

The sound of an engine starting made Sean's heart sink. He was way too far from the Jeep to make it before a vehicle would close the distance. Veering off of the road, Sean made an arc towards the Jeep. His mind raced. He knew he was moving away from the immediate danger of the approaching vehicle, but diminishing the chances that they would reach their own vehicle in time for an escape.

In seconds, headlights swept across the desert road, and the grumble of a V-8 being gunned filled the night air. Streaking for the nearest rock outcropping, Sean slid to the ground, gently depositing Sienna in the process. Freeing one of the .45s from his waistband, he stuck his head out from beyond the rock. As pleased as he was to see the chase vehicle fly by on the road, he was equally disappointed to see it careen to a stop near where he had left the Jeep. Shouts from the road told him that now he would face pursuers from two directions.

In the sliver of moonlight, he looked at the face of Sienna. He thought of how much she must have been through. "I'll get you out of here," he promised, swallowing hard, having no idea how he was going to make good on that pledge.

Focusing his attention on continuing toward the Jeep, he pulled on Sienna's hand while readying the pistol with his other. Keeping his body between the girl and the road, Sean tried to maneuver them as best as he could through the sporadic shadows. In the headlight beam of the chase vehicle, he could see three men scanning the terrain. Ten feet away from them was the Jeep and their most likely route to salvation. Further ahead of where Sean and Sienna stood was a small cluster of cacti – the only other cover in the area between them and the bad guys.

"Sienna, you see that group of cactuses over there? I want you to run over there as quietly and low to the ground as possible. When you hear shooting, get as flat as you can. If I tell you to run, you need to take off that direction," he pointed, "The highway is that way. Otherwise, I'll come and get you."

Sienna looked at Sean for a moment and hesitated. She didn't want to be alone anymore, she wanted to stay right by this man's side, but she nodded anyway. With a quick look towards the road where the kidnappers were fanning out to widen their search area, she ran as fast and low as she could before squatting near the stand of cacti. Sean positioned himself for cover fire if they heard or saw Sienna run. They didn't.

Sean took in a deep breath. He didn't like his options, but he knew Sienna's life depended on him getting them away. Squaring up the first kidnapper in his sights, he gently began pressing on the trigger. Before he could pull it taut, a twig snapped to his right, alarming Sean to a gunman closing in. The man saw Sean and began raising his pistol. Sean squeezed off a shot, hitting the man in the chest and dropping him to the ground. Suddenly, footsteps seemed to come from all directions. Sean's cover given away. He knew he would soon be overtaken. "Sienna, run!"

The kidnappers searching along the road were quickly on top of Sean's position, one trailing after the girl. Sean gave up his spot to roll into position, snapping off a shot hitting Sienna's pursuer in the leg, sending him to the ground. A shot fired behind Sean, clipping him in the side. Clawing at the ground, Sean tried to curl near the small rock that he had used for cover, determined to take as many of the kidnappers out as possible before they inevitably overwhelmed him. Holding a pistol in each hand, he waited for the next target or the next unseen shot to take him out. From both sides, he could hear men closing in around him.

Readying each pistol, swinging his head from side to side, Sean's senses burned, trying to give him the maximum amount of warning. He was surprised as the sky lit up from all directions. A black helicopter screamed across the horizon, massive searchlights flooding the desert floor. A pair of shots flashed from an open door as a marksman peered through the bay. The sound of Humvees rocketing down the dirt road and across the rocky terrain added to the chaos. In seconds, the whole area was filled with dark-clothed men with high-powered semi-automatic weapons swept the area. Only twice needing to empty their chambers as two kidnappers made final stands, three more collapsing to their knees, less than fifteen feet from Sean's position.

Sean, too, swung his guns upside down on their trigger guards and allowed the agents to relieve him of the weapons. His most significant relief was seeing from the glow of one of the Humvee's massive lighting, Sienna being swooped up by one of the commandos. The sight nearly brought Sean to tears as the girl's ordeal was finally over. The scene was so surreal. Sean hardly felt that he was a part of it. Sitting on his knees, his hands laced behind his head, he watched as a small army descended on the scene. A second helicopter swung overhead, circling once and landing softly on the road. The SUV with Sienna in it passed by and stopped short of the new arrival helicopter.

Sean's wrists were tied tight by plastic zip ties, and he was stood up by a pair of the agents. Passing several kidnappers being assessed for wounds and mortality by gunpoint, he was led to the road where a black Ford was waiting for him, the rear door open. Placing a hand on Sean's head, an agent began to guide him into the vehicle. "Wait!" a little voice called out. Both the agent and Sean turned their heads to Sienna, leaving the embrace of a man who had exited the helicopter and streak across the road toward the car.

Breathless, Sienna looked up at the agent, "You can't take him. He's a good guy!"

The commotion attracted the attention of several men in suits, including the one that had been hugging the girl. Sienna looked up at a man wearing a suit, his tie undone, hanging limp from his neck, and exclaimed, "Daddy, he saved me...twice!"

"He what?" the man gasped, looking at Sean, he wrinkled his brow, "Who are you?"

"I was looking for Clarissa Lamraillo in Mexico when I found Sienna. We had nearly escaped together when our vehicle was struck. The kidnappers stole her here to the abandoned hotel where I tracked them," Sean replied and then smirked, "But mainly, I'm just a guy who seems to have a knack for being at the wrong place at the wrong time."

"I'd say the right place if you ask me," the man said and held his hand out to Sean before realizing that his wrists were bound and pulled his hand away, "I am Ambassador Gutierrez. Sienna is my daughter. You saved her life."

Looking at the agent holding Sean, Gutierrez asked, "Can you release him, please?"

"I'm afraid not, sir. Like it or not, this man is an international fugitive who is being sought for the kidnapping of Clarissa Lamarillo," the agent replied.

"Ah, you must be Sean Kendall," the ambassador smiled, "I am afraid I must insist in his release. The charges you speak of do not exist against him. Mrs. Lamarillo returned to Mazatlan this afternoon. She absolved him, and in fact, the Secretary of Commerce is requesting his return to Mexico for rescuing his wife."

The agent stared at the ambassador, his face utterly flush in bewilderment. "I'm gonna have to run this by my superiors," the agent said and called to a fellow agent to watch over Sean.

In minutes, the agent returned. With a shrug, he whipped a blade from its pouch and quickly sliced through the zip ties holding Sean's wrists together. "The story checks out, Mr. Kendall, you are free to go…though the State Department would still like to see you in the next twenty- four hours for debrief."

"With a ride, I'll head to Lackland Air Force base right now. I'll be glad to speak with them there," Sean agreed.

"Even I am not being allowed to fly over the border. It would be my honor to have our helicopter take you," Ambassador Gutierrez offered.

Sean looked at him and his daughter, "It would be *my* honor. Your daughter is an incredible young lady, the true hero in all of this."

Sienna beamed and grabbed both men by the hand, "Then I'm ready to go."

Seventeen

The Bell Ranger helicopter settled down on the pad. Sean thanked the ambassador once more for his hospitality and removed his headset. Turning toward Sienna, she was already unbuckled and ran headlong into Sean with outstretched arms. Pressing her head into Sean's chest, she squeezed tight.

Looking down, Sean returned her embrace. He was unsure as to what to say, but was surprised with the emotion that welled up inside him from the young girl's affection. Patting her on the back, Sean pulled away and gave a quick nod to Ambassador Gutierrez as he slipped out of the helicopter.

Two marines met Sean immediately and ushered him inside the base's main barracks. Wilkins was waiting inside the doorway. "Mr. Kendall, I would swear that you have nine lives, both physically and politically."

"If I only had nine, I'm sure I'd be dead," Sean retorted, half under his breath.

"The senator is sleeping. I hope you understand that I chose not to wake him."

"That's fine. I'd like to get an update on Miranda, Adam and Laura," Sean replied evenly.

"Shouldn't you just get some sleep, you've been through a lot," Wilkins suggested, and somewhat tongue-in-cheek added, "And perhaps a shower?"

"A shower, definitely."

"How about some food? You must be famished," Wilkins offered.

"The rescue crew gave me some MRE squeeze tube stuff. Not so tasty, but filling...I'm fine, thank you," Sean replied, "So, what is the latest on my friends?"

"How much do you know?"

"I know they crashed in their evac helo from Mazatlan. I know that when the good guys got there, they were gone," Sean said.

"Unfortunately, we don't know much more than that," Wilkins shrugged.

Sean seethed with Wilkins' nonchalant response, but tried to understand that everyone had had a long couple of days – and he was up at nearly four in the morning.

"A shower would be good," Sean admitted.

"I'll make sure you are taken care of, Sean," Wilkins replied, "You did, after all, return a hero."

"Hero? The marines, or feds, or whoever had come – saved me in the nick of time. They're the heroes," Sean grumbled.

Tug singled out one of his men. Garibaldo was second-generation American, but through his grandmother learned Spanish as a close second language. Turning to two of his former Special Ops guys, "Get Raines."

In moments, a haggard Adam Raines was plopped onto a steel folding chair. In front of him was an inexpensive digital video camera. Garibaldo clicked on the "record" button. In his most harsh Mexican accent, he announced, "I have three American terrorists that fled from Mazatlan. I demand counsel with a representative from the American government. If you do not comply, I will behead them one by one." Sliding a machete from a sheath strapped to his back, the hooded Garibaldo approached Adam.

Slumping, Adam used his grossly fatigued appearance to avoid the camera. He couldn't help but peer up in his peripheral vision. Seeing the maniacal mercenary approach with blade drawn, Adam reacted. His entire being thinking of his wife somewhere locked in the bowels of their decrepit quarters, he hurled his body forward.

Everything was going to plan, Garibaldo was surprised when the powerful man locked two strong hands around his wrists. In an instant, Garibaldo was on the ground staring at the very blade he was wielding only moments ago. From either side, a pair of by-standing mercs snapped into action and slammed the big man to the ground. The machete fell forward, smacking Garibaldo in the face with just enough force to slash a crude slice down his nose an upper cheek.

With a kick, Adam launched one of his attackers across the room, only to be rewarded with a barrage of knees to his midsection and punches to the face. Unable to resist, Adam succumbed to unconsciousness.

"Good damn enough for me," Tug growled, "Lean him in the chair and start again. And Garibaldo, don't bleed through that damn mask. Can we get him a new one?" Spinning his head around at the crew that had huddled near the doorway, one ran off to find a new balaclava to hide the young merc's new scars.

Resetting the video, Garibaldo approached the unconscious Adam with renewed vigor, pulling the machete free, he brought it sharply down against the wall, mere inches from Adam's neck. It

was only Tug's repeated insistence that he not harm the hostage –
this time – that prevented him from completing the act and removing
Adam's head from his body.

Senator Johnson entered the situation room, excited to have a
large cup of coffee thrust into his hand. Awoken by an insistent
young marine and afforded three minutes to shit, shower, and shave
as he had been instructed, he felt a little out of sorts. The stress, both
physical and emotional over the last few days had taken their toll on
him, though no one near him could tell. "What's going on?"

Base Commander Richards greeted him, "We received this
video in the last few minutes. I believe you know this gentleman.
Can you identify him as one of the lost civilians on evac flight Helo-
Bravo?"

Pressing the play button, the commander, turned towards the
Senator. He studied the senator's face as he watched the video of the
terrorist state his demands and bring the wicked blade within inches
of taking the American's life.

"It's Adam Raines," Johnson identified softly, "Is he alive?"

"Sir, we've replayed the video several times before you
arrived," rewinding the recording and playing it back, he zoomed on
Raine's midsection, "You can see his chest expand and contract right
here. He appears to be unconscious but breathing. He has been
roughed up a bit but is still alive."

"So, they want a list of Mexican extremists released from
U.S. prisons. Any link amongst who they requested?"

"You are very sharp, Senator. No, that is one of the unsettling
things about it. Several of the names listed on the recording are from
feuding factions. NSA intel says that they would never be linked
together. They're not even all from Mexico. Some are from other
Central American countries, including rival drug families. Our guys

think this is a bogus request, but we can't figure out why," the Commander Richards replied.

The senator pulled away from the graphic image on the screen. Rubbing his chin, he tried to tie in all of the previous events of the last few days. To his surprise, the links did not add up. Most of the military responses from either government did not either match their public statements, and much of Mexico's reactions were initially predicated on a kidnapping that did not really occur. And now, this latest "terrorist" demand and the foiled kidnapping that Sean intervened on – Mexicans kidnapping the Mexican ambassador's daughter. A sickening thought crossed his mind, "Maybe this whole thing is bull shit. Rival groups on either side of the border, unwittingly with the same goals of driving conflict between the two countries…"

"With all due respect, Senator, what the hell are you talking about?" Richards scowled.

"Look at the events that we actually know who was behind. Americans against Americans, Mexicans against Mexicans, *framing* the other for their actions," Johnson decried, "Look at who had something to gain from the U.S.-Mexico tensions – the Mexican drug cartels top the list. Second would be the extreme wings of our country that don't like the idea of our government pairing up with any of our neighbors."

"This is a serious theory, Senator, though not one without merit," Richards admitted. "If this is all true, both militaries have engaged in wrongful actions."

"Not necessarily so. If we begin to cooperate now, we show our partnership in taking out nefarious organization on either side and, in fact, is the best way for both countries to come out of this," Johnson countered, "But, I do not want those captives to be collateral."

"Come with me, Senator. I think we need to get on the line with Washington."

Alex Santos stopped his car along the highway. Craning his head under the windshield, he watched as the third helicopter flew overhead, this one a Super Puma, a VIP transport helo occasionally used by Mexico, but not by the U.S. Something was wrong. Each had flown towards the safehouse. Moments later, a parade of vehicles tore by at high speed. The Drake Hotel was a busted operation. As the last vehicle passed, Santos turned the wheel of the car headed back the way that he had come.

Regrettably, he unsheathed his cellphone and punched in the necessary numbers. As the call was answered, he spoke plainly, "The Drake has been compromised. The entire operation has been scrubbed on this end."

"What the hell do you mean? What happened?" La Costa yelled into the phone.

"It came down as I approached. Never even got to the site. It looks like the feds are all over the scene," Santos explained, "What are my counter orders?"

"Find the American and kill him."

"*Which* American?"

"The one who got to Lamarillo's wife, and the ambassador's daughter the first time around," La Costa said. "He's probably the one behind this. We tracked him to the border and lost the trail at Sonoyta."

"If he's here, I'll find him."

La Costa slammed the phone down. His plans were unraveling, and he was running out of chips to play. Now it was time to start making a mark in case his border war lost its momentum. He had a shortlist of high impact targets that he would like to see fall – the American, Lamarillo, Gutierrez, President Marshall, Senator Johnson.

Retrieving the phone, he placed a call. "Reyes, it is time to change our tactics."

The Mexican Army Colonel pushed the earpiece further into the canal to try and isolate the conversation away from the shelling his men were conducting, "What do you mean change tactics?"

"The war is going to end soon. My intel has the two sides beginning to realize that rogue groups have propagated it. Disband your team and send them back into their ranks, except keep a handful of your top, most loyal men," La Costa declared.

"What do you have in mind?"

"Target elimination, starting with Lamarillo."

Even a couple hours of sleep rejuvenated the exhausted Sean Kendall. Though his body cried out for more time in the military cot, his brain was turned on and ready to get some answers. Slipping on his shoes, the only articles of clothing that were his own, he left the small airbase room. The olive BDU trousers and brown t-shirt that he wore were welcome gifts by his military base hosts. He found the clothes surprisingly comfortable and was thankful to be out of sweat and desert ravaged outfit that he had been wearing.

His arrival the previous evening had been such a rush; he had no idea of his whereabouts. Instead, he let his nose lead him the way towards a strong pot of coffee. Walking through the stark hallway, he found a well-lit room with a mix of Air Force and Marine personnel scattered tucked into a few of the tables. To the wall nearest the door, a bank of coffee pots and cups nestled in between a refrigerator and a microwave.

The men at the tables ignored Sean as he grabbed a paper cup from the stack and poured a cup of coffee. Adding a thimble of nondescript creamer, he left the room and began roaming the halls. Reaching the end of the first section, he sprang open a set of double doors blocking the hallway. Two well-armed marines immediately confronted him.

"I'm sorry, sir, no civilians beyond this point. Please proceed back beyond this set of doors," one of the sentries said.

"But, I need to…"

"Sir, those are strict orders. If there is someone you need to reach, there is a phone in each of the bunk rooms. That is where you should stay unless under escort."

Knowing the guards had no say and would stand by their commission, Sean relented and doubled-back. He would use the phone in his room to try and ring Wilkins or Senator Johnson. He wanted to get an update on Adam, Miranda, and Laura, as well as see if he could find out that Ambassador Gutierrez and Sienna made it home safely.

Sipping his coffee, that to Sean's taste buds reminded him of the smell of freshly paved asphalt. He retraced his steps back to his room. Swinging the door open, he was almost startled to see a figure sitting on his bed.

"I see you have survived trouble once again, Mr. Kendall."

"Rachel! What are you doing here?" Sean stammered as Rachel rose from the bed and gave him a solid hug.

Her arms still around him, she shared, "You call me for help, we send in the marines, and I don't hear back from you. I don't mind pitching in, but I want to be kept in the loop." Pulling away, she looked her friend in the eyes.

"I'm sorry. It was a whirlwind. Things went crazy at the hotel and then the feds or the marines or whoever showed up and…"

"I know. I had to find out my own way, thank you very much," Rachel smiled, "I came down here to see if I could keep you out of additional trouble."

"I'd stick to your regular job. It seems like these days trouble is all around me," Sean retorted meekly.

"That's what we love and hate about you, Sean – you can't help but to stick your neck out for others when they need you."

"Yeah, well, it's a line of work I'd like to get out of," Sean replied.

"I'm not sure at this point you can. I'd settle for alive and out of jail," Rachel, "How are your friends?"

"I don't know. I was on my way to try and find an update when I was told to return to my room. You have any pull around here?" Sean asked.

"On the base? No. This way out of my jurisdiction. I do have a few people in D.C. we can try and chat live with. Can your man Wilkins get us a conference room with a phone?" Rachel asked.

Sean shrugged, "Maybe, but couldn't Johnson get us in?"

"I don't think so. I tried when I arrived and found out you were sleeping. They are barely letting the elected officials in at this point," Rachel informed.

"Wilkins, it is," Sean replied, holding his hand out toward the doorway.

Together, they snaked their way through the halls towards the media center where Wilkins ran support for the Senator that he served. Nearly a dozen similar aides sat sleepily at individual desks, either answering phone calls or pecking on laptop keyboards. Rachel made a beeline for one who was staring at the wall, seemingly sleeping with his eyes open, "Excuse me, can you tell me where to find James Wilkins? He's Senator Johnson's aide."

Snapping his head in their direction, the exhausted man looked at them with dark red eyes, "I think I saw him head down the hall, just passed the press pool doors is a small lounge. Probably there grabbing a cup of coffee. Had a few myself." Lazily, the aide pointed his hand in the direction of a wastebasket on the side of his tiny desk. The can was overflowing with discarded coffee cups.

Thanking the man, the two followed his instructions down the hallway. A pair of guards stood sentry by the press doors, ensuring that the newshounds did not sneak through and into the political quarters. Continuing passed, Sean and Rachel found the lounge area. There they found a man sleeping on a couch, and a woman slumped, head down on a table, fast asleep. Wilkins was nowhere to be found.

"Let's try outside, maybe he needed some fresh air," Sean suggested, nodding towards a pair of double doors at the far end of the lounge. Pushing the lever carefully not to wake the sleeping pair, Sean nudged the door open and held it just wide enough for Rachel to follow. Closing it just as carefully, he peered around what appeared to be a courtyard. A marine at the far end eyed the two. He too guarded a door leading into the press pool quarters.

Pivoting, he peered down the length of the building in the opposite direction. Ending at a fence that overlooked one of the runways, Sean thought he could see a figure watching a squadron of F-22 Raptors one by one roar down the runway. Leading Rachel in that direction, the two strode towards the figure as they too watched the impressive jets take off into the night sky.

As the last Raptor angled its way into the stratosphere, Sean heard the figure speak. He must have been talking over the roar of the F-22s, because as the thunder of the afterburners subsided, the man was practically yelling into a cellphone he held to his ear. Recognizing the voice as Wilkins, Sean was about to get this attention when he heard the Senatorial aide call into the phone, "I've done my part. I've stuck my neck out way too far for you already, and your operation is failing! The word from the front lines is that Marshall has already spoken to President Lopez, and they are going to meet for a joint press conference to call your little coup a pathetic terrorist plan."

Sean and Rachel exchanged glances and froze in place. They couldn't believe what they were hearing. The aide continued, "I supported you. I even allowed some very nice people to get hurt, and it seems all for nothing. Now, I just want it to go away. We need to cut the cord, and I am doing it now. Passing you the advance information about Marshall's conference in the morning was my final act!"

Wilkins slammed the clamshell shut and whirled around towards the building. He stood in horror as he saw the two people observing him. Stammering, he blurted, "Sean, it's good to see you. Feeling refreshed?"

Sean stared at him quietly for a moment, collecting his thoughts and trying not to overreact. "I am feeling better. Thank you. I'd be much better if I knew Miranda and the Raines' were okay," Sean sighed and then held a hand out towards Rachel, "This is Rachel York, she is the Regional Director for the Department of Interior out of Seattle."

Rachel and Wilkins exchanged handshakes. "Trouble? You seemed upset on the phone," Sean pried.

"Oh, uhh, just domestic issues at home, nothing to burden you with. You have enough on your mind. Let's go get that update on our friends," Wilkins replied casually and tried to move past, towards the door to the lounge.

He stopped as Sean stood steadfast and blocked his path. "You've done so much for me, fill me in on your call, maybe I can help," Sean insisted.

"Really, it is just personal stuff," Wilkins again tried to brush Sean's inquiry off and then snapped, "I'd like to keep it that way."

"I'm not sure that is possible, Wilkins. I think you need to tell us what is going on," Sean declared.

The senatorial aide looked angry as he glared at Sean and then over at Rachel. "I have to get back to the Senator, excuse me."

"That is a great idea, you can fill him in too," Sean said.

Wilkins stopped in his tracks, turned and looked squarely in Sean's face, "You don't know what you are getting yourself into, Mr. Kendall."

"It's what you've gotten into that is the question," Sean said, "Passing on executive secrets, getting good people hurt...would those people happen to be my friends, Wilkins?"

"That wasn't supposed to happen!" the aide blurted, and the courtyard fell into silence for several moments as the three tried to piece together the crossroads that had seemed to arrive at.

"But it did," Sean said softly before his voice changed rapidly to a snarl, "Who were you talking to?"

"I can't tell you that!"

"Oh, but you can!" Sean grabbed Wilkins by his shirt collar and wrenched him close so that their eyes were directly in front of each other, "You are now responsible for their lives. If anything..."

"Sean! Stop, not here," Rachel snapped, placing a hand on Sean's forearm. Casting her glance towards the Marine at the far doors, which had taken an interest in the commotion.

"Fine, let's find a nice conference room," Sean growled, releasing Wilkins with a rough shove towards the lounge.

As they reached the door, Wilkins suddenly ran towards the Marine. "These two are from the press pool! They were harassing me for information!"

Sean sprinted after him, but was stopped short by the Marine's palm smashing him in the forehead. His feet swung out from under him as he landed on his back. Sean could hear Rachel pleading with the Marine, who had called in for back-up and drawn his sidearm.

"Ma'am, stop where you are," the Marine barked, flashing his firearm briefly at her before returning it on Sean.

"This is a mistake. I am going for my I.D. I am the Regional Director for the Department of the Interior. I …Mr. Kendall, who you have there, and I work very closely with Senator Johnson. We were trying to find his aide when we overheard him talking about the attacks. We think he was somehow involved, or at least sharing secret information," Rachel declared, slowly pulling her credentials from a pocket on her jacket.

"We'll take care of this inside, ma'am," the marine said as two more soldiers joined him.

Rachel opened her lips to continue her pleas, but stopped short, realizing that the marines were only going to follow protocol. Instead, she watched in silence as the two who joined the first pulled Sean to his feet and marched him along the sidewalk. The guard that approached them initially escorted Rachel. Sean scanned the courtyard, but Wilkins was nowhere to be seen.

Senator Johnson leaned against the conference table, looking at President Marshall through the flat screen monitor, "Mr. President, I in no way advocate giving in to terrorist demands. What I *am* asking for is to buy some time. Connect them with an envoy and try to gain some information as to where the American hostages are being held."

"Rick, I know you wouldn't be asking if these folks weren't important to you. And after all that has happened over the course of that last few days…the last few weeks, I would like to do anything to prevent the loss of more American lives," President Marshall replied, "You know as well as I do, the analysts agree that the request is bogus. The groups they requested have no connection with one another. In fact, they don't even like each other."

"I know, I've been thinking about this," Johnson agreed, "But I might have a way to make this more palatable. First, these people were working with me, essentially part of my delegation. Second, Raines *is* a federal agent. Third, they are connected with *rescuing* the Mexican Secretary of Commerce's wife and the daughter of a Mexican ambassador."

"Who exactly are these people, Rick?"

"Very special people, sir, very special people," the senator replied.

"Your third argument gives us our best shot. I'll give President Lopez a call. This could be a good thing to join forces on," Marshall conceded.

"Thank you, sir."

"Rick – two things," President Marshall said, squaring his face directly into the camera that was broadcasting him to the Lackland, "First, we've known each other too long for this 'Mr. President', 'sir' stuff. Second, if we get your friends back, I want to meet them personally. Lay eyes on this motley crew you claim have been so integral."

"You got it," Johnson beamed as the screen transitioned from a view of the Oval Office to the Air Force seal. As he opened the door to the conference room, he found two marines waiting in the hallway.

"Sir," one of the marines spoke, "Would you be willing to follow us? There has been an incident."

"What sort of incident?" Johnson queried/

"I'm afraid we're dispatched to get you, not speculate as to why, sir."

The senator began to appreciate what his friend President Marshall had felt with the constant denotations of respect. However, he knew with these professional soldiers, it was part of their doctrine. Nodding, he followed the men to the Military Police compound. Led inside, he stood outside of a closed-door where a lance-corporal met him.

"Thank you for coming, Senator Johnson," the lance-corporal said, extending his hand.

Shaking it, the senator looked curiously at the man, "What is this about?"

"Sir, one of our guards found two people in the secured courtyard molesting your senior aide. My men interceded and brought them into custody. They demanded to speak to you." His hand on the door, he nodded as a guard pressed the code for the latch. Swinging it open, he found Sean Kendall and Rachel York sitting side by side across a small wood table.

"Sean!" Senator Johnson exclaimed and then with his face twisted in utter confusion, "Rachel York? What is going on?"

Instantly, Sean and Rachel launched into a hasty diatribe before the lance-corporal cut them off. "You two will have your say!" the soldier bellowed, turning he asked, "You know these two, Senator?"

"Yes, yes, I do. I am confident they have a good explanation of what happened," Johnson confirmed, and then with a puzzled brow, "Where is Wilkins?"

"He left the scene. My men have not seen him since. He has full clearance…"

Waving the lance-corporal off, Johnson requested, "Give me a moment?"

"Of course, sir," nodding to the MPs standing guard, the lance-corporal followed them out of the room and closed the door behind him.

"Sean, I'm getting used to seeing you in these situations. Ms. York, it a pleasure, but do you two mind telling me what is going on?" the senator cast a stern glance at each and sat down across from them.

"I wouldn't have believed it, if I didn't hear it for myself," Sean replied softly.

"Heard what?"

"Wilkins, I don't know who he was talking to, but he was telling someone of the President's intentions. He didn't seem to agree, and it sounded as though it was echoed on the other end," Sean said.

"That is classified information, not to have left the Situation Room, I'll talk with him," Johnson shrugged.

"I believe it may be worse than that," Sean sighed, "It sounds as though he may have been working with someone who was initiating the conflict."

"What? You must have overheard wrong, out of context. James Wilkins has been part of my team, a friend, for over a decade!" the senator bellowed.

"It's true, Senator. I heard it that way as well," Rachel York said, breaking her calm silence. Knowing that Sean had a closer relationship with the senator, she wanted him to take the lead, "Furthermore, it seems as though he may have been privy to the attack on Miranda and the Raines'."

"I...I can't believe that," Senator Johnson pushed away from the table and stared at the wall, rubbing his eyes. After a minute of reflection, he returned his gaze at the two across the desk, "So, where is he?"

"He took off when the MPs stopped us," Rachel said flatly.

"If I were him, I'd either be sucking up to you to try and negate our story, or I'd have left the base and ran like hell," Sean replied.

"Hmmm, you're probably right," Johnson agreed, rubbing his chin, "I just don't understand why he would do that. And why he wouldn't just come talk to me."

"Either scared, didn't think you'd understand, or he knew he was wrong, but felt he had no other way," Sean suggested.

None of the scenarios seemed to improve Johnson's affect. He had a sullen, almost sad look about him, a look that generally becomes someone when they uncover betrayal.

Seeing this, Sean tried to quell the negative emotions of his friend, "We've all made mistakes believing we were doing the right thing..."

Rachel scoffed loudly, "You're the poster child of that sentiment!"

Ignoring her interruption, which he had to admit, brought a slight smile to the senator's face, "I think we have to believe that Wilkins had the country's best interest...your best interest at heart. He was just flawed in the implementation and the path to do so."

"That's good of you to say, especially if he did have anything to do with Miranda and Adam being shot down and taken hostage," Johnson replied. Suddenly, he was snapped back into the action-oriented man Sean knew him to be, "We may have a way to deal with the terrorists that have them."

Sean leaned closer as he listened to the senator's plan, "We can attach your efforts in rescuing Clarissa Lamarillo and the Gutierrez child to them, and have the Mexican authorities deal for their safe return."

"Because the U.S. will not deal with terrorists," Rachel cut in.

"Exactly," Senator Johnson confirmed, "President Marshall agreed that is the only way. We found a way to make it a political win for both countries."

"What if the terrorists don't abide by any arrangements set forth?" Sean asked.

"The fact the terrorists request was deemed bogus by the Intelligence analysts, I am quite certain that they will not, however, if we can demand continued confirmation of our friends' good health, then we buy us more time at least," Johnson replied.

"Delay at this point is the most we can offer," Rachel agreed.

Sean didn't like the answer, but this time, he knew that he was powerless to help. With no leads to go on, he knew that Miranda and crew could be anywhere in North America.

Eighteen

Tug prepared the video. The Mexicans bargaining for the Americans' lives was a surprise. Enough so that he was curious where that path might lead. More importantly, he was sure that he could spin this to his advantage. If the Americans were on the hook and the hostages were killed, they become another sad statistic of the border war. If the Mexicans are on the hook and they fail to bring back these anointed American heroes, the wildlife officer and his companions become fodder for the anti-Mexican crowd - mission accomplished.

Nodding to one of his men, he sent him off to retrieve all three prisoners. He would agree to the exchange. Make it a significant public display out on a tarmac on some crappy Mexican runway. When the hostages were in view of the cameras, they would meet a very nasty death, leaving the Mexican *federales* standing by idly by with their hands in their trousers.

His years of training also told him that any time the plan changes, things typically go wrong. Intuition nudged him to make this his final task of this mission. Before he could take the next step, his scrambled phone rang. Pushing the button, he grunted, "Yes…".

"Tug, it's Rhinehart, I have another request for you. Our mutual benefactor is on the line with us."

"Gaskill, this is Billings. Our friend in Washington has a loose end we need your help with."

"I have gone as far as can be considered prudent, Mr. Billings," Tug replied.

"You are probably right. This is your get-out-of-town final assignment," the oil executive suggested, "We have a figure who is unraveling. He has enough information to bring us all down, including yourself. Important enough for me to speak with you personally."

"Who is it this time?"

"A Washington insider we had aligned with inside a rival senator's camp. His name is James Wilkins. We have made this one pretty easy for you," Billings declared.

"How so?" Tug asked suspiciously.

"We invited him to my yacht offshore for refuge. He is taking a skiff out of Brownsville in about four hours," the tycoon replied.

"Very well. I assume I will be arranged easy access?"

"Wide open. There will be another seven zeros in your account."

Clicking the sat-phone off, the mercenary glanced at his watch. If he wanted to get to the yacht in the Gulf waters before his target, he would have to leave immediately. Given the U.S. – Mexican border tensions, he needed to prepare for delays as well. Glancing at the video equipment, he decided he would have to hand over the remaining duties to his next in charge. A little disappointed that he would not be there in person to see the irritating Fish and

Wildlife officer disposed of, his professionalism pushed him forward.

Grabbing the unprotected line, a measure he felt would add to the authenticity of the hostage-taking emanating in America. Tug called back the Mexican Embassy. "Senor Gutierrez, I have thought about your terms, and I find them acceptable, though we need to do this thing my way. I'll pick the exchange point. I'll need to see my comrades alive and well, and then I'll turn the Americans loose."

The ambassador tried to keep the conversation going for as long as possible, hoping to get some clue for who or where the call was coming from, "As long as the location is on Mexican soil…".

"I'm sure as hell not doing this in the States!" Tug bellowed.

"Good, because we would not be able to deal. Now, we are expecting a revised list of prisoners," Gutierrez said, "We cannot deal with the Americans, especially not now."

"I have already thought of that. I demand that Carlos Leoni, Ezdrubiel Carlion, Pancho Sanchez – a life for a life," Tug replies, looking at a site he found on the internet regarding militant drug lords that were currently in Mexican custody.

"Those are all killers. This is going to take some time."

"You don't have any time! I expect to make the drop by sunset, or there is no deal," Tug shot back.

"I will do nothing without proof that the Americans are still alive," Gutierrez demanded.

"I will send you one last video. You will find it posted online in twenty minutes, entitled 'AmeriMex Relations'. You will know the time as we will have a news channel on a television in the background," Tug added.

"I'll see the video, and then we will talk again," Gutierrez agreed.

"No, see the video and bring the wrongfully accused Mexican patriots to the abandoned airstrip south of Nuevo Laredo exactly ten minutes before sunset or the American infidels will be executed!" Tug hung up the phone.

Further believing that this whole Mexican ran operation was a farce, he knew it was time to bail. Giving his right-hand man last-minute instructions, he gathered the few things he wanted to travel with and left the building. One thing was for sure. He would bill his employers extra for this added US-Mexico tension bonus.

Adam Raines kept himself busy in his tiny, dank cell. Alternating between sit-ups and push-ups, he tried to keep the blood flowing through his body. He found the exercise was a tremendous help to his psyche, keeping him rational in his thoughts. Especially to retard the agonizing feeling of being so close to his wife yet being unable to help her. One thing he knew, if Tug wanted them dead at this point, they would be. The question was, what sort of bargaining chip could they be? A wildlife officer and his spouse would scarcely get a dial tone with the feds. Tug had to be making a personal plea, but to who?

Hearing the click of the lock, he fell to the floor, slumped as though the abuse that had been delivered to him had been too much, and the experience weakened him. A shaft of light sliced into the dark room as the heavy metal door creaked open.

"Let's go! Up on your feet!" the guard yelled into Adam's room.

Adam lifted his head wearily, acting as though that had taken all of his strength. "Damn, you're soft for such a big guy!" the guard cursed and walked into the room to lift him.

Watching, Adam waited for the guard to swing his weapon behind his back and reach down to lift the wildlife officer off the ground. Striking quickly, Adam grabbed the guard's arm, yanking him forcefully to the ground, a tactical move using both the imbalance of the guard leaning over and an attack pulling him in rather than pushing away caught the man by complete surprise.

Immediately on his feet, Adam snatched the assault rifle from his victim and delivered a fierce blow to the back of the guard's head with the butt of the gun. A second guard, had been holding Miranda in the hallway left his charge to investigate the commotion Adam's cell. Bursting through the doorway, he squared off with Adam in a stand-off, each with the muzzle of high-powered assault rifle aimed at the other.

Cautiously, the sentry held the gun in one hand with his index finger wrapped around the trigger and began to lean into his shoulder-mounted radio to request help. From behind, Miranda hurled herself into the room, driving her body into the back of the guard. Staggering slightly forward, the guard let his arms swing upward to hold himself upright. Adam struck quickly, driving the stock of his assault rifle into the sentry's chin. Another blow knocked the guard's weapon free before Adam delivered the final knock out shot alongside the man's temple.

Flashing a momentary grin of appreciation and approval, the big man's face fell into one of concern, "That will not buy us much. We need to get Laura and find a way out immediately."

"They were holding her in the cell next to me. It's right down this hall," Miranda replied, liberating the weapon from the guard that had left her side, she stood behind Adam who had snatched a set of keys off the first guard.

"Let's go," Adam whispered as he peered into the hallway. Miranda pulled the cell door shut to both slow down the two fallen men returning to action, but also alleviate suspicion for anyone walking by Adam's cell.

Pointing the way with the assault rifle, Miranda guided Adam to where Tug's men were holding Laura. Keys already in hand, Adam reached the door and began inserting each key into the lock until he found the correct one. Swinging the heavy steel door open, he used the light from the hall to see into the dark room and find his wife. Crumpled into a corner, she looked up at her husband, her frightened eyes morphing to a surprised smile.

"How did you…" she asked before Adam shook his head and put a finger to his lips. Nodding, she followed her husband out to the hallway where Miranda was keeping watch.

Unable to resist a soft chuckle, Adam leaned towards Miranda and flipped a switch on the M-4 assault weapon, "You might want the safety off".

Miranda flashed a sheepish grin, which turned quite sour, "I really don't want to have to use this."

"But if you do, just squeeze the trigger and point it roughly in the direction of the bad guys," Adam replied. Pausing, the wildlife officer looked down each direction of the hallway, trying to decide which way was out. Before he had a chance to determine, the latch to the door on the far end of the hall rattled wildly. Tucking behind a corner, Adam urged the ladies back with his arm.

"Carlos, Carlos…what the hell is taking so long? We need to get that video out!" the man down the hall called out.

Hearing a heavy sigh, the trio listened to footsteps pause outside of Adam's cell and then proceed quickly to the open door of the room Laura had been held. "What the…" the man cursed as the sound of him clicking off the safety on his weapon rang through the corridor.

Approaching the open cell cautiously, the mercenary pulled a flashlight from his pocket and shined it into the dark room. Adam wasted no time sliding into the hall just behind the hostage-taker and pressed the muzzle of the M4 into his neck. "Not a sound, not a movement," Adam warned, "Set your weapon and your radio down. Step over them and into the back of the cell."

After a brief hesitation, the terrorist complied with Adam's orders. Behind him, Adam closed and locked the door. "Aren't you afraid of him yelling for help?" Laura asked.

"Not really, I figure they put us down here for a reason. No one can hear anything from this section of the building, that's why they didn't bother to gag us," Adam replied.

"The bigger problem is there are bad men upstairs waiting for us. More are going to come looking, and they are not all going to be so conveniently disarmed," Miranda warned.

"I think there is a back way. When they put me in the cell, I saw some of the men disappear that direction," Laura pointed beyond where the terrorist held her hostage.

"Let's give it a try, it's better than up the stairs into the hornet's nest," Adam agreed, leading the way. In the far dark corner of the corridor, stood a heavy steel door. The smell of stale cigarette smoke grew strong as they reached the door. With Miranda facing to his back and Laura aiming one the M4s toward the door, Adam again cycled through the set of keys. Finding one that slid into the lock mechanism, Adam took a deep breath and turned the handle.

Swinging open the door, the trio met with a blast of sunlight. Squinting, Adam moved forward. Taking one step, he steadied himself as he realized that his foot was hovering in midair. The concrete landing jutted out from the building and stopped, leaving a five-story drop into a large body of water. Behind him, Laura gasped as she grabbed at her husband's shirt to pull him back.

The two started to turn back when Miranda shrieked from behind them, "Someone's coming!" Popping out through the door, she saw what the Raines' were contemplating, "We don't have a choice!" Before her counterparts could respond, she closed the door and leaped off of the platform, landing with a massive splash into the dark waters below.

Adam and Laura looked at each other in shock and bewilderment, "She's as crazy as Sean!" Hesitating, he turned back towards the door, ready for a fight he pulled up his gun and then let it drop, "But she's right."

"You're not that good of a swimmer," Laura warned.

"I know...," Adam replied. Grabbing his wife's hand, he followed Miranda into the water below the platform.

Senator Johnson was in the situation room with several other officials, including a special envoy to President Marshall. The bank of screens shared mixed images throughout the U.S. and Mexico, some fighting still ensued, though the message of cease-fire and a return to peace seemed to be predominating. Johnson, alternated between the live video feeds and the text that scrolled along one screen. There, the all-points-bulletin of James Wilkins flashed among other vital individuals who the feds now sought after.

Below the wall of large flat panel screens, dozens of analysts scanned their multi-screen desktops and monitored phone lines interagency memoranda. One pressed his earpiece closer to his head and popped out of his seat. Grabbing a transcript he printed, he brought it to the commanding officer standing among the policymakers in the observation room. "Sir, we just intercepted a call from a landline in Texas to the Mexican ambassador. There was a request for hostage exchange, including the individuals who were shot down during their extraction from Mazatlan."

Snatching the transcript, the senior officer began scanning the page. The analyst chimed in, "And there is more, sir. Our software matched a voice. It belonged to a formerly classified special ops soldier named Tug Gaskill. Now listed as rogue – extremely dangerous, plays for all sides."

Senator Johnson's head swiveled to the man talking. Tug had Miranda, Adam, and Laura. His heart sank as he knew the methodical mercenary would not let his captives live. His best hope was that the feds could find Wilkins and somehow extract information that could lead them to the hostages. He knew that long shot was unlikely to pay off. Tug was too good at what he did to be caught.

Sean paced back and forth along the fence line of the runway. He would instinctively glance up with each fighter, bomber and cargo jet that roared past. Waiting and helpless did not sit well with him. The fact that his best friend and the woman he loved were in trouble, and he had no way to help ate at him incessantly. As he pivoted to make another pass, a hand grabbed at his arm.

"You're going to wear a hole in the ground," Rachel York warned, pulling gently on his arm to force him to face her. "You need to quit beating yourself up. This thing has the attention of the top military and agency brass."

"I'm not sure how strong my faith is in the system anymore," Sean shot back.

"They haven't locked you up yet, I'd say that's something," Rachel snapped back sternly.

Sean's initial response was an angry glare, which quickly changed into a laugh, "I'm not sure who's point you just proved."

Smiling back at him, Rachel squared up to Sean and looked him straight in the eye, "*I* still have faith." Suddenly, she leaned in close, enough so that Sean could feel her breath on her chin, her eyes still locked with his.

Motionless, Sean seemed frozen in place as his alluring longtime friend hovered close to his lips. More curious than interested, he studied the warmth that linked the two, as she closed in to what was dangerously close to a kiss, a voice called from the barracks. Rachel snapped erect as Sean looked past her shoulder. "Senator Johnson has asked me to locate you, Mr. Kendall, if you would, please follow me," a soldier called.

Nodding, Sean pulled away from Rachel and walked towards the waiting Marine. Rachel looked up into the sky, releasing a light sigh before she turned and followed. The marine held a sharp pace through the corridors and turned abruptly into a small meeting room. Senator Johnson nodded from the table he sat at and quickly dismissed the soldier.

As Sean and Rachel sat down in chairs across from the senator, Johnson lowered his head slightly as spoke softly, "Sean, I am very conflicted in sharing this information with you. In fact, it is far against my better judgment, but I know if I were you, I would want to know."

Silence engulfed the room, as Sean and Rachel too leaned in slightly as the senator spoke, "One of our analysts picked up a transition to Ambassador Gutierrez. The voice on the other end was identified as Tug Gaskill. He claimed to be holding Miranda, Adam and Laura hostage. He was demanding a trade in the small Mexican town of Falcon. His demands included a random set of dissidents that plucked off of an internet search."

"He won't make the trade," Sean declared flatly.

"No, he probably won't. His style is for impact, not results. He is probably working with the factions that are desiring border conflict, and he is using your...*our* friends as bait," Johnson agreed.

"He likely isn't even around anymore," Rachel agreed.

"His M.O. has been to abandon his crew and have them all taken out when things go wrong," Sean admitted.

"Our intelligence says that too. They are sending teams to the site in Mexico, oddly enough, they have triangulated where Tug made that call," the senator shared.

"That is just what he wanted. A raid, no one makes it out alive, hell...probably filled the place with explosives to guarantee annihilation," Sean shrugged.

"Does the CERT team know that?" Rachel asked the senator.

"I let them know that would be his way," Johnson nodded.

"He won't be there," Sean declared defiantly, "He would use a scrambled phone unless he *wanted* to be found. No, he is long gone – either back in hiding or off to his next assignment."

"Seems early in the game for him. He usually waits it out until the eleventh hour," Rachel mused.

"Maybe. He almost got caught the last time, maybe he has learned his lesson," the senator shrugged.

"I don't believe people like him do learn. I think he is off to something else," Sean said, tapping at the table, suddenly, his head shot up, "Wilkins, does anyone have a line on Wilkins?"

"I haven't heard yet. I am sure I can...why?"

Sean looked hard at the senator, "Whoever is pulling the strings is not going to let him walk away. I am not going to believe that all of this coincidence. Tug has been involved in this whole thing. The helicopter was not random. It was targeted."

Johnson began to counter, before sitting back in his chair and sighing, accepting that Sean might very well be right. "I'll check with the situation room." Leaning across the table, the senator tapped the Polycom.

In a moment, the phone was answered, "Special Agent Morrow."

"This is Senator Johnson. I am in room 318. Any updates on the APB for James Wilkins?"

"Hold, sir, I will transfer you to the analyst desk."

"Agent Zigler."

"Agent, this is Senator Johnson. I wanted to get an update on the whereabouts of James Wilkins."

After a brief pause, the agent came over the speaker, "Yessir, we have a call from Wilkins to an unknown line. The transcript states that he is heading for a port near Brownsville, Texas. The call came in about an hour ago."

"Thank you," Johnson pushed the off button on the Polycom phone system.

"I'm going to Brownsville," Sean declared, pushing away from the table.

"You don't know Tug will show up there!" Rachel cried.

"Maybe he won't. But Wilkins has information on what happened to those I care about. I have more questions for him!" Sean spat and stood up, turning towards the door.

"The feds are going to be all over him," Johnson pleaded.

"Then I guess I need to intercept him before he gets there. You will help me," Sean replied sharply.

The senator paused before nodding a reluctant agreement.

"I'm coming with you," Rachel insisted.

"No. I have hurt too many people with my involvement. I can't put any more people at risk," Sean declared, glancing back towards the senator, "Can you get me a car and off this base?"

"I'll have it arranged."

Miranda, a competitive swimmer while in college, was the first reach the bank on the far side of the salty inlet. Only as she reached up to pull herself out, did she realize her compatriots were not alongside her. Looking back towards the warehouse they had leaped from, she saw Adam laboring, not even a quarter of the way across. Laura was slightly ahead, encouraging her husband along.

Taking long, easy strokes, Miranda streaked back to her friends. "You guys alright?"

"We're fine," Laura gasped, "Adam is clumsy and slow, but he'll be okay."

"The other problem is that time is not on our side," Miranda warned, looking up at the third-story door they had jumped from, "Let me help you, Adam. Just lean on your side and kick slowly, I will provide the power." Grabbing the big wildlife officer's hand, Miranda glided through the water as Laura kept pace beside. As they reached the bank, they could hear the shriek of metal being torn open. The mercenaries had jimmied the door that they had escaped from open.

"Under that dock!" Adam called softly as he again began swimming on his own. The two ladies followed suit, and they were soon in the decrepit pier's shadow.

Miranda looked cautiously at the building they had just fled, seeing a pair of men strain their eyes in all directions of the waterway. Turning back to her friends, "I think we can climb the bank on the other side of this dock and not be seen."

Slowly, trying not to create too many ripples, the trio made their way to the steep slope. Grasping at the thin foliage that lined the waterway, they pulled themselves from the water and crouched as low to the ground as they could. Surveying the area, Adam saw that they were in a primarily abandoned section of dilapidated buildings. Yet, scarcely a block away, the sounds of traffic gunning their engines through an intersection could be heard.

"We need to get one street up, but let's move a block further away from the bad guys before we risk exposing ourselves," Adam suggested, "Move quick and quiet, don't even look back."

Quickly, they shuffled along the abandoned street, sticking as close to the shadows as they could. Even as they ran towards the next turn, they could hear voices yelling from the hostage site. "They'll be after us in cars soon!" Miranda called.

"Turn here!" Adam yelled as he wheeled down an alley, escorting his wife gently with an outstretched arm. Their hearts racing, they ran down the dark lane toward what they hoped would be sanctuary of traffic on the next street. Nearing the end of the alley, a police car rolled to stop behind traffic. Behind them, Adam could hear the sound of a vehicle's brakes grinding to a halt. Knowing it would be the kidnappers closing in, Adam picked a discarded malt liquor bottle resting on the ground and hurled it at the police cruiser, just as it began to move forward.

The police car came to an abrupt stop, and a bewildered patrolman stepped out, "What the hell…" he started as he watched the soaked trio sprinting towards him. Seeing a pair of armed men making their way through the alley behind the odd group, the policeman drew his weapon, "Get down!"

Adam, Laura, and Miranda took a few more paces before ducking to the sides of the alley. The officer leveled his gun at the armed pair moving towards him, "Stop and drop your weapons!" Scarcely getting the words out, gunfire exploded through the corridor. The officer wheeled as a bullet met its mark in his chest. Falling to the ground, he opened fire down the alley.

Adam urged Laura and Miranda to keep crawling toward the end of the alley, where they could duck around the corner, out of harm's immediate path. As he passed the patrolman, Adam grabbed a handful of the officer's shirt and pulled him around the corner as well. "You have another weapon?" Adam asked.

The officer looked at Adam as if he were crazy, "I can't…"

"If I wanted you dead, I'd have left you in the alley," Adam barked.

"In the trunk, a shotgun, you'll need this key," the officer declared, pulling a lone key on a ring out of his pocket.

Snatching the key, Adam darted to the patrolman's car, still sitting in the middle of the street. Popping the trunk, he turned the key in gunlock that held the shotgun in place just below the rear sill. Wasting no time, Adam pumped a shell into place and strode to the alley where one of the gunmen neared the end. The mercenary leveled his automatic towards Adam, but before he could get a shot off, Adam cranked a shot out of the barrel and pumped a second round into position. The gunman pulled back as his accomplice put on the brakes and retreated, letting loose a few errant shots into the air.

The streets were suddenly filled with the sounds of sirens responding to the "officer down" call that the patrolman had been able to declare over his shoulder-mounted radio. In moments, half-dozen police cars slid to a stop outside of either end of the alleyway, more closing in.

Adam tossed the shotgun into the open trunk of the patrol car. He returned to the group as he watched the mercenaries move to the center of the alley before being flanked and then overtaken by dozens of officers. Turning to the patrolman sitting next to Miranda and Laura, Adam thanked the man.

Pulling apart the Velcro tabs of his flak jacket, the policeman extended his hand to Adam, "I hear you are the ones we have been looking for."

"I'm glad you found us," Adam grinned.

"I think you found me," the officer corrected, still inspecting his bruised chest.

"Yeah, I guess you're right. Sorry about the bottle, I'm not sure I had an alternative," Adam laughed.

"I get that," the policeman nodded.

"Did the police get them?" Laura asked.

"The two in the alley, yes. The others, we'll have to wait and see," her husband replied.

"We had Officer Rawlings report the warehouse too," Miranda said.

"Good. I just hope they're able to catch Tug," Adam agreed, wondering where his nemesis had taken off to."

James Wilkins turned his sedan down the coastal highway. He was torn on whether to take the time to swap vehicles or just speed towards what he prayed would be refuge. Harold Billings had been a long-time supporter, but Wilkins was not sure he felt he could consider Billings a loyal friend. Loyal to the cause, yes. A faithful ally, yes. But now Wilkins was an expendable figure in the organization.

He began to think about what he would do if he were Harold Billings. Suddenly a pale wash swept down his body. He knew exactly what he would do – lure him into a safe place in which to terminate the threat. A boat sitting offshore in the Gulf of Mexico would be just such a place. With this realization, Wilkins took the next road leading away from the coast. He wasn't sure where he was heading, but moving straight into a trap was not where he was going.

Now, a whole new list of priorities tallied in his head. He had to ditch the car, lose his credit cards, access as much cash as he could without raising too much suspicion. Pulling into a gas station, scarcely a quarter-mile from the coastal highway, Wilkins filled his tank and used the station's ATM to extract as much as could.

Confounded by his bank's one-thousand dollar limit, he turned to the attendant. "You, the owner?"

The kid in the soiled red cap stuttered, "Ah, no, sir. That's Barney. He's in the back office."

"Can I see him?"

"Uh, sure, I guess," shrugging, the attendant shuffled into the back of the store.

In moments, an older, though equally soiled man stepped out, eyeing the man in the starched dress shirt and suit pants warily. "Can I help you?"

"I have a quick business proposition. I need to get some money out, but the machine only lets out so much. Do you have a credit card machine?" Wilkins asked.

"Well, yeah, for folks with expensive repairs..."

"Good, I'd like to run a charge for ten thousand. I'll give you a grand off the top."

"Are you serious? Sounds illegal," the man's suspicious countenance intensified.

"I assure you it is not. I have several forms of ID. You can call it in if you like," Wilkins added. He wondered if the feds had cut him off yet, though they might also keep his credit open to make tracking him easier. Glancing out the window as the man weighed his decision, "Whose truck?"

"That's mine! A 1985 Ford Bronco, thing can run through anything," the boy replied.

"I'll tell you what, if your boss can run another card for the same, I'll give him another grand and you five for the truck," Wilkins bargained.

"Six."

"Done," Wilkins smiled, turning to the owner, "What do you think, boss?"

"Alright, but I'm calling the charges into VISA directly," the man agreed.

Nodding, Wilkins handed over two of his Platinum cards and turned to stare out of the window. Despite the air of calm he displayed for the yokels, his inside were eating him up. He expected a parade of black vehicles to close in on him any second. He focused on his breathing, forcing his body to retain as normal functioning as possible.

"Hey, mister, what are you gonna do with your car?" the boy asked.

"It's a company car. I just quit, they can come get it," Wilkins grinned and then pushed his story forward, "I'm heading down the coast to Port Isabel. A friend's got a boat there. I think I'll join him on his charter business."

"Right on," the boy nodded as his boss stepped in with a handful of cash.

"I had ten thousand in the safe, but I only got five hundred in the drawer, that's gonna leave you short," the owner said, "I can pay Walter here when I go to the bank and square up my cut, but I ain't got the other two thousand."

"Fifteen hundred," Wilkins corrected, "I tell you what. Top off the tank on the Bronco, and we'll call it square." Wilkins did not want to stay in this spot any longer. He just wanted what cash he could grab and get the hell on the road.

"If you're sure…"

"I'm sure," Wilkins snapped as he held his hand out for the keys to the old four-by-four.

Nineteen

Tug Gaskill drove straight for the harbor. A small boat waited to take him to the yacht, where he would wait for the senatorial aide. He didn't mind this side job. It was a great stop off before heading for exile. He had pushed his luck to the edge with his involvement in the border war. It was, without a doubt, time to disappear.

Turning on the coastal road, he went through the steps of the plan. Not that this was a tactical challenge. It was just his way. Being meticulous is what helped him stay alive to this point. The fact was, the mercenary almost felt sorry for the hapless aide. No doubt sticking his neck out to impress his superiors and stepped in a pile of dung. Typical Washington weasel didn't stand a chance against a well-trained mercenary with the deck stacked in his favor.

Passing an intersection, he maintained a consistent speed to avoid any undue attention. The only factor untold in this scenario was who would get there first. Tug had left instructions for the bureaucrat to be liquored up in the event he was not there first, and it appeared as though that would be the case. Either way, another quick million, and he would be mere miles from international waters.

Sean pushed the Ford sedan to its limits. The open Texas highways allowed him to gobble up miles in enormous sections. The highway patrol was not at all concerned with traffic infractions given the events of the past several days. As he closed in on the harbor town of Brownsville, he wondered what he would find. If he had been able to follow a tip on where the senatorial aide had gone, then so could others. Weaponless, he would have to be very cautious as he closed in on his target.

Suddenly, the phone that Rachel had acquired for him began buzzing at his hip. Flipping the clamshell open, he called "hello" into the mouthpiece.

"Sean, its Rachel. I just got a call from an agent in my office, Wilkins unloaded his credit card at a gas station just northwest of Brownsville, according to the report, the last exit before entering."

"When?"

"Not more than forty-five minutes ago. You should be right on his heels," the Regional Department of Interior Director informed Sean.

"I think I just passed it," Sean said, "Maybe I still have time to catch him before he boards the boat."

"You might," Rachel agreed, "But, I wonder why he would pull off there. So close to town, why not get to where you are going and scope out a place to get money then? Or if he was heading to a haven, wait for his backers to support him."

"Maybe it dawned on him that his backers weren't going to support him," Sean mused.

"That's what I am thinking. Put myself in the shoes of whoever he was working for, I probably am not letting him ride off into the sunset," Rachel agreed.

"Where does that exit take you?" Sean asked.

"Away from Brownsville and towards Baton Rouge."

"Louisiana isn't a bad choice of a place to hide. I'm going to turn around and check out that service station and see if we can corroborate what our suspicions are," Sean replied.

"What if we are wrong? What if he just wanted cash for his escape and didn't want to withdraw from the place he was using as his launching pad?" Rachel second-guessed.

"Maybe. Any way you can have that harbor patrolled?"

"I think so. Between Johnson and myself, we ought to be able to have eyes on the ground, and if possible, satellite coverage shared with the border sweeps," Rachel replied.

"Ms. York, you never fail to amaze me."

"You too, Sean. But you also never fail to frighten me to death, either. You be careful out there, do you hear me?"

"I'll do my best...," Sean said, closing the phone.

Slowing the sedan, he angled slightly towards the emergency lane before pulling the wheel into a hard turn, forcing the car to cross the median and head back the way he had come. A few miles clicked before he saw the exit. Swinging the car down the off-ramp, he made his way to the service station that Rachel had informed him.

Beside the garage, sat the very vehicle that the Lackland's security cameras had picked Wilkins up fleeing in. "Guess I got the right place," Sean mumbled to himself, bringing his vehicle to a stop. Eyeing Wilkins' sedan, he found it empty aside from a crumpled map and candy bar wrapper.

"May ah help you?" a voice called form the service station door.

Sean turned to see a large man in coveralls, chewing vigorously on some unknown substance, staring at him.

"Ya need some gas, mister?" the man asked.

So focused on catching up with Wilkins, Sean was caught off guard with the very natural question, "Uhh, sure. Yeah, go ahead and fill it up."

"Sure thing," the attendant said, casting Sean a wary look.

"This car," Sean began, noting a snap reaction in the young man who had just unscrewed the gas cap to Sean's borrowed sedan, "Did you see the gentleman who was driving it?"

"Aw, man! I knew it was too good to be true!" the attendant declared, then his eyes widened, "Are you a cop?"

"No, why would you…," Sean began before he started to piece the situation together, "So you *did* meet the man."

"Yeah, I did. He bought my truck and left me this car. Now what am I gonna do?"

"Far as I am concerned, you can keep the car. What I want to know is if the man told you where he was headed," Sean affirmed.

"Not really. He was in a big hurry. He got some cash, paid me for the truck, and took off."

"Towards Brownsville?"

"No, the other way, towards Corpus Christi," the attendant replied.

"What did your truck look like?" Sean asked.

"Aw, it was a sweet, brown Bronco with a four-inch Pro-lift kit riding a set of thirty-fives…"

"I got it," Sean cut in, "Was it fast?"

"For a short while. If you ran her too hard, she'll overheat. If you keep running her hot, she'll blow a rod," the attendant responded.

"Thanks. What's the highway like that way?"

"Straight and boring. He'll need to stop for gas near Kingsville. After that, it's a straight shot to Corpus."

Sean handed the attendant a handful of twenties and jumped back into the Ford Interceptor the base provided.

When the helicopter landed, Miranda was surprised to see the party that had gathered near the tarmac to welcome them. Leading the entourage were Senator Johnson and Rachel York. The one person she so desperately wanted to see was not there. Sighing deeply, she tried to stifle the sinking feeling that she felt in her chest.

Smiling weakly at Adam and Laura, she could see that her friends had recognized the same vacancy in the crowd. Instinctively, Adam squeezed his wife's hand. Leaving his seat, he leaned into the cockpit and tapped the pilot. Motioning his fingers in the rotation of the rotors, he lipped, "Keep it running."

Returning to the ladies, he walked them away from the helicopter and towards the crowd. They each exchanged hugs with Senator Johnson and Director York. As Adam leaned in to squeeze the DOI Regional Director, he whispered into her ear, "Where is he?"

"He's after Wilkins, somewhere near Brownsville town."

"Wilkins? What the…," Adam frowned, "Is he in trouble?"

"Maybe."

"Let's go," Adam said casually, taking her elbow and swinging her towards the waiting helicopter. Peeling away, he hugged his wife and pulled Miranda close, "Sean's after Wilkins, I'll let the Senator explain things to you. I'm going to go with Rachel and make sure he comes back in one piece."

Silently, the exhausted women watched the wildlife officer and bureaucrat jog to the helicopter. They both knew that there was no arguing with this direction. Instead, they supported each other as the Senator led them into the barracks where he found a private room to bring them up to speed.

"What's going on?" Adam asked as the Bell Ranger helicopter lifted off of the ground and screamed eastward.

"Sean overheard Wilkins talking on the phone. It was clear that he was somehow involved in the recent events at the border, with Sean in Mexico and with your helicopter being shot down," Rachel replied directly.

"Wilkins…involved?" Adam frowned.

"We found it hard to believe too, but when Sean confronted him, it became quite clear," Rachel shared.

"And then the weasel bolted."

"He bolted, and who else would go recklessly chasing after him?" Rachel added.

"Our buddy Sean," Adam let out a brief grin, "But why not just have the feds go after him?"

"They are. We have satellite feeds being scoured now, trying to pick up Wilkins' car, we are monitoring his credit, cellphone…"

"But no agents," Adam interjected.

"We have none to spare right now. There is a team waiting for Wilkins in Brownsville. We'll redirect them if Sean reports any findings contrary to what we currently know," Rachel added.

"If you and Sean have an idea, so will the bad guys. They'll be all over him," Adam mused.

"That is accurate and dangerous," Rachel agreed.

Once more on the open highway, Sean pushed the sedan to its limits. Despite Wilkins owning a half-hour lead, Sean had hoped to close the gap with his car's faster high-end speed. Glancing off of the road for a moment, he watched the needle climb well into the triple digits. The semi-barren landscape whizzed by outside of his window, the few features that existed melted into a blur.

Which each mile that clicked on the odometer, he hoped to see the taillights of the old Ford Bronco. The race for Sean was desperate. If he couldn't catch up to Wilkins by Kingsville, he might never find him. He wanted information on who Wilkins was working for. It was evident that they wanted him and his friends dead. He had to find out who was behind the attacks.

At the far end of the horizon, he watched a small dot begin to grow. As the Interceptor closed in, Sean could discern the shape of a full-size SUV. Feeling his pulse quicken, Sean hoped that he had caught up to his man. As the SUV's features became increasingly clear, he recognized it as a late model Chevrolet. Disappointed, he never let off the throttle as he nudged the steering wheel to bring the car alongside and past the truck.

Cursing, he gauged the miles. He still had time to catch up, he hoped. Flowing over a light rise in the road, Sean eyed another vehicle up ahead. Again, he reeled the object in. Another SUV, this time, Sean was confident this was the one. First, he identified the vehicle as brown and raised. Then the full truck came into view. It was a Bronco from the eighties. Sean finally allowed his foot to back off the accelerator as he closed in. Slowing the vehicle to seventy-five miles per hour, he figured that was the peak range that Wilkins was comfortable driving the big, bouncy rig. Following the SUV closely for a few moments, Sean pondered what his next step should be.

Wilkins decided for him as the Bronco sped up. Steadily increasing another fifteen miles per hour, the SUV tried to pull away. Heeding the attendant's description of the truck's breakdown point, Sean just had the keep the pressure on. Increasing his speed to match that of the Bronco, Sean tailed the vehicle relentlessly. At the first sign of a change, Sean backed off of the accelerator. The Bronco seized and began to swerve violently as white smoke began to seep from the engine bay. Suddenly the big SUV lurched and spun sideways, causing the raised behemoth to flip side over side on the pavement.

Sean squeezed hard on the brakes, stopping his vehicle quickly behind the Bronco. He collected himself as he took in the scene, putrid smoke drifted by from the overtaxed tires digging into the asphalt. Ready to launch out of the car and grab his prey, Sean was stopped in his tracks as a bullet slammed into the windshield of the sedan. Lifting his head after instinct dove it down beneath the dashboard, he saw the shape of Wilkins' upper body poking through the passenger window of the overturned truck. In his hands, a high-powered hunting rifle readied for a second shot.

Cursing softly, Sean jammed the sedan into gear and pressed his foot hard on the accelerator. The borrowed vehicle lurched forward in a squeal of tires and slammed violently into the undercarriage of the overturned Bronco. Wilkins, and the gun he was holding, flew backward into the air. Having braced for the collision, Sean recovered quickly, brushing glass fragments off of his shoulders. Sliding out of the driver's seat, he sprinted for the area where the Senatorial aide had flown. Sean found Wilkins slowly crawling towards the rifle, fifteen feet from where he had landed.

Dashing to the weapon, Sean planted a heavy foot on the barrel of the gun, beating Wilkins by a solid body length. Instinctively, the aide turned away from Sean, looking for a direction to flee.

"You think you can outrun me?" Sean warned. "You have some explaining to do, and I don't mind this being a painful process for you."

The senator's aide hesitated, not fully knowing what to do. Finally, he relented and sat up, facing his captor, "What are you going to do with me?"

"I'm going to take you back to the base, and I'll let the professionals decide how to extract the information from you," Sean replied, "Unless, that is, you feel like openly sharing with me on our ride back."

"Who in the hell do you think you are? You are naïve civilian. You have no idea what in the hell you are doing or what you are up against!" Wilkins snarled.

"Maybe, but I know what side I'm on," Sean replied.

Tired of the discourse, he strode towards the weary bureaucrat. Surprised, he was momentarily overtaken as Wilkins lunged forward, grasping his hands tightly around Sean's throat. More annoyed than overcome, Sean's arms sliced upward, breaking the desperate aides hold. A determined glare crossed his face as his emotions towards this worm of man exploded. Suddenly, rational thought and concern to get Wilkins back to the base as unharmed as possible were gone. Sean delivered several crushing blows with his fists dotting his opponent's face and head, finishing with a sidekick to the solar plexus sent Wilkins careening backward into the crumpled SUV.

The rage quickly flushed out of his system, and Sean calmly walked over to his fallen enemy. Grabbing Wilkins by his shirt, Sean hoisted the limp administrator up and tossed him over his shoulder. Moving back towards the Interceptor, he hoped the car would still run after using it as a ram against the massive SUV. Starting to lay Wilkins down in the back seat, Sean changed his mind and headed for the trunk. Lifting the lid, he dumped the senator's aide in the well and slammed the trunk shut.

Moving quickly, washed clean of emotion, Sean returned to the driver's seat of the Interceptor. Turning the key, the ignition spun, but failed to ignite. Cursing, Sean slammed the steering wheel with his fists. Popping both the hood and the trunk lid, he remembered the gun that Wilkins had fired at him. Jogging once more around the SUV, he froze as he saw a familiar face staring back at him.

"Looking for this?" Tug Gaskill grinned, patting the hunting rifle with his hand. Slinging the gun over his shoulder, he drew his pistol, "Move over to our friend, will you?"

Rolling his eyes and sighing to himself, Sean complied. As he walked forward, he felt Tug's eyes burn through him. "Sounds like you lost once again…"

"What are you talking about? I am holding a gun to your head," Tug scoffed.

"Once more, you couldn't hold the wildlife officer and a couple of girls!"

"What…" Tug stifled his surprise as he shook his head, "Too bad you won't have the same opportunity."

"If you're going to kill me, just do it already," Sean baited, more interested in the reaction than giving in to his execution.

"Oh, I will. First, I want to put you in the market. Might as well make a few bucks off of the experience."

"Yeah, money. How much did it take for you to turn on your country?" Sean lobbed the pointed question.

"My country turned on *me*! I was infiltrating for them, and they left me for dead when things went wrong!" the mercenary bellowed.

"Is that how it happened? You didn't know the risks when you went Special Ops? Or was it just a convenient excuse to sign with the devil and not take the hit to your conscience?" Sean retorted.

"You don't have any idea. You're what, maybe forty, and living off your 401k that my men died for!" Tug lobbied back.

"You make more on a single hit than I have in my retirement. That's just it. *Money* wasn't what motivated me," Sean defended.

"Soldiers fight for freedom. Well, mine comes at a cost. There is no real freedom from a soldier in this country. We sweat and bleed for pennies while pansies like you cash out of your retirements and coast through the rest of your life. We deal with memories, pain, and trauma."

"Oh, so now this is your just your way of supplementing your pension…" Sean was cut off when the butt of Tug's pistol slammed down on the back of his head. Sean dropped to his knees and fought to remain conscious. He turned his head to see the mercenary poking at Wilkins with his gun.

"He dead?" Tug asked, looking back.

Understanding that Tug was sent to kill him, Sean admitted, "Yep. He tried to escape, I didn't mean to, but I killed him."

Sean, if he escaped, wanted to get Wilkins back to the base alive so that he could be questioned and hopefully give up who was backing him.

Tug nodded and started to walk away to Sean's relief. Suddenly, the mercenary swung back towards the trunk and squeezed off two shots from his .45 caliber pistol. Seeing the look of shock on Sean's face, he smiled, "My employers are going to want to see *my* bullets in him if they are going to pay me."

Sean felt sick to his stomach and suddenly very helpless. Nothing seemed to be in his control. He had fought Tug before, but on his knees in the middle of a deserted Texas highway, he felt completely vulnerable. He thought of Miranda, never really having the chance to show how much he cared for her. He thought about his friends, Adam and Laura, who had become his family. He even thought about his ex-wife and his former in-laws, wondering if they knew how much he cared for them despite the divorce. He wondered how his beloved country would turn out after the tragic events of the past several days.

Helplessness gave way to anger. Suddenly, the one thought that consumed Sean's mind was to go out fighting. Taking in a deep breath, he prepared to strike out at Tug and accept whatever became of his attack. Almost as soon as he flinched, Tug stopped him with a boot to the face.

"Son, if I wanted you dead right now, you'd *be* dead," Tug laughed, "Don't get me wrong, your time is coming. I need to contact my employers and add you to the tab. If you're dead already, I don't have much to negotiate."

Sean's instincts were to fight. His death sentence was written. Still, a stay of execution could lead to a better opportunity. A twisted laugh from the mercenary broke his thoughts, "I like your trunk idea. How 'bout you hop into mine. Should be real comfortable." Motioning with his gun, the mercenary herded Sean to the rear of his car. Reluctantly he climbed in with Tug's persuasion. The lid slammed shut, engulfing Sean in blackness.

"Well, do we go towards the coast or the detour that Sean was exploring?" Rachel asked Adam. The wildlife officer's face twisted as if the decision seared him with pain.

"I don't know. We haven't heard with him since he was last called," Adam replied over the intercom system of the Bell Ranger helicopter.

"That doesn't mean much with Sean, does it?" Rachel sighed.

"No. No, it doesn't," Adam admitted, "His hunches have a weird way of panning out. If he chose to go detour, I think we should too. Besides, you have tons of personnel in Brownsville, and they haven't reported anything of interest."

"Open range it is," Rachel agreed and instructed the pilot to turn north and follow the rural highway.

Through the expansive helicopter windows, all Adam could see was vast fields of golden wheat and grazing land for cattle. The only structure for miles was the gas station that had come up in the report. Seeing a Sheriff's vehicle parked out front, Adam leaned on Rachel, "Looks like the police got to the station, looks quiet from here."

"I'll get a report," Rachel replied and asked the pilot to hover.

Adam watched the deputy talking to two very animated men in front of the station. Beyond that conversation, Adam could see nothing else out of place.

"The sheriff's deputy reports that two men fitting Sean and James Wilkins' descriptions had been by. Each within the past hour or two. It sounds like they both headed north," Rachel reported.

"Then let's get moving!" Adam roared.

The pilot nodded and pushed the yoke forward, sending the swift helicopter screaming along the highway. The barren landscape flowed by, almost as featureless as treadmill rolling along its track. The interstate had been closed at its northern point at the start of the border skirmish, traffic had not yet begun flowing back along the southerly route, so when vehicles were spotted on the highway, the occupants of the Ranger each straightened to attention.

"That's gotta be them!" Adam bellowed.

As the helicopter roared closer, the details of the vehicles became more evident. An SUV clogged the road, tipped on its side. The car that Sean had taken from the base was nose into the underbelly of the truck. A third vehicle was parked in the ditch a mere fifty yards from the other two. A man was just about to climb into the driver's seat.

"Was that your man?" the pilot called.

"No!" both Adam and Rachel chorused.

"I can't be sure, but that looked like Tug Gaskill," Adam said as the helicopter rocketed past and then banked sharply to swerve back to the scene.

The man near the driver's door raised a gun and fired off several shots toward the helicopter. Two distinct "pings" rang through the cockpit as a pair of bullets found their way into the fuselage. "That's Tug!" Adam confirmed. Then in horror, he watched as the mercenary strode confidently to the rear of the car and pointed his pistol at the lid of the trunk.

"Oh no! Sean might be in there!" Rachel screamed.

Sliding open the cockpit door, Adam grabbed an M16 assault rifle from the stand and let loose a volley of shots in the direction of the mercenary. The hasty attempt failed to hit its mark as Tug levied a barrage of his own into the trunk of the car.

"Get this thing down!" Adam bellowed.

Squatting by the open door, before the chopper could get with fifteen of the ground, Adam leaped out of the cockpit and rolled onto the dusty ground below. Tug had swung back towards the helicopter, but had to replace the clip in his gun. Before he could slam it into place, Adam was able to get off two well-placed shots. The first plunked the mercenary in the shoulder, narrowly missing his bowed head. The second caught Tug in the hip, shattering his bones and sending him sprawling to the ground. The pistol rolled out in front of the mercenary.

Adam strode forward, leveling the assault rifle square at the forehead of the rogue military specialist. Rage coursed through him, causing his finger to tense on the trigger while his brain fought the debate whether to squeeze or not. Suddenly, the rear passenger door of the sedan flew open, and Sean Kendall flew out, tackling Tug as the mercenary was trying to swing the hunting rifle slung over his shoulder into position. Sean's athletic body slammed into Tug with tremendous force, Sean's shoulder driving into the mercenary's head, sending him sliding across the roadway. Snatching the rifle, he was able to wrench it from Tug's grip.

The mercenary pulled his bloody face off of the pavement and glared at Sean. Slipping a knife from his belt, he lunged at Sean, but his attack was cut short as a series of bullets pierced his chest and head. Lifeless, the former Marine lie dead at the hand of another. Instinctively, Adam scooted the knife away with his foot.

Looking at his friend, Adam asked, "You alright, partner?"

"Wilkins is dead."

"I figured, but how about you, I thought you were in the trunk," Adam asked.

"I was," Sean replied weakly before letting the slightest of a grin escape, "When I heard the shots out there, I popped through the rear seat. My company used to use those cars. They have a slot for skis and stuff to fit through. I used that to get out of the trunk."

Adam laughed, "Being a skinny runt paid off for you."

"I guess it did," Sean grinned.

Behind Adam, Rachel York appeared. "Sean, you're alright!" Running up, she spread her arms around her friend in a rare show of affection.

"I'm alright," Sean cooed, accepting his friend's hug.

Twenty

Stepping out of the helicopter and onto the tarmac, Sean couldn't stifle the grin as he saw Miranda for the first time in what seemed weeks. Exhausted, both physically and emotionally, the sight of her gave him renewed energy. Walking quickly to her, he exchanged quick hellos with Laura and Senator Johnson so that he could devote his full attention to her.

At first, the two stared at each other in silence, feeling the warmth of their embrace seep into their souls. Finally, Miranda spoke first, "I'm so glad you are okay. I was…"

"I know. So was I," Sean helped as she choked, "I was worried about you too. It sounds as though you guys had quite the adventure."

"We did. I didn't think we were going to make it. Oh, Sean. Tell me it's over," Miranda pleaded, burying her head into his arms.

"I think it finally is," Sean consoled, "Tug was the one coming after us. He can't hurt us anymore."

"Good, maybe we can get our lives back."

"If I have one. I seem to be adding whole other countries to putting me on their "most wanted" list," Sean shrugged.

"I have been talking with Rick. The Mexican government has completely pardoned you. Clarissa Gutierrez has confessed to her part in her own abduction," Miranda shared.

"How about here at home? I violated I don't know how many conditions in my commuted sentence."

"You're a bureaucrat, now Sean. You're *supposed* to have a checkered past," Senator Johnson broke in, "Listen, I don't want you to worry about any of that right now. Go on inside, shower, have medical check you out, spend some time with this beautiful woman. I'll keep the dogs at bay for a while, though the Department of Justice will want a full de-briefing."

Sean nodded as his friend walked away. Wrapping his arm around Miranda's waist, he began the walk towards the barracks. "You two coming? They're going to want to poke and prod you too, big fella."

Adam grinned at his friend, "I know. I volunteered to go first to give you a break. Use your time wisely, will you?"

"They're not letting us out of here tonight, let's meet in a few hours, and we'll find someplace good to eat around this base," Laura added.

Colonel Reyes tipped up his glass of premium tequila and basked in the late day sun. La Costa was on his way to meet him. He knew this visit would be one of recognition and reward. He wasn't sure if he would be allowed to remain at his post. He covered his tracks the best that he could. His team abandoned the gear that had used and lit up the armory with more C-4 than he had ever seen in one place. He had faith in the loyalty of each one of the troops that he had entrusted to the mission.

Hearing a knock on his door, he paused to straighten his uniform, shuffled his cigars on his desk, and made his way. Snatching the handle, he swung the door wide. Holding his chest out proudly, he welcomed his guests. Peering past the four men on his stoop, he asked, "Where is La Costa?"

"I'm afraid he couldn't make it, Colonel. Instead, he sent us to offer his appreciation," the man in front replied.

Disappointed and confused, the Colonel shrugged and held his arm out for the men to follow. "Can I get you a drink?"

"No, sir. But before we proceed, there was one request. Would it be possible to get a list of those in your regimen?"

"Of course, I'll print a list from my office," Reyes agreed.

"Excellent," the one who had done all of the speaking replied, and then gave a quick nod to one of his men.

The man followed the colonel down the hallway. The sounds of a printer were followed with the crisp sound of a bullet flying through a silencer. The man reappeared with a piece of paper. Nodding to the crew, the one in charge circled his finger in the air, "Light it up!"

Several incendiary devices were planted strategically throughout the house. They were designed to burn slowly with intense heat that would eventually catch the rest of the house on fire. The time it took for the house to completely engulf in flame was enough for the four men and to leave the building and be well on their way, long before attention was attracted to the colonel's home.

"You must be exhausted. Why don't you sit with me? I want you close," Miranda suggested as she watched Sean gently rapped at her door.

"I'm afraid to fall asleep," Sean said as he took his place alongside her on the stiff mattress, "I don't want to let you out of my sight."

"Then wrap your arms around me and don't let go," Miranda called.

"I can't begin to explain how good it feels to be with you," Sean said.

Pulling her lips against his, Miranda muttered, "Then don't talk."

The knock on the door rattled the both of them. Miranda and Sean had both fallen asleep locked in each other's arms. "Guys, it's Adam. Got news for you. freshen up and meet us in ten minutes."

"News? What news? Where do we…"

"We'll come back and get you."

Rolling back towards Miranda, he placed a soft, lingering kiss on her lips. "News."

"I heard. Good, I hope," Miranda nodded.

"Me too," Sean agreed, "I guess we fell asleep."

"I guess we did. It felt good…to be with you," Miranda purred and then with a more serious look, "Sean, I know we have had our issues. But I think I realize they are *our* issues, to work out together, not alone."

Putting both arms around his neck, she looked at him dead in the eye and continued, "It is hard for me. I worry about you. I never know what you are going to do next, if you're going to be okay. But I also think that is what is so wonderful about you. You do what your heart knows is right, regardless of the consequences. You can't help but to jump in the fire when there is someone who needs you. That is very admirable, even attractive, really, but it's also terrifying."

"I imagine. It's unfortunate the hurt you have been through since we've met. Honestly, my life was pretty boring before you came along," Sean smiled, and then he too turned serious, "I didn't think after my divorce, that I would ever utter these words…I love you. I have since the day you nearly knocked me over at the coffee stand. It's strange. Half of the things that I've done, I've done because of you. Because you make me selfless. You make me want to do more. When I moved to the North Cascades, I had no one to worry about. I had a few good deeds that I tried to implement, but really, I was just taking care of myself."

"You're not the run from things type," Miranda said.

"No, I am not. That's not why I moved out there. The truth is, I had nothing left to fight for in my own life."

"I think that might be what scares me. What happens when that life is shared," Miranda asked.

"I don't know. Guess it depends how many terrorists come after us," Sean smiled.

"I love you too," Miranda turned serious once more, "Enough to understand you and to want to be with you, kryptonite and all."

Wrapping her arms around him, she pulled him tightly. Weeks, maybe months of emotion poured into that hug. An almost dizzying feeling coursed through her. Anger, sadness, and unbelievable joy swirled around her. The danger, her cousins, the politics, the romantic fire-lit picnics in Sean's living room, the smells of his cologne that cling to her clothes after they've been together all collided into a strangely content feeling. All of this was over, and she could enjoy this man.

Senator Johnson and Rachel York were waiting for the foursome as they laughed their way down the hallway. A great weight seemed to lift off of all of them, and now they were just regular civilians of the United States of America. Seeing the dignitaries alongside the senator, the gravity of taking the law into his own hands – repeatedly – begun to sink in. Dozens of men in dark suits flitted about, several members of the military, Department of Defense, and Department of Justice that Sean recognized from previous meetings with the senator and from television stood nearby.

As the four neared Johnson, the sea of officials parted as another entourage came from the nearby room. Among this new group was a tall, confident African-American man. Sean recognized him. This was President Marshall. A circle formed around the senator and the president.

Marshall scanned the group and singled out Sean. "You must be Mr. Kendall."

Extending his hand to accept that of the president's, Sean responded, "It's a privilege, sir."

"Hmm, did you vote for me?" the president cocked a curious but friendly look at Sean.

"No, sir. But I might if I get a second chance. I admire how you handled the situation with Mexico," Sean admitted.

"Fair enough. I'll see if I can't give you your chance," Marshall laughed, "However, you know, felons can't vote in this country."

"Yessir."

"What are we going to do about that?" Marshall ruminated, "I have been briefed in full as to what had happened in Mexico. What happened *here* in the past couple of days. What happened in Portland and Seattle this past year. You have been quite busy in what most would consider, a rather unusual life."

"Yes sir, I suppose that it has been a rather challenging set of circumstances," Sean agreed.

"Senator Johnson is quite an advocate on your behalf. Secretary of Commerce Lamarillo and Ambassador Gutierrez are as well. Ms. York has painted a picture that in nearly every incident, your options were to follow the rules and allow others to get hurt or to bend a guardrail or two and be a good American citizen. I don't know how we can penalize you for standing up for the rights of this country and her citizens. Speaking with President Lopez feels the same way after hearing your efforts with his people as well."

The president studied Sean carefully, "I hereby pardon all of your charges. My office is working with the Attorney General as we speak to provide the proper paperwork."

Holding out his hand once more, "Mr. Kendall, it is *my* honor to be meeting *you*. All of you. Mr. Raines, a heroic former serviceman, Mrs. Raines, and Ms. Shaw, for your bravery in tremendous circumstances, and I have to imaging putting up with these two. Please, if you are ever in D.C., do let my secretary know. I would love for you to be my guests. Now, if you'll forgive me, I am due to leave for a meeting with President Lopez at an "undisclosed location"."

Half of the crowd moved away with the president, leaving the core group left with themselves. Senator Johnson addressed his friends, "Let's celebrate. I'll buy, and I don't think we'll have any trouble getting off base tonight."

Walking with Sean, Johnson said, "Well, with the full pardon, I guess you don't work for me anymore."

Sean looked up at the senator with a thoughtful glance, "No, I suppose I don't."

"I could still use you. Who else could get blamed for kidnapping a dignitary's wife only to get a ringing endorsement from him ultimately?"

"I think we've had a few politicians in our country that would have offered an endorsement to anyone who would have kidnapped their wives," Adam grinned and was quickly reprimanded with a backhand from Laura.

"Perhaps," Senator Johnson conceded, "I could use your honesty in my office. I could use your judgment."

"You know, I didn't vote for you either?" Sean reminded the senator.

"Maybe more of us politicians need to consider balance and explore all sides of a debate. What do you say?" Johnson pressed.

"I'm honored by your offer Rick, can I think about it?"

"Sure. You've been through a lot," changing the subject, the senator added, "I don't know about you guys, but I could use a drink. Let's go."

As soon as the sun rose the next morning on the east coast, President Marshall addressed the nation on every standard channel. "We have been through a lot over the past several weeks. We have lost loved ones. We will all mourn those who have fallen to the tragedies our nation and our neighbor's nation have faced.

I stand before you this morning, a proud man. I am proud of my country. Every one of you listening, for facing the terrorists, not with the fear that they prescribe, but with solidarity and strength. That perseverance, instead of panic, allowed us to confront the enemy and respectfully counsel our neighbor to put an end to the violence. Instead of being saddened, my heart is enlightened with the strength this nation has shown over the past several weeks.

Instead of cleaving the longstanding relationship with Mexico, we have found a way to join and become more reliable partners. Where there was blame and malice, sprang respect, bravery, and support. I am not going to tell you that all of our trains have been righted, but I will say that we are able to get back to the table and continue talks with Mexico. We have emotional debates on either side how best to manage our border. That is the beauty of this country. We get to share our thoughts as well as our fears. In the end, we generally find somewhere in the middle is the best way forward.

For those who have lost, I ask that you respect them. Love them. For those of you who can, return to your normal lives. Share your thoughts with others. Write your congressmen. Seek counsel from your clergy. God bless America."

"Just listen to that nonsense! That man is the end of our civilization. Somehow, he has made this mess a win for his campaign. It is time for a change. We saw enough anger in the streets. The time is right. It is time for you, Senator Small, to run for president of the United States," Harold Billings declared as he cursed the flat screen on the wall of the senator's private office.

"I've been waiting for this day for some time. I can't believe we lost the last election with that dolt from Alabama," Small agreed.

"He was afraid to cut to the quick, but at the same time, broaden his platform. We will have the best financial staffers to assemble your economic package. The military will be yours, evangelists…"

"That's great. We always get them. How about the independents. That is where the race is won," Small countered.

"We keep the pressure on. The attacks don't stop. It looks like Marshall averted this crisis. What if he didn't? What if his soft-actions lead to more violence?" Billings suggested.

"I still love my country…"

"I'm not suggesting you don't. I am suggesting that we need to take drastic actions or this country you love won't exist anymore!" Billings bellowed.

"Fine, what's next?"

"The Mexicans are small potatoes, and they don't have the history or the firepower to really get the Americans excited," Billings mused.

"Then what? Raise the Iron Curtain?" Small wrinkled his nose.

"Anytime an outsider attacks the U.S., then everyone bans together. Even the worst president can look good under those times. The one thing that will rattle U.S. citizens is attacks from the inside."

"What are you suggesting?"

"Whatever it takes to fracture the U.S. populous. We need to make them *want* the change that you can bring. Well placed attacks that show Marshall's team cannot handle it. Events that show he has taken our country backward. Hundreds of years backward. Senator, I think it is time for the confederacy to rise again!"